"Who Will Win, Fawn? Will I Turn You Into a White, or Will You Make Me Over Into an Indian?"

"As long as we are together, we will both win," she answered.

Nathan's face lowered and she raised her lips and kissed him in the wonder of new love. His growing passion made him pull her to him and his kisses seared her soul as she responded. He had loved this woman almost from the first moment he saw her. He had been tormented by the memories of her lithe body.

Fawn ran her hand over his chest and felt the hard muscles beneath the soft leather of his shirt. His hand stroked her face and her hands upon his body were turning his blood to flames as he pulled her tightly against him.

"Are you sure, Fawn? A man can only hold back just so long."

Dear Reader,

We, the editors of Tapestry Romances, are committed to bringing you two outstanding original romantic historical novels each and every month.

From Kentucky in the 1850s to the court of Louis XIII, from the deck of a pirate ship within sight of Gibraltar to a mining camp high in the Sierra Nevadas, our heroines experience life and love, romance and adventure.

Our aim is to give you the kind of historical romances that you want to read. We would enjoy hearing your thoughts about this book and all future Tapestry Romances. Please write to us at the address below.

The Editors
Tapestry Romances
POCKET BOOKS
1230 Avenue of the Americas
Box TAP
New York, N.Y. 10020

Embrace the Wind

Lynda Trent

A TAPESTRY BOOK
PUBLISHED BY POCKET BOOKS NEW YORK

Books by Lynda Trent

Embrace the Storm
Embrace the Wind

Published by TAPESTRY BOOKS

An *Original* publication of TAPESTRY BOOKS

A Tapestry Book published by
POCKET BOOKS, a division of Simon & Schuster, Inc.
1230 Avenue of the Americas, New York, N.Y. 10020

ISBN: 0-671-49305-1

First Pocket Books printing June, 1983

10 9 8 7 6 5 4 3 2 1

POCKET and colophon are registered trademarks of Simon & Schuster, Inc.

TAPESTRY is a trademark of Simon & Schuster, Inc.

Printed in the U.S.A.

To our children,
Kim, John, Steve and Vance.
Because they are.

Embrace the Wind

Chapter One

FAWN RAN THROUGH THE FOREST, HER HEART THUD-ding painfully and her breath a ragged fire in her throat. Not far behind she could hear her pursuers. Their angry war cries stirred her to run faster even though she was stumbling from weariness.

The long fringe of her doeskin ceremonial dress caught on the high brambles and low hanging branches, but she dared not head for open ground. In a fair race the seasoned warriors would be upon her in moments. Instead, she kept to the under-brush and tried to remember the wily escape routes of the fox, her secret totem.

A swiftly running stream appeared before her and she leaped into it. It would be easier to follow the water's flow downstream, but the Indians would expect that since they must be aware of her exhaustion. Fawn forged her way against the flood, her feet tingling from the icy cold of the spring thaw. She kept to the rockier patches as much as possible and prayed that the quick current would sweep away any mud she stirred in her wake.

The stream broadened and curved. With the Indians' shouts fainter now, she assumed they had gone in the opposite direction, but she dared not slow down. This was still the hunting grounds of the Arapaho tribe and they were familiar with every inch. As soon as they found no sign of her downstream, they would be on her trail again.

Just ahead, the protective cover of the woods alongside the stream gave way to an open meadow, but she continued on against the swift current. She knew she was clearly visible in the water to anyone nearby, but she couldn't risk following the river's banks. The long grasses that bordered the stream would leave her trail as clearly as a marked sign.

Above the meadow the stream narrowed again and became deeper. Once more huge trees hugged its banks, their dense foliage blotting out the sunlight as their limbs arched together high overhead. The water was above her knees here and it was increasingly difficult to run against the current. Still she pressed on.

Suddenly she heard the war cries again. She jerked her head around to stare in fright at the way she had come. They had overtaken her so easily! To the spur of ever nearer shouts she plunged on in the icy water. The stream took another sharp curve, and off to her left, near the bank, was a dead tree, half submerged in the water. Leaves floated lazily on the surface as the water eddied about the hulk, and in the deep shade from the trees overhead the inky water was almost opaque. It was her only chance.

Fawn waded to the huge log and again cast a fearful glance over her shoulder. Already she could see Walking Tall, the son of her late husband and the new chief of the tribe. He was bent over as he ran, studying the sides of the river. His face was streaked with white mourning paint, as was her own, and he looked as fierce as a wolf.

Curling her long auburn braids around her hand so they wouldn't float, Fawn took a deep breath and dove beneath the fallen log. The water closed over her head silencing the blood-freezing cries of her former friends and family. She opened her eyes and through the dimness saw the mossy underside of the log and its great, hairy roots.

Her heart was pounding from terror and exertion, her lungs demanding air, but Fawn forced herself to go beneath the log. Using her hands to guide her, she eased up the back side. The trunk was revoltingly slimy beneath her fingers, but she made herself stay close.

On the other side she dared surface just long enough to gasp a lung full of air. The warriors were so close now she could hear their footsteps. Silently she went under and hoped the great tree would hide her.

Her fear was so great that she was no longer

aware of the icy chill of the water. She had called upon all her willpower and stubborn determination to remain beneath the tree and overcome her growing need for air. A dull roar began in her ears and bright flashes sparked beneath her eyelids. Still she waited. When she could bear it no longer, she threaded her way through the roots and, still under water, worked her way as close to the bank as possible. She could see a slight overhang above her where the tree had pulled the earth apart in its fall. Grasses fell over the side like a green waterfall, nearly touching the water. There was enough space between the water and the overhang for Fawn's head to surface.

Above and behind her, she heard the warriors of her tribe arguing. Walking Tall was positive she was nearby, possibly upstream. Storm Dancer, her stepbrother, was equally sure she had gone downstream and had crossed over the rocky shoreline and into the pine trees. Although Walking Tall was now chief, he had been so for only a few hours, and the braves were not yet accustomed to his rule. On the other hand, Storm Dancer was a hunter and rarely wrong about a trail. Almost all the warriors agreed with him that a woman would choose the easier path downstream, and head for the pines, which would make the trail harder to follow.

Fawn forced herself to breathe silently through her mouth and beseeched Walking Tall's totem to send him down river.

After what seemed to be an endless discussion, Walking Tall was persuaded, and the band of war-

4

riors padded off in a nearly soundless run. Now that their prey was out of sight, and possibly earshot, they no longer wasted their breath in war cries.

Fawn waited until the men were well gone before she submerged and swam through the roots and out from under the tree. She lay her palm on its scaly bark and silently thanked it for its protection. Then she started against the current again, half swimming, half wading.

At last she found a place where she could safely leave the water. A gravelly shoal fingered out into the water and led to a jumble of flat granite. She gratefully waded across the stream and stepped out onto the rocky ground. She took off her dress and wrung it out into the stream as she shivered in the cool wind. When the braves didn't find her in the pine woods, Walking Tall might persuade them to search upstream again. She could not afford to leave a wet trail behind her.

She kicked off her moccasins and rolled them in her dress. Taking a deep breath, she started out over the flat rocks, her bare feet leaving no wet trace. She couldn't stop shivering, but she did her best to be careful so she wouldn't lose her balance and fall, or even worse, sprain an ankle. Clasping her clothes near her body, she hurried to the far side as quickly as she could. To her great relief, she found a forest of towering pines.

Quickly she redressed and forced her wet shoes back onto her feet. Any drops they left here would disappear into the golden brown carpet of needles that had fallen from the ancient trees. She had no idea where she might be, but since she knew her tribe was uphill, she followed the downward slope.

The forest was a broad one and relatively free from undergrowth. Her way was easy and she moved with good speed, her moccasins leaving no trail behind her. At the end of the pines, she skirted a small meadow of wild flowers and again set her course downhill.

By dusk, Fawn knew the warriors had stopped their search and returned to their village. The cremation of her dead husband, Chief Many Rivers, had to be accomplished before sundown or his angry spirit would haunt the tribe, and Many Rivers had been feared even in life. Fawn wondered if the funeral pyre would end their pursuit, or if her stepson would swear revenge because she had shamed his father. She knew his motive was not a great love he bore for Many Rivers, but disapproval of his father's choice for a wife long before it was clear that the match was an unhappy one.

When Fawn had been informed by Walking Tall that she was to follow Many Rivers to the Great Hunting Ground, she had argued that his first wife had already preceded him and that *she* could tend to his needs! Fawn had only been joined with him for two months, and she saw no reason at all to end her life in order to serve a man she had detested. But her arguments had fallen on deaf ears.

The forest opened onto a rocky cliff and Fawn stepped out to look around. Never, as long as she could remember, had she been so far from the tribe. She had also never been alone. Not really. On occasion she had gone apart from the others to sit out her cycles, but there had always been other women in the same condition; and they had waited together and enjoyed the respite from serving the men. Now as she gazed over the edge of the cliff and saw the hazy depths so far below, she felt a sickening dizziness.

Could a woman live alone? The Shaman frequently lived apart for long periods of time while he waited for the Great Spirit to speak, but the Shaman was a man and carried weapons. Fawn had not had time to grab a weapon, though she knew how to use one, had it been necessary to help defend her tribe. She had only the small knife she used for household chores that hung at her side. It was large enough to skin small animals, but would be of little use in bringing down game or defending herself.

She sat on the cliff and confronted her fears. It would be foolish to join another Arapaho tribe for they would immediately turn her over to Walking Tall. She might find a band of Utes. She spoke enough of their language to get by, but of course they were not of the People. Nor were the Shoshone, who occupied much of the territory to the east and were the sworn enemies of the Arapaho besides. Fawn's thoughts turned to the valley below and the small settlement of whites that Many Rivers had called Bancroft. She assumed this to be their tribal name. But to go to them was even more unthinkable, because they were her own deadly foes. A white man had shot and killed her father— by accident he had said—only about a month before she had been wed to Many Rivers, and since then hatred for them had grown in her heart. No, she could not go to the whites.

That left her a life of solitude. Fawn looked down where an eagle was soaring in tight circles in search of food. Her spirit greeted his and she saw his lesson. The eagle had no tribe, yet he survived. She sighed. The eagle also had a lifelong mate and was equipped with sharp talons, a rending beak, and the gift of swift and noiseless flight. The thought occurred to her that this sign might be more meaningful to a weaponed warrior.

The sun was dropping low in the valley beyond and the sky's blue haze was softening to rose. Soon night would fall and she could no longer stay on the cliff. Fawn got to her feet and cast one more look at the chasm below. She had overcome her fear. Perhaps she could survive after all.

She went back into the woods in search of a safe place to sleep. She carried a flint in her pouch, but she dared not make a fire, not when she didn't know who might see it. Her dress had almost dried, but with the air cooling rapidly as the sun set, it was clammy against her skin. The wet moccasins had rubbed raw spots on her heels, and she knew her feet would be even sorer tomorrow.

Fawn had never slept outside and she wondered how the warriors endured it. Boys were taught these survival skills, but girls were trained only in household crafts. If she slept on the ground would she be eaten by a bear? If she slept in a tree would she fall out and be eaten by a bear anyway? None of the trees nearby had accommodating limbs, so she decided to take her chances on the ground.

Night was falling fast now, and she felt curiously light-headed. At times she shivered with a deep chill, while at others she was as hot as if it were midday. Hoping her fevers were only from fatigue, Fawn made herself a nest of sorts in the dry pine needles. Her bed pricked her, but as she lay down she became too dizzy to rise again. If she were eaten by a bear, so be it; she could do no better for herself tonight.

Fawn awoke from the restless half-sleep that had plagued her all night. When she opened her eyes, the trees loomed above her in wavering fuzziness. She became aware of her surroundings so slowly that she was uncertain which was nightmare and which was reality. She licked her dry lips and squinted to bring the forest into focus.

By the brightness of the light filtering through the thick leaves, she judged it to be well into morning, perhaps nearly noon. Painfully she straightened her legs and shivered with a sudden chill. At last she sat up and huddled miserably on the forest floor. Maybe, she reflected dismally, being eaten by a bear would have been preferable.

With shaky hands she loosened her braids and ran her fingers through her hair. The dark, auburn masses tumbled well below her waist. As she worked the tangles out, she wished for the comb her stepbrother, Storm Dancer, had whittled for her on her name day the year before. At last her hair lay smooth and shiny along her slender back. She parted the strands as well as she could and braided them into two thick plaits, then bound them with rawhide thongs.

Knowing she could rest no longer, Fawn caught the nearest tree trunk and pulled herself to her feet. Once erect, she swayed feverishly as she tried to recall her route from the previous day. Downhill —that was it. Weakly she pushed herself away from the tree and made her feet walk forward.

The pain of the blisters helped clear her head, and she knew she needed to find water. She was burning with fever and her mouth felt like hot wool. She wasn't hungry, but instinct told her she needed food, even if she found only berries.

Fawn was hardly aware of leaving the pine grove and entering a thicket of aspen and alders. Only when her feet became wet did she realize she was wading in a creek. Numbly she looked at the water, then bent and scooped some into her mouth. It felt uncomfortably cold on her tongue, and she fought down a wave of nausea. Plodding on, she left the creek and crawled over an outcropping of fissured granite, not knowing where she was headed but dimly aware that each step took her further from Walking Tall's tribe and the certain death that awaited her there.

By midafternoon Fawn faltered on in a dream-like trance. Exhausted, she struggled up a low hill and had just reached its crest when she stumbled, rolling over and over down the grassy slope until her head hit a pair of leather shod feet. She lay there unconscious.

The huge man started in surprise and his hunting knife was already poised to fight when he identified the leatherclad figure as that of a woman. Wary of an Indian trap, he rolled her over and looked hard at her face.

"Good Lord," he gasped. "It's a white woman!"

Chapter Two

NATHAN STODDARD KNELT BESIDE THE UNCONSCIOUS woman and felt for a pulse as he stared cautiously in the direction from which she had come. She was dressed in a midcalf-length ceremonial dress and ankle-length pants, fringed and encrusted with brilliantly colored beads and dyed porcupine quills that he knew couldn't be the garb of a slave woman. Her face was caked with a heavy white paste that signified mourning, but her hair was still uncut. What she was doing here, he couldn't fathom.

She must have been running from the Indians, he guessed. Nathan slipped his arms under her knees and shoulders and lifted her with little effort.

She appeared to be a rather tall woman, but Nathan was a giant of a man with powerful arms and legs as thick as tree stumps, and he carried her as easily as if she were a child.

His horse, a dun gelding of uncertain temperament, was tied to a sapling not far from where the woman had fallen. When he saw Nathan approaching, he whickered softly, but he rolled his eyes in consternation at the unconscious woman. As Nathan came nearer he shied away, straining to break the leather reins that tethered him.

"Be still, damn you," Nathan growled. "Blamed fool horse."

The animal pricked his ears and slackened the tension in the reins. He allowed Nathan to lay the woman over the saddle but nipped at Nathan's leg as he mounted behind her.

Nathan lifted the woman to a sitting position and let her lay against his broad chest. Even through her clothes he could feel the feverish heat of her body. He looked back again the way she had come and strained his ears to catch any sounds of pursuit. Only the normal stirrings of the forest could be heard.

He gathered the reins tighter and nudged the horse forward. In spite of the double load, the animal moved eagerly into a smooth trot as he picked his way through the trees.

Nathan's cabin lay downhill to the east along Wolf Creek. Nestled in a grove of tall Ponderosa pines, it wasn't far from a cliff that presented a striking vista of the Rocky Mountains. Behind the cabin was a barn and several outbuildings, among them a smokehouse and a tanning shed.

He rode beneath the pines, his horse's hooves making little noise on the thick carpet of needles. He felt a welcoming tranquility from the stand of pines near his cabin, almost as if they were glad to have him back. Inside his huge frame, Nathan housed the soul of a poet—a fact he went to great lengths to conceal from his friends. No man was quicker to fight or harder to overcome than Nathan Stoddard, and only a few were as sensitive to the colors of a sunset or to the beauty of the majestic Rockies.

Riding to the cabin, Nathan dismounted and lifted the still unconscious woman off the horse. Her head rolled against him and lay on his shoulder, her breath warm against his neck. Nathan was surprised at the protectiveness this aroused in him.

"You poor thing," he rumbled in his deep voice. "Lord only knows what you've been through."

He shouldered open the door and carried her inside. The horse poked his head in to follow, but Nathan spoke to him sharply and the animal backed out. "Damned horse," he muttered. "Acts like he thinks this is a barn." He went into the small bedroom—a luxury few mountain cabins afforded —and lay her on his bed. He had built the bed wide and long, for his own comfort. In its midst, the woman looked somewhat lost.

She moaned and a chill violently shook her. Nathan pulled up a bearskin cover and tucked her into its warmth. Still watching her, he struck a flint to the dry tinder in the hearth and blew on it to produce a flame. He lay a couple of logs on the andirons and dusted his hands on his pants.

He strode back into the cabin's main room to get a black iron cooking pot, then headed to the stream to fill it. His horse followed like a large dog, occasionally biting at him and missing by mere inches. "Horse, I've never seen anything like this," Nathan said conversationally. "She just came out of nowhere, fell down, and rolled into my legs. Now what do you suppose a white woman was doing way up there? Her beadwork is Arapaho." The horse snorted as if in comment, and Nathan rubbed its velvety nose. "My guess is that Chief Many Rivers captured her, but I haven't heard any news of a raid in several years."

Nathan stood and carried the pot back up the gentle incline to the cabin. The horse dogged his footsteps. "Wherever she came from, she's in a bad way. Her skin's as hot as a cheap pistol. Wait here," he told the horse as he went inside.

She still lay as he had left her, and Nathan put the water over the fire. After another long look, he went back to the horse. Without bothering to take the reins, Nathan walked to the barn, the horse right behind him.

"She's still asleep," he informed the animal. "I sure hope those savages didn't hurt her bad. From all I can see she has a fever, but that's about it." Once inside the barn he went to the animal's side and began to loosen the cinch. The horse flattened his ears and snapped at Nathan's arm, his strong teeth clicking audibly.

"You damned horse," Nathan complained. "One of these days you're going to misjudge and get me, and there's going to be hell to pay!" He pulled off the saddle and blanket as the horse kicked at him. Nathan ignored the huge hoof that barely missed his leg and carried the saddle and blanket into the small tack room.

He tossed the saddle onto a wooden sawhorse and lay the blanket over it, hairy side up to dry. Going back to the door he patted the horse, who was sticking his head inquisitively inside. He unbuckled the bridle's chin strap and pulled the leather off over the animal's ears as the horse opened his mouth to release the bit. Nathan looped the bridle over the saddle horn.

"Back up," he said to the animal, who was now half inside the room. The horse snorted and shuffled out into the barn. Nathan got his brush and began currying the buckskin coat as he talked. "I'm not too sure what to do with her, Horse. Once she's well enough to travel, I mean. I guess I'll take her down to Bancroft and see if anybody there knows of her family." He brushed until the horse's wheat-colored body gleamed evenly in the dim light of the barn. Then he brushed the tangles from the black mane and tail.

Nathan hung the brush on its nail and went back into the tack room. He opened a bin and scooped up a bucket of horse feed. "Go get in your stall," he ordered the horse.

Horse flattened his ears and bowed his proud neck as he trotted the length of the barn and waited for Nathan to open the gate. There were four stalls along the wall, all open to the pasture. Two of the stalls were occupied by mules, and Nathan paused to scratch one of the dark brown heads.

"Hello, Stewart," Nathan greeted the mule. "Are you ready for supper?" One by one he fed the animals and patted each briefly before shutting the tack room and leaving the barn.

Nathan walked quickly back to the cabin and into the bedroom. Sitting on the edge of the bed, he put his hand on the woman's forehead and was appalled by the searing heat. Maybe washing the thick paint off her face would help. He wet a cloth in the warm water and began to dab at the white clay. The paint was caked on her skin, but Nathan's gentle fingers and the warm water took effect. When the paint was removed, Nathan sponged the woman's face with cool water, hoping to bring down her fever.

She was the most beautiful woman he had ever seen. Her nose was straight and finely sculpted, and her lips curved gracefully as if she were accustomed to smiling. Eyebrows as delicate as birds' wings arched over her eyes, and her forehead was high and smooth. Her skin was tanned and flushed with fever but it molded softly over high cheekbones and a jawline and chin that might be described as stubborn. Her throat was long and slender, and he could see the pulse beat in the hollow of her neck. Two thick braids of the deepest shade of red, tied with leather thongs, fell onto the pillow.

Slowly Nathan uncovered her and loosened the lacing at the neck of her dress. He was reluctant to take such liberties with her, but bathing just her face wasn't enough to break the fever. He hoped she would understand.

Carefully he removed her moccasins, frowning at the angry red blisters on her feet. It would be a while before she could wear shoes comfortably. He untied the drawstring at her waist and pulled off her pants. Her legs were graceful and long, her ankles delicate. He eased the dress up over her head and lay her back onto the bed.

Her breasts were fuller than he had expected, and her waist slim and firm before rounding into the swell of her hips. Although she was slender she didn't appear to have been starved. He rolled her over onto her stomach and frowned again. Dark bruises marked her back and the gentle curve of her buttocks. Someone had beaten her quite recently.

Nathan got fresh water and began to sponge her back. The water was much cooler than her fevered skin, and when he touched her, she jerked away.

"There now, ma'am," he said in a soothing voice as he would to a frightened animal. "I'm not hurting you. We just need to bring down this fever."

He ran the cloth over her again and this time she lay still, although he was certain she had never really regained consciousness. The texture of her skin was silky and fine, and he felt stirrings of excitement in spite of himself. She was a real lady, not like the floozies at Prairie Belle's down in Bancroft, or the hardened wives of the miners who still worked the dying gold town. How had she happened to be here on the mountain? he wondered. Lately a wagon train of settlers had arrived in Bancroft and were staking claims to homestead the valley. But he had just come from Bancroft, and there was no talk of a missing woman. He ran the washcloth over her graceful back and down the curve of her hips. She was definitely the sort that would be missed.

After a few minutes Nathan rolled the woman over onto her back and continued his ministrations. He found it much more difficult to remain detached as he sponged the hot flesh of her breasts. The rosy nipples tightened as if in eagerness when he touched them, and she moved her head restlessly on the pillow. Nathan had never been known for celibacy, but he was certainly not the sort who would take advantage of a helpless woman, either. He hastily turned her over again and returned to the safer area of her back.

For over an hour he continued sponging her back and face. Gradually she became cooler and her breathing deepened into the rhythm of genuine sleep. He put his large hand on her brow and then felt the tender skin along her ribs. Both were cooler, and she seemed to be resting easier. Gently he drew the bearskin up and gazed down at her for a few more minutes as questions raced through his head. At last he stood and went into the other room to prepare his supper.

For three days the strange woman drifted in and out of fever. Even when she was cool, her eyes remained closed in a half sleep. Twice she mumbled words, but he couldn't hear them well enough to make sense of what she said. He made her a broth of meat and onions and gave her frequent sips of boneset and snakeroot tea. When he put the spoon to her lips, she swallowed obediently, but she still lay in feverish delirium most of the time.

Nathan had made a pallet for himself in front of the fire where he could hear her if she called out. Even though his bed was large and she would be unaware of his presence, he couldn't leap the bounds of propriety and sleep beside her. He stayed close to her, sponging away her fever, feeding her as much of the liquids as she would take, and leaving her alone only when absolutely necessary.

Fawn blinked and opened her eyes. The woods had mysteriously disappeared, and for a few sickening minutes she thought she was back in Many Rivers' wigwam. Her brain felt foggy and her thoughts moved slowly, as if they were trying to run under water. Under the mossy log in the icy stream. She closed her eyes and struggled to recall if this had really happened or if it were part of the strange dream she seemed to be having.

She opened her eyes again and tried to focus on her surroundings. Gradually the fuzzy brownness took shape and she noticed the wall was made of squared timbers. Felled trees? Where was she? Awareness was flooding over her now, and she saw the chair beside the bed where she lay. Her clothes were folded neatly on the seat. She moved her hand over her stomach and felt her bare skin. Her eyes opened wide. Where was she!

Her body ached. All her muscles were sore and she moved slowly. She turned her head and saw rafters above her and a door opposite the bed. Shifting further, she spotted the fireplace and the man who knelt beside it. Her eyes dilated in fear as she took in his ruddy blond hair and the buckskin clothing that molded his large body. A white man! The enemy!

Without taking her eyes from the man, Fawn reached out and groped at her clothing. Would it be there? Her long fingers found and curled around the handle of her knife. It wasn't large and powerful like a brave's, but it was as sharp as a whetstone could make it. Keeping her eyes on the man's broad back, she raised herself from the bed.

Silently, she swung her legs over the side, and as her bare toes found the wooden floor, she carefully stood. The room seemed to whirl about her and her knees were alarmingly weak, but she tightened her grip on the weapon. One good stroke. That's all it would take. As she eased off the bed, the mattress of corn husks rustled faintly.

The man half turned when he saw her movement, and a look of astonishment crossed his face. Fawn gave a shriek and hurled herself at him. The man moved quickly and grabbed her wrist just as the knife plunged down toward his throat. He stopped the wickedly gleaming blade a hair's breadth from his neck and caught her to him.

Fawn was weak from illness, but she had a will born of fright and desperation. Wordlessly she fought the man, using her teeth and feet to aid her. He cried out as she bit his arm, and he grabbed her hair to force her away. Still he held her hand and refused to let go even when she hit him in the stomach as hard as she could with her other fist.

Before she could strike again he shook the knife free and threw her onto the bed. He pinned her down and held her as she fought to get away.

"Be still!" he ordered. "What in the hell are you trying to do?"

His voice was deep, like a bear's, and his words were incomprehensible. Fawn fought harder. "Let me go!" she demanded in the tongue of the People.

Nathan pinned her hands above her head and waited until she stopped struggling. She lay panting beneath him, too weak to continue fighting. "Lady, what's gotten into you?" Nathan demanded. "You're acting like some kind of wild Indian, coming at me with a knife like that!"

Fawn glared up at him and tried to make sense of his words. Some were familiar, but she couldn't catch their meaning. They sounded like the language her real mother had used—long, long ago. "Turn me loose," she ordered.

He frowned. She was speaking Indian! The shock of it nearly made him lose his grip on her. "Why are you talking like that?" he asked in confusion.

She struggled again, then lay still as she tried to regain her breath. "You're heavy! Turn me loose. If you let me leave I won't harm you or tell my brother where you are!" It was a desperate gamble, but he might believe it. After all, who had ever heard of a woman being alone in the woods?

Nathan frowned. She was speaking a dialect he didn't know. Arapaho, maybe? Shoshone? "Be still. I won't hurt you," he said in halting Ute. It was the only Indian dialect he knew and he had learned very little of it.

She stopped fighting and looked up at him warily. "You speak Ute?" she said. He had mispronounced the words so badly she wasn't sure if she had heard him correctly.

"Some." Her accent made the words almost unintelligible and he concluded she was not very familiar with that language. "What tongue do you speak?" he asked haltingly as he continued to hold her down.

Although he had not hurt her, Fawn felt a quiver of fear. His face was so near hers and it was so unlike all the faces with which she was accustomed. Not only was the hair on his head a strange yellow, but hair of the same color grew on the lower part of his face. She had seen a man with a moustache once, but never one with a beard. And his eyes were as blue as a summer sky with flecks of silver in

23

their depths. Again his deep voice rumbled the indistinct words, and she struggled to interpret them. "I am of the People," she said arrogantly.

"What people?"

"Arapaho, of course," she said indignantly. "Turn me loose!"

Nathan suddenly became aware that he lay upon her and that she was naked. Blushing, he cautiously released her. "Be still!" he warned.

Her angry green eyes glinted fire but she remained still. He flicked the covers over her and sat on the edge of the bed. "Where did you come from?" he asked in English. "Why do you speak Arapaho?"

She frowned and looked from his lips to his eyes.

"Do you understand me?"

"I do not speak that tongue," she said in Ute. "It is the language of my enemy."

Nathan stared at her. "Did you say enemy? But you're white! It must be your language!"

"I am Arapaho!" she confirmed indignantly.

"Lady, nobody ever heard of an Indian with red hair and green eyes! You're as white as I am," Nathan argued, slipping back into English. "I ought to know!" He gestured at her body and although she didn't understand the words, she caught his meaning and pulled the covers tighter around her.

Nathan frowned and tried to figure out what to do next. He had not expected this unlikely development. "My name is Nathan Stoddard," he said slowly in English. He gestured at himself and repeated, "Nathan."

Slowly she took her arm from the cover and pointed at him. "Nathan?" When he smiled and nodded, she motioned toward herself. "Fawn."

"That's your name?" he asked in Ute.

"Fawn," she repeated in Ute.

He pointed at her and said in English, "Fawn."

She nodded uncertainly. In the dimness of her memory the English word seemed to mean the same as the Indian word for her name, although it was shorter. She had no idea what his name meant for it had sounded the same in both English and Ute. "Nathan?" she said again.

He nodded and grinned. Somehow he didn't look quite as frightening now, and she relaxed a bit. The exertion had tired her and she lay back onto the pillow.

"Sleep now," he said first in English, then in Ute.

Fawn tried to stay awake. He had not yet harmed her, but he was still the enemy. One did not sleep in the bed of one's enemy. But her body was treacherously weak, and her eyes closed in spite of her fears.

Chapter Three

FAWN RAISED HER HEAD AND LOOKED CAUTIOUSLY around the room. The large man was no longer there, and a light rain peppered the glass windowpane. She concluded that she must have slept a long time for hunger made her stomach rumble. She sat up, testing herself. Feeling almost well, though weak, she decided this might be her best chance to escape from the white man.

Being careful to make no noise, Fawn searched for her knife. It no longer lay on the floor where it had fallen, nor were her clothes still on the chair. She stood and wrapped the bearskin blanket around her to cover her nakedness. Through the doorway she could see another room. Perhaps her clothes were in there.

As she padded lightly across the floor, she was aware not only of the soreness of her bare feet, but also the strange feel of wooden planks beneath her. It felt odd to be inside such a large enclosure. Even Many Rivers' spacious wigwam had been only half the size of this room. Yet the man called Nathan seemed to live here alone!

She had made no sound as she crossed the room, yet Nathan looked up when she approached the doorway. "Good morning," he said cheerfully. "Care for some breakfast?"

She had no idea what he had said, but the smell of frying meat drew her toward the fire.

"Where is my knife?" she asked in Ute.

"It has been taken away." Nathan's Ute was sketchy and he hadn't phrased the words exactly right, but he saw by the flash of anger in her eyes that she had understood.

"Give it back. It belongs to me." Fawn lifted her head regally and clutched the bearskin.

"So you can cut my throat? Sorry, ma'am. I'm not that big a fool."

"Talk Ute!" she commanded.

He sighed, "Miss Fawn, you've got to learn English." Then he added in Ute, "The knife is gone."

"Where have you hidden my clothes? Is it white man's way to steal from a helpless woman?"

"You weren't so helpless yesterday when you tried to cut my throat. Your clothes are over there." Nathan nodded toward a shelf on the far wall.

"Where are my moccasins?" Fawn asked, lifting her foot out from under her bearskin cover.

"You don't need them now. Your feet are still so sore that you're limping. I'll give them back to you when you're well enough to travel."

"Travel?"

"To leave here. I'm taking you back to your people."

A spark of fear lit her deep green eyes. "To my people? You would give me to them?"

"It's where you belong," he said firmly.

"No. They will kill me. They expect me to go with my dead husband so that I can see to his needs."

Nathan studied her face. Had he misunderstood her words? Ute was not an easy language. "I don't know what you're talking about. Speak slower."

She gave him an exasperated look as if he were being particularly obtuse. "My husband has died, and his son, Walking Tall, hates me and will kill me if I go back."

"Your son is Walking Tall? Many Rivers' boy? It can't be. You don't look old enough."

"He is not my son. He is my husband's son." She glanced uneasily around the cabin. "And don't speak his father's name, lest his spirit overhear you and settle here."

Nathan stared at her. "Many Rivers is dead? Since when?"

"Several days ago. Now Walking Tall is chief." She came closer to him and looked up at him beseechingly. "You won't send me back, will you?"

"To the Indians? Of course not!"

"But you said you were going to send me to my people," she said in confusion.

"You're not an Indian. You're white! I meant I would take you to Bancroft and see if anyone there can trace your real family."

"I am Arapaho!" she stated indignantly. "They are my real family."

"Then why is your skin white?" he countered. "No, ma'am, you're a white lady all right."

"I am not, and don't tell me that I am."

With a long fork Nathan fished the bacon out of the pan. He saw her eyes follow it hungrily, so he cut a thick slab of bread to add to the plate and gave it to her. "Eat," he said.

Fawn took a slice of bacon warily, as if she feared it might be a trap, but hunger was stronger than caution and she ate it quickly.

Nathan sat opposite her and leaned his forearms on the table as he watched her. "Why do you say you're an Indian?" he asked.

"Because I am," she answered in surprise. "My father was Elk Tooth and my second mother was Clouds Passing."

"Your second mother?" he asked. "Did I hear you right?"

"Yes. My first mother, my real one, died when I was very young, and then my father married Clouds Passing."

"Do you remember what your real mother looked like?"

Fawn's forehead puckered as she struggled with

a vague recollection. "She was tall and her hair was lighter than the People's. It was brown, like an elk."

"Then she was a white woman."

Fawn shrugged. "Perhaps. She spoke a language I no longer remember. My father, Elk Tooth, told her to talk to me only in Arapaho, but she did not always obey him."

"Was Elk Tooth your real father?"

"No," Fawn said sadly. "I wished he had been, but his only true child was my brother, Storm Dancer. It was a sorrow of my father's that he had only one child and me." She raised her chin defiantly, "But he was very proud of me and treated me as his own."

Nathan wondered who her real father was. Obviously Fawn didn't know, but clearly he must have been white. It was a sad story. Fawn's mother probably had been pregnant when she was captured by Indians. It must have been her condition that had saved her life.

Nathan cut her another slice of bread, but hesitated. "You spoke English once and you can learn to do it again. The word for this is bread."

Fawn grabbed at it and glared at him.

"Bread," he repeated calmly, holding it beyond her reach.

She faced him stubbornly and repeated the Indian word for the food.

"Nope," Nathan said. "Bread."

Fawn tightened her lips and glared at him.

"All right," Nathan said with a shrug, "if you're

not hungry." He got up and took the bread with him.

"Bread!" Fawn snapped and held out her hand.

He grinned and gave it to her. "That wasn't so difficult, was it? You'll soon be speaking English as well as anyone," he told her in Ute.

Fawn refrained from answering, but she rebelled silently. This was obviously not the time to try to escape.

For the next few days Fawn rested and regained her strength. The bout of fever had left her weaker than she had realized, and she had postponed her escape attempt. She wasn't sure when she stopped her planning, but the need to get away had faded as her health returned. The only thing that concerned her now was that Nathan might any minute decide that he wanted her physically. So far he had made no demands upon her, and for that she was grateful. But why he hadn't puzzled her. Could it be that white men did not feel the urges that braves did? Many Rivers had never given her pleasure in their sex, but she had heard other wives describe the same act in glowing terms. Would she be able to find pleasure in Nathan's arms?

Nathan asked her to join him by the fire after they finished their supper, and she cautiously agreed. As she stared at the flames dancing across the log, she felt his eyes upon her. Turning, she saw him look quickly away. Fawn moved uneasily. Was he about to take advantage of her? She gauged the distance to the door in case she needed to escape.

But he only sighed as if he had something weighing on his mind. Perversely, this made Fawn feel drawn to him. *Why* didn't he want to touch her? she wondered.

The firelight flickered over his amber hair and emphasized the vivid blue of his eyes. Fawn pretended to ignore him as she watched the movements he made. He crossed his arms over his chest, propped his feet against the chimney, and leaned precariously back in his chair. His sleeves were rolled up to his elbows, and the fire and lamplight burnished the fine hair on his arms to gold. His hands looked powerful even when he was at rest, with square palms and strongly formed fingers. Veins rippled under his tanned skin and muscles broadened his forearms. He was a large man and magnificently made. Fawn found she was actually wishing he would touch her.

Embarrassed at the improper channel her thoughts were taking, Fawn looked quickly back to the fire. She was aware that he was watching her again and she blushed awkwardly.

The silence was making her tense, so Fawn cast about for something they could talk about. "Will you have more?" she asked, indicating a smoke-blackened coffee pot.

"Coffee. Yes," he said quickly, as if he, too, had been wanting to break the silence. He leaned forward and handed her his metal cup. "Would you like some?"

She shook her head. She had tasted some the day before and found it unpleasing. Carefully, she poured the steaming black liquid into the cup and passed it to him. Their fingers touched and she started. A tingle raced across her hand and up her arm. Quickly she pulled back.

Nathan studied her thoughtfully. "Did you burn yourself on the cup?"

"No."

He leaned back and carefully sipped the hot coffee. "We've been having good weather for this time of year," he ventured after a while.

"What?" She was still having some difficulty understanding his accented Ute.

"Not much rain. We've had very little bad weather."

"Oh. Yes, that is right." She felt a thrill at the sound of his voice. The words mattered little, but the timbre seemed to trigger an emotional response deep within her. "Soon meadows will be green and filled with flowers," she said in Ute and sign language.

Nathan nodded. Again the silence lengthened, and they both stared at the fire as if seeking inspiration.

Why does he not touch me? Fawn wondered silently. Does he find me so unattractive? She became embarrassed at her thoughts and hastily reassured herself that she was glad he had not tried to dishonor her.

He shifted in his chair and Fawn was instantly aware of every fiber of her body. Suddenly it occurred to her that he might be sleepy and that he couldn't go to bed as long as she was in the room.

Abruptly, she stood and he looked at her in surprise. "I am going to bed now," she said.

"So early?" He got to his feet as well and looked down at her.

Fawn nodded. She was unaccustomed to seeing anyone much taller than herself, and found that she had to tilt her head back to see Nathan's eyes. She liked that. "Yes," she said as her eyes were captured by his. "I will see you tomorrow." For a moment she seemed unable to tear herself away from the magnetism of his gaze. But then he smiled and stepped aside and the mood was broken.

"Sleep well," he said with determined cheerfulness. He watched her leave the room and close the bedroom door behind her before he sat back down. Leaning forward, he rested his elbows on his knees and stared at the fire. All day he had been unable to keep his eyes off her, and then when he tried to talk, he seemed to say only dull, inconsequential things. All his life he had been known as a glib talker with a quick and ready wit. Yet somehow this mysterious woman made him tongue-tied and bashful. It was very confusing.

For the next few days, Fawn rested and gathered her strength. Her feet were healing rapidly, faster than she wished. As soon as she was able to travel, she would have to go, and she was becoming more and more reluctant to leave.

Nathan sat with her often, and gradually they talked more comfortably. He taught her English words when her Ute failed her, and she found the language easy—more proof, as he said, that it had been her first language. As he became accustomed to her presence, he appeared more relaxed and his sense of humor returned. Often Fawn missed the intent of his jokes, but laughed along with him. Even if she didn't understand the words, she could follow what he said. Fawn soon looked forward to their conversations. Never had she talked to any man so freely, except her brother and father, and she liked it. She enjoyed hearing his deep voice, and his laugh was infectious. She too talked more openly, and soon she noticed she measured her day by his visits with her. So often did he stop whatever he was doing to talk to her, in fact, she wondered how he ever got anything else accomplished.

Yet the more she enjoyed his company, the more she worried at night when the cabin was still and her thoughts kept her awake. Soon she would be strong enough to travel—already she felt much better than she admitted—and then she would have to go away.

On the day Nathan returned her moccasins, Fawn held them as if she were almost afraid to touch them. She had hoped he would not yet know she was well enough to travel. And, unless she had misunderstood his garbled Ute, he still planned to take her to Bancroft and turn her over to the whites. She had heard terrible tales of what happened to Indians at the mercy of whites. Especially Indian women.

After the door closed, Fawn stood frozen for a

minute. He had told her to get ready and that he would be waiting for her in the barn. His face had been almost without expression and the sparkle she had so often seen in his eyes was gone. He must be angry with her. But why? She didn't want to leave Nathan and she certainly didn't want to give herself to the savage whites. But obviously he wished to be rid of her. This knowledge stung, and she felt tears gather in her eyes. Angrily, she blinked them away. She wouldn't stay where she was unwelcome.

"Get ready," he had said. What was to get ready? She was already dressed in the one garment she now owned, and her only other possession, her knife, had not been returned to her. Fawn seemed frozen in place, incapable of moving from the spot. Unable to accept that she was to be cast out again, she turned her thoughts to the dress she wore. The soft doeskin felt good against her skin and the silky fringe moved sensuously with each motion of her body. She had sewn the beads with the porcupine quills and was very proud of her handiwork. Few maidens in her tribe had had such a fine dress for their marriage, but then it had been many years since the chief had taken a wife. It had been a matter of pride to her to be well dressed on such a momentous occasion. The dress was also to have been her funeral shroud, though no one then could have guessed it would be necessary to use it for that purpose so very soon.

Fawn touched the glass beads her brother had brought her from the trading post at Fire Bluff. She had sewn each of them with a prayer song for a happy marriage. What had gone wrong? Had she not directed her prayers to the Great Spirit? Her marriage to Many Rivers had been anything but happy. She tried guiltily to summon up some good memory of him in case his spirit was passing by, but she failed. He had died while beating her, and she felt only relief that he was gone.

Fawn reluctantly sat on the edge of the bed and pulled on her moccasins. Although they had become stiff after her escape through the river bed, she found them as soft as they had been when she had first made them. Nathan had evidently been working on them without her knowledge. She couldn't imagine a man being willing to do such a thing, but she was pleased. She had a lot of walking to do and had dreaded the thought of recreating the blisters on her feet. She stood up and looked around the room again. It might well be the last time she ever saw a white man's house from the inside. She wanted to remember it, for she wasn't going to Bancroft as Nathan seemed to think she was. On the mantle she saw a gleam of gold and she hesitantly picked it up. It was a small, flat, circular object. One side was gold, the other bone white with tiny black figures painted on it. Nathan had called it a watch, and she had often seen him look at it and twist the small knob. She supposed it held some magic for him and she could feel it tick as if a tiny heart beat somewhere inside. Gently she lay it back down and let the tips of her fingers caress it.

She would miss Nathan. For all his fearsome appearance and rumbling voice, he had been kind.

At least he had been until today. Today he had made it clear that he wanted her to leave.

Fawn set her jaw stubbornly and walked out of the cabin. To her left she saw a row of small outbuildings, the larger of which she guessed to be the barn. How strange, she reflected, that even the white man's animals lived inside a house. Their spirits must be very weak indeed. But such matters were no longer her concern. Nathan was not in sight, and that was all that mattered. He might try to stop her and force her to go to Bancroft. She didn't want to argue with him.

With determination, Fawn struck out across the yard. Huge pines hid the sky, and beneath her feet the fallen needles were soft and silent. She wasn't at all sure where she was going, as long as it wasn't to Bancroft. Perhaps she could find a dry cave to use as a shelter and live on fish and berries. Without her knife she knew it would be harder, but she was sure she could fashion another out of a piece of flint.

Because she had to go somewhere, she went west. The sun shone on her back instead of in her eyes, and would until at least midafternoon, and the land was clearer in that direction. Before she had gone far she heard the sound of someone following her. Contemptuously, she didn't deign to turn her head, nor did she run. It had to be Nathan—no Indian would ever make so much noise.

"Where are you going?" he demanded when he caught up with her.

"I am leaving," she answered frostily in a mixture of Ute and English.

"I can see that, but where are you going?"

"I will find a cave and live in it as the Shaman do while waiting for a vision. You need not concern yourself."

Nathan caught her arm and brought her to a stop. "You can't go live in a cave like a wild animal. You're a woman!"

"I know that. Perhaps I will live anyway." She tried to go around him, but he stopped her again.

"Listen, Miss Fawn . . ."

"Fawn," she corrected.

"Fawn. I can't let you go off on your own like this. It's not safe."

"What could be less safe than going to Bancroft to be given to my enemies?"

"They aren't your enemies, they're your people," he said in exasperation.

"A woman has heard stories," she answered in the formal Arapaho phrasing. "They will kill me as surely as would Walking Tall, and for less reason."

"They would not."

"An Indian knows these things," she replied firmly and shouldered past him.

Nathan walked beside her a few feet, then stopped again. "If you're dead set on not going to Bancroft, then stay here."

"Here?" she asked doubtfully. "With you?"

"That's right. I have two rooms. You can take the bedroom and I'll sleep in the other room, just like we've been doing."

She looked at him closely. "This is the way it is with whites? You sleep in separate places? How can I be your woman if we do not sleep together?"

"I'm not asking you to be my woman," he protested quickly. "That wouldn't be right. I just don't want you to wander off and get yourself killed."

"Why don't you want me for your woman," Fawn demanded, her pride bruised by his rejection. "I am widow to a chief. Look at me! Am I not young and strong? I have many sons here!" She slapped her stomach as if in support of her claim.

That she might have children back in the tribe had never occurred to him. "You have babies?" he asked gesturing in a stair-step fashion with his hand. "Children?"

"Of course not!" she replied haughtily, "I was only married two months."

A sigh of relief escaped him. Nathan had no desire to tangle with the Arapahos, but he couldn't have left her children in their midst. "Fawn, I want you to come back to the cabin and stay with me until we can figure out what to do."

"As your woman?"

"No. Not as my woman."

She paused. It made no sense for her to attempt to survive in the woods alone, nor did she want to try. "It doesn't sound . . ." She struggled for a suitable word in Ute or English, but had to settle for one in her own tongue, "proper. You are not my brother nor my father nor my uncle. Why would you want me to live with you and not sleep with you?"

"Now don't get me wrong," Nathan said. "I find you mighty attractive. In fact you're just about the prettiest lady I've ever seen. But I don't want to marry you or anybody else."

"I see. You are a Shaman. A holy man," she said with sudden insight.

Nathan grinned. "No, ma'am. I'm surely not that." He took her arm and turned her steps back to the cabin. "My people don't marry except for love, generally, and they can only have one wife, so they choose very carefully."

"I understand," she nodded sagely. "There was a man in our tribe who had two wives. There was no peace in his home. He Whose Name I Cannot Speak was against taking more than one wife, but the other man was willful and did it anyway."

"'He Whose . . .' You mean Many Rivers?"

Fawn nodded. "That is the one. You are wise to choose your mate carefully. We called the unlucky husband Man Climbing Two Trees." She smiled up at him and two dimples appeared unexpectedly in her cheeks.

Nathan laughed. "Then you will stay with me as a sister until we can think of somewhere else for you to live?"

"Perhaps. An Indian is like the wind. Who

knows where we will decide to be tomorrow or next week? We do not put down roots like trees and white men. I will stay with you for a while."

"Many Rivers has camped in that same place for years," Nathan argued, using sign language to augment his words. "That seems pretty root bound to me."

"Tomorrow they may be gone," she said philosophically. "Who can say?"

They crossed the yard and Nathan pushed open the door of the cabin for her. "If I give you your knife back will you promise not to stab me with it?"

Fawn hesitated. She had sworn a blood oath against whites. Could she have a weapon in her hand and not use it? This white man was no longer her enemy. She had no desire to hurt him, much less kill him. Was her totem growing weak? "I will promise," she said at last.

"It took you long enough to decide," he grumbled.

"I wanted to be certain of my heart before I gave my pledge. You see, I have sworn to kill all whites that I can, and an Indian never breaks his word."

"Never?"

"Never. You will be safe with me," she assured him solemnly.

Nathan looked down at her. She was tall for a woman and gracefully slender. Her jade green eyes were gazing earnestly up at him, her head was lifted regally. In the dim light of the cabin her hair looked darker and she could almost have passed as the Indian she claimed to be. He looked away and, after pausing for a moment, retrieved the knife from a box on a shelf beside the fireplace and handed it to her.

"Thank you," she said with dignity. "My father made it and I would not want to lose it."

"Your father? Elk Tooth?" He walked with her outside to sit on the bench under the pines.

"That was his name."

"I gather he's dead since you won't say his name."

"Yes. He was shot nearly three months ago. That's why I married my husband."

Nathan raised his eyebrows in question.

"My mother, Clouds Passing, was too old to remarry, and we were to move in with my step-brother, Storm Dancer. But Storm Dancer's wife has a sharp tongue and is quick of temper. I'm afraid I don't care for her. Besides, three women are too many for one wigwam. I married my husband so I would have my own home."

"Why didn't Clouds Passing have to die when Elk Tooth did?"

"He was not a chief," she explained. "Is it the custom among your people to kill all widows?"

"No, of course not. Did you love Many Rivers?"

"I did not. In a matter of weeks I came to hate him. He was cruel to me and liked to see my pain. Had I known what marriage to him would be like I would never have married him." She looked at Nathan proudly. "More than one warrior asked for my hand. I made a foolish choice and repented of it too late."

"Is Many Rivers the cause of those bruises on your back?" Nathan demanded grudgingly.

Fawn looked at him silently for a moment, then said, "Yes. He often beat me."

Nathan scowled. "There's no reason good enough for a man to hit a woman. Let alone to beat her the way he did you. I've seen men look better than that after a barroom brawl."

She flushed with shame but kept her head erect. Nathan must have spent more time with her than she had thought. "I was disobedient. He had a right to chastise me."

"That's the stupidest damn reasoning I ever heard," Nathan thundered. "Don't you ever let anyone treat you like that again!"

She looked at him with interest. "White men do not beat their wives?"

"No real man would hurt a woman!"

She sat back, pondering his last statement. "I, too, have always thought this way. I believe you would make a good husband," she told him. "Some woman will be lucky when you take her to wife."

"I told you I don't want a wife," he reminded her. "So don't get any funny ideas."

"Funny ideas? What do these words mean?"

He thought for a while, then shook his head. "I can't say it in Ute. What I mean is, don't get any notion that I might marry you."

"This woman doesn't need or want a husband," she reassured him. "Once was enough. I will be your sister."

"What I would really like is for you to be my friend."

She smiled at him and again the dimples appeared. "We will see. I don't know you very well, and an Indian makes friendships for life."

He grinned. "You must know some Indians that I don't know."

"Yes," she answered quite seriously, "I am certain that must be true."

Chapter Four

FAWN KNELT ON THE FLAT ROCK AND PUT HER HOOK into the quietly drifting river beside the cabin. Slow ripples fanned out from the string, distorting the reflection of white clouds and azure sky. A breeze ruffled the long needles of the pines behind her and the trees made a soughing whisper. The sun felt warm on her back. The day was perfect for fishing.

Nathan sat a little way off and was watching her. "I thought Indians just reached in and grabbed the fish," he commented.

She glanced at him over her shoulder. "Why would you think such a silly thought?"

"I don't know. I guess I heard it somewhere."

"This way is better." She angled the hook with its wriggling worm into the shadows of the rock and wrapped the string around her palm. If there was a fish in the area, he was likely to be hiding there. At least that's where she would hide if she were a fish. "Come, fish," she whispered low. "All is safe. You may eat now."

"Why are you talking?" he asked as he tossed his own hook into the water. "You'll scare all the fish away."

"I was only reassuring them that it's safe to take the worm. Otherwise they may not bite."

Nathan sat down on the grass and propped his cane pole against his leg. "I always heard that talking would drive the fish away."

"That's because you use English. You must speak to them in the language of the People." She patiently held the string in her hands and waited.

"Arapaho?"

"Of course."

They sat quietly for a while. From his position, Nathan had a good view of Fawn perched upon the grey granite boulder. Her braids hung below her waist and in the sunlight they gleamed with a reddish hue. Her skin was tanned to a pale gold and it made her teeth seem very white when she smiled. The doeskin dress fit her loosely, but he could see the swell of her breasts and hips beneath the soft fabric. Unbidden, he recalled how she had looked when he had undressed her. Nathan moved uncomfortably.

"Ha!" Fawn exclaimed as she pulled a twisting trout from the water. "Look! Here is our supper!"

Nathan went to her and took the large fish, then

held out his hand to help her off the rock. She ignored it and slid to the ground.

"Is it not beautiful? I think it is big enough for both of us."

"Nearly," Nathan conceded. "Look! My pole is jumping!" He ran to grab the pole as it was pulled toward the water. He hauled back and landed another trout. "Now I know we have enough," he said holding it up proudly. He looked from it to the fish Fawn held. His was easily two inches smaller.

She laughed. "My Indian words lured the larger fish!"

He grunted and turned his fish to see if the other side looked longer. It didn't. "You made so much noise you scared off the big one."

Fawn only laughed again and took the fish from him. "Do not fret, Nathan. Perhaps next time you will catch the larger one." Smiling maddeningly, she bent to kill and prepare the fish for cooking.

"What do you think you're doing?" he asked, taking the knife from her.

"Do white men eat the head and tail?" she asked in surprise. "It wouldn't taste good."

"I'll do this. You go put the greens on to boil."

She shrugged. "I was going to do both."

He pulled her to her feet and put her knife back in her beaded scabbard. "I will take care of the fish."

"All right," she said doubtfully. As she walked away she called back over her shoulder, "You must choose your woman very carefully, Nathan, and not get a lazy one. For if you do half her chores and do not beat her, she will become insufferable and idle."

Nathan watched her go, then he grinned.

Fawn dug a hole and buried the remains of their meal, then carried the dishes to the river. Kneeling on the grassy bank, she scooped sand and water into the cooking pot and scoured it with a hank of grass.

Nathan came out of the cabin, stretched, and wandered down to join her. "Do you want me to do that?" he asked.

She gave him a scornful look and didn't answer. Under her fingers the old black pot was taking on a cleanliness it had not known in years. "Your totem must be very powerful," she commented, "else you would have become ill from all I've scrubbed out of this pot."

"Do you mean it wasn't clean?" he asked as he looked over her shoulder. "I wash it out every night."

"It takes more than merely sloshing water in it," she scolded. "You must scrub it. Hard. Like this."

He sat on a large flat rock and watched her. The sun was now low in the sky, and the fingers of pink and mauve clouds that were stretched across the heavens were reflected faithfully in the smooth water. The ruddy glow also lay on her cheeks, giving her skin a look as rosy as the blush of a peach. The fires in her hair were banked in this light and her abundant braids were Indian dark.

"Do you recall your white name? What did your real mother call you?"

Fawn sat back on her heels and looked across the water as she thought. "Eliz . . . Elizabeth. I think it sounded like that." She rinsed the pot and took up a dish. "I don't like that name. It has no meaning and therefore no strength." It occurred to her that his name, too, was meaningless as far as she knew and that what she had just said might have hurt his feelings. "Tell me of your name, Nathan. What does it mean in your language?"

"Well, it doesn't mean anything as far as I know. It's just a name."

She looked at him as if she were certain he must be teasing. "You must have many brothers and sisters for your parents to have run out of names."

He grinned at her. "I have two brothers and three sisters. Their names don't mean anything either. I'm named after my grandfather."

"How sad," she commiserated, "to never have a name with strength. Do you suppose that is why the whites have tried to take so much of our land? Perhaps if your names had meaning you would be content."

Nathan frowned. "I haven't taken any of your land, Elizabeth . . ."

"Fawn," she corrected firmly. "And I meant the ones in Bancroft. Once my father said there were beavers and elk in that spot and now only dirty buildings are there. This is what I am told, for I have not seen it myself."

Nathan nodded. "I have to admit he's right. Bancroft is an eyesore. But as for myself, I prefer to live close to nature." He looked around at the pine forest and the river. "No civilization for me. I like it outside in the clean air."

Fawn looked meaningfully at the cabin and the neat outbuildings that flanked it. "Outside?"

"For my people, this counts as being outside. Are you sure you don't want me to help you?"

"Yes."

The hour was late, and the sun seemed to be resting on the tree tops along the ridge of the mountain immediately to the west. It melted lower, and jagged silhouettes of branches and leaves partially obscured the huge orange orb. The pink clouds deepened to rose, and streaks of gold illuminated their edges. Behind them the sky deepened to a pansy blue, then darkened to violet.

"It's a beautiful sunset," Nathan commented. "Tomorrow morning let's walk over to the cliff and watch the sunrise."

"Why?"

"Because you can see it come up beyond the far mountains. You can see the air turn blue, then pink, in the valley."

She looked at him over her shoulder. "I didn't know men thought such things."

"They do. Or at least they do if they have eyes to see and a brain to think. Otherwise they go through life without ever living."

"You sound like an Indian," she said in surprise.

"Let me teach you the word for sunset," he said tactfully.

"It's 'sunset,'" she replied, using the word of the People.

"That's Arapaho. Say 'sunset.'"

"My word is prettier."

"But you need to learn more English. If we ever have company that can't speak Ute, they won't know what you're saying."

"I say some English," she defended herself.

"About every third word," he countered. "Say 'sunset.'"

She tightened her lips in the way he was beginning to recognize. "Sunset," she said in Arapaho.

"Do it right. You're not even trying."

"I will say it in your tongue if you will say it in mine."

Nathan sighed with resignation. "All right. Just this once. Say it again."

She repeated the word and he dutifully said it after her. "Very good," she praised. "Sunset," she said in English. "Now you know your first Arapaho word. Soon you will learn more."

"The idea is for you to learn English," he protested.

"For each word you learn of Arapaho, I will learn one of English." She turned back to wash the last dish and her ramrod straight back clearly indicated her stubbornness.

She picked up the dishes and when he tried to take the heavy pot she rapped his knuckles. "I will not touch your weapons. You will not touch my pots."

"Sounds fair to me," said Nathan, who detested cooking almost as much as he hated cleaning up afterward.

Night had gathered beneath the trees and only the glow of firelight from the cabin's windows guided their footsteps. The tops of the bushy limbs sighed and sent a heady aroma of evergreen through the forest.

"Tomorrow night it will rain," Fawn announced.

"Why do you think that? There is hardly a cloud in the sky."

She glanced back at the sliver of moon that could be glimpsed through the branches. Its points were tilted to pour out the rain water and there was a halo around it that encompassed one star. "It will rain by sunset tomorrow." She threw him a superior smile. "Indians know these things."

"But you're not an Indian," he countered.

"I am Arapaho. You need not insult me." She jerked her chin up proudly.

"Forgive me," he heard himself saying in Ute. He frowned in the darkness. Was he turning her into a white woman or was she changing him into a brave! He decided he must watch her closely.

Fawn put away the dishes where she had found them and sat on the bear rug while Nathan put another log on the fire.

"Don't you want to sit in a chair?" he invited. "It's a lot more comfortable."

"No. I like to feel the ground beneath me."

"You're sitting on a wooden floor, not the ground."

"I am pretending. At least the floor is close to Mother Earth."

Nathan pulled up a chair and took out his whittling knife. He got a chunk of maple about the size of both his fists and sat down. Propping his feet on the side of the fireplace, he began to carve the wood.

"What are you making?" Fawn asked curiously.

"A bowl. Some friends of mine down the mountain had a baby and I'm making her a bowl and spoon."

"She must be a very large baby to need such a great bowl," Fawn teased.

Nathan held it up and looked at it closely. It did seem rather large now that she mentioned it. "I'm going to carve flowers or something on the outside," he decided. "Besides, I don't want her to outgrow it too quickly."

"She won't," Fawn affirmed. She sat cross-legged and watched him under the guise of studying the carving. The golden firelight made his face as bronze as any Indian's but his blond hair and beard fascinated her. Was his hair as soft as hers, or was it wiry and stiff like a horse's mane? She found herself wanting to touch it. She had almost become accustomed to his appearance, as alien as it was, but his eyes were so startlingly blue. Never had she seen eyes that color, and she couldn't help but wonder if he could see the same colors she did.

Wouldn't they be tinged with blue, like the pebbles seen through the reflection of a lake? What a shame, she thought, to see everything in hues of blue!

Also he was so large! She had seen white men before, though usually from a distance. One named Charley Three Toes came to their village regularly with his Ute woman, Pale Moon. His eyes were light in color, she recalled, but not a true blue. And he was small—shorter than she was. Her thoughts made her angry. It had been Charley Three Toes who had shot her father. He had said it was a hunting accident, and because he was the emissary to the whites, Many Rivers had begrudgingly accepted his explanation. But she knew better. If it were not for Charley Three Toes her father would still be alive, she would not have had to marry Many Rivers, and she would not have been exiled from her people.

Perhaps, Fawn reflected, the Spirits would accept her blood oath for Charley only, rather than for all whites. She had come to like this white man in front of her. But could a blood oath be altered? She had no idea. To her knowledge, no woman had ever sworn one, and none of the braves had ever told her the rules that might apply.

"I have decided not to kill you," she said with sudden resolve.

Nathan started and peered down at her. "Say that again? I didn't know you were still planning to."

She drew her knees up and laced her fingers

around her legs. "I swore a blood oath to kill all whites."

"*All* whites? That's a mighty tall order." He looked at her searchingly and leaned forward to rest his elbows on his knees. "Why would you want to do that?"

"A white man killed my father."

"I didn't know that. I gather he was never punished?"

She shook her head.

"Why not settle for the one who shot your papa and leave the rest alone?"

She decided the English word must mean father and she nodded. "That was my decision."

"Who was it? Maybe I know him." He looked at her with interest. No wonder she had been so difficult to befriend at first. She had good reason to see his people as the enemy.

"I think not. He is like dirt. A man like you would not know a man like him. Besides, he is of your people and you might warn him. I understand this. I would do it myself for one of my tribesmen. Even for Red Eagle who beats his horse, though I consider him to be dirt also."

"I see. If we do run across this man, will you tell me? He should be put in jail if he killed someone."

She pondered for a moment. "I will tell you, but I will also kill him. A jail is not enough. For an Indian it would be, but a white man's spirit is accustomed to cages." She gestured at the sturdy walls and roof.

"You don't like my cabin? It's a lot nicer than

most. There are two rooms and several windows and there's a fireplace in each room. The roof doesn't leak and there are no chinks for the wind to blow through."

She nodded. "All these things I dislike. But I do like the floor. On rainy days there will be no mud."

Nathan leaned back in his chair and slowly stroked his beard. "You sure enough think like an Indian," he said at last.

"It is as I have told you."

"I don't know what I'm going to do with you. The Indians don't want you and you don't want the whites. What will become of you?"

"I don't know, Nathan," she answered sadly. "It worries me a great deal."

Chapter Five

FAWN FOLLOWED NATHAN TO THE TANNING SHED and watched him salt down the green-dried hides. Stacks of elk, deer, and wolf skins stood almost as tall as his knees. While he pulled each one back, Fawn tossed rock salt on the one below. The shed had a pungent aroma that Fawn found very unpleasant.

"Why do whites need so many hides when they dress in wool and cotton?" Fawn asked.

"Some of these hides will go to make shoes or boots, some for coats or gloves. The nicer ones like fox or ermine will be used to trim ladies' cloaks."

"Ermine?"

"That's the English name for a weasel wearing a white coat," he smiled at her.

"You must be a very great hunter to have all these pelts. Perhaps I was wrong about the white man's skills."

"Game is plentiful," he said modestly. "And I have good traps."

"Traps?"

"That's one over there. The spring's broken, and I brought it in to fix it."

She went across the room and picked up the metal object. It was quite heavy and looked threatening with jaws large enough to swallow her arm up to the elbow.

"Be very careful if you go downstream," he cautioned her. "I've set them out by the water holes."

Fawn frowned. This trap looked like evil to her. "How does it work?"

"The jaws are forced open against the strong spring and cocked with the trigger there in the center. When an animal steps on the trigger, it clamps onto his leg."

"That's cruel!"

"I don't relish that part, but it's necessary. I check my traps every day, but some trappers don't. I don't want an animal to starve to death."

She tossed the trap from her. "That is just like a white man! No Indian would use such methods."

"Of course they do. They just use tree limbs instead of metal."

"Not Arapahos!"

"Even Arapahos," he informed her.

"My father used only live traps and he apologized to each animal before he killed it!"

"Your father wasn't a trapper."

"This is true," she admitted reluctantly. She kicked at the broken trap with her toe. "Is there no other way?"

"Nope."

Fawn looked around. The cured hides were folded in thick bales along one wall, ready to be carried to Bancroft or Fire Bluff to trade. She picked up one of several deer skins that lay on top of one of the bales. "May I have two of these?" she asked him.

"Sure. Why do you want them?"

"This woman would like to use them," she said in the formal manner that indicated she would brook no further questioning on the matter.

"Well, then. They're yours." He grinned at her as he dusted the salt from his hands and went outside to test the dryness of the skins that hung on drying racks behind the building.

Fawn was still getting used to Nathan's easy-going attitude, and she wished that she hadn't been so abrupt. She picked the best two hides and followed him. She watched him work for a few minutes. "This is much as we would do it," she approved. "Could I use that stretcher to scrape the hair from my deer skin?"

"Go ahead. There's a scraping knife in that tool box on the shelf. It's just inside the door."

She got the large, flat-bladed knife and knelt to run leather thongs through the slits in the outer edge of the hide. When it was stretched taut on the wooden frame, she started removing the hair by working the knife against the grain.

"What are you going to make, another dress?"

"Not yet. Perhaps later."

Nathan got another knife from the tool box and started scraping the underside of a wolf skin. It needed to be free of all meat particles before it would cure properly. They worked in silence for a while.

"You sure don't seem to mind working," Nathan commented as he looked over the progress she had made.

"Should I?" she asked in surprise. Work was so much a part of her life that whether she liked it or not had never occurred to her.

"No, no. That's fine." He glanced at her from the corner of his eyes. She looked quite happy over there, working under the shade of the large pine. Nathan knew several men who had Indian wives, and the one quality they all seemed to share was laziness. Reason told him this couldn't always be the case, but experience had affirmed that it was. Also missing in Fawn was the servile attitude, common to the Indian wives. Fawn was as haughty as royalty, as he supposed she was in a way, as widow of a chief. Not only that, but she kept herself neat and clean. Even though it was late afternoon, her hair was as smoothly braided as it had been that morning.

Nathan frowned as he turned back to the hide and began scraping harder. For days now he had found her foremost in his thoughts, and recently the mere sound of her voice had been enough to send his pulse racing. He couldn't understand it. This was not the sort of feeling he had experienced toward any other woman, and this made him uneasy. Other pretty faces had aroused passion in him, certainly, but this was something more. Something that felt uncomfortably permanent. Like love. Nathan scowled and scraped more tissue from the hide than was necessary. He didn't want to fall in love. Especially not with someone like Fawn, for he suspected he might never recover from it.

Still, he glanced at her from the corner of his eye. She liked to talk and was very beautiful and cheerful, all the things he liked in a woman. He tested the thickness of the hide with his fingertips and pretended nothing else was on his mind as he surreptitiously glanced at her again. Yes, he decided. She certainly was more pleasant company than old Charley Three Toes, his drinking and carousing companion.

Charley had a Ute wife named Pale Moon, a silent mountain of a woman who moved only when Charley told her to move and who rarely spoke. Neither she nor Charley were given to bathing, and although Charley was handy to have around in a fight, neither was very smart. Nathan tried to remember the last time he had seen Charley and Pale Moon. It had been sometime last summer down in Bancroft. Old Charley should be coming along before too much longer.

That gave Nathan a moment of concern. Auburn hair and green eyes notwithstanding, Fawn had Indian written all over her. As soon as she spoke, Charley would be on his back about being a squaw man.

Nathan had lived on the mountain for nearly five years and although he had never particularly agreed with the rampant prejudice against the mixed relationships, he knew that when word got out that he had an Indian woman living under his roof, he would be the object of ridicule by many. It was a curious thing that even though Charley himself had an Indian woman who lived with him, he seemed to find great pleasure in lambasting anyone else who chose to do the same. Charley would never accept that Fawn was in truth a white woman. He frowned uneasily. He had never been particularly bothered by people's opinion of him, but he didn't want Fawn to be hurt. Perhaps if he got Fawn a gingham dress she would look less Indian.

Fawn finished scraping the hide and released it from the stretching frame. She had seen the thinness of his cotton shirt and knew a thorny branch or a large bramble would tear it to shreds, and his skin as well. What Nathan needed was a good, strong, leather shirt, such as braves wore. She had often made them for her father and brother, and she knew she could make one for Nathan if she used one of his shirts as a pattern. Perhaps she would even sew a row of fringe across the shoulders. Storm Dancer had had one like that and it had made his shoulders look awesomely broad. She glanced covertly at Nathan. His shoulders were already as broad as any man's could be. She smiled as a warm feeling spread over her.

The sun was sending long brown shadows across the billowy carpet of pine needles. By now the flat rock beside the river would be in the sunlight. Fawn folded the unwieldy hide and carried it back to the cabin. Later it would give her something to do as she sat beside the fire. She took the large cake of soap from the bowl on Nathan's washstand and went down to the river.

As she had expected, the rocks were warm from the afternoon sun and lazy sparkles glinted in the broad expanse of the slow-moving water. Fawn unbraided her hair and lay the thongs that had held it on the rock. She kicked off her moccasins and felt the cool grass kiss her feet. Without hesitation she removed her pants and pulled her dress off over her head. She paused for a minute, testing the temperature of the water with her toes. It was cold, but not unpleasantly so. A warm breeze gently wafted across her bare skin, making her nipples tighten with a pleasurable sensation.

Raising her slim arms, she made a shallow dive into the water and surfaced well away from the bank. She reveled in the feel of the cold water against her skin and the warmth of the sun on her head. Her long, thick hair spread behind her like a cape and swirled luxuriously as she swam.

The river here was wide and deep and the

current was slow, but she could hear a faint rattle of rapids not far downstream. Over her head a hawk glided noiselessly, and she wondered what he must think to see her far below in the water. Small fish, too young to be cautious, nibbled at her toes and fled when she kicked out.

Laughing with the sheer joy of youth, Fawn dove under water. She opened her eyes to see the rubble-strewn bottom far below. Large brown rocks covered with dark green mosses were embedded beside emerald-furred tree trunks. Fawn rolled to her back. A school of minnows drifted between her and the sun as if they were a flock of miniature birds.

Letting the water lift her, Fawn rose to the surface and breathed deeply of the warm air. She had felt grubby after scraping the hide, but now she seemed to be clean inside and out.

Slowly she swam to the river bank and reached for the soap. It had a much different feel from the pumice the Indians used and when it was wet it became slippery and hard to hold. She remembered how odd it had seemed the first time she saw Nathan lather his face and hands in the wash bowl. Soap had become one of her favorite discoveries. Stepping out of the water, she lathered her entire body, enjoying the feel of the suds and the fragrance that reminded her of the smell of the tall pines around the cabin. She rubbed the soap into her hair and scrubbed it clean.

Carefully laying the soap back on the rock, Fawn

dove back into the water. The bubbles slid from her as if by magic and she looked back to see them floating like a cloud on the slowly drifting water.

She swam out to the middle of the river where the depths kept the water uncomfortably cold. For a while she treaded water and looked at the small cabin on the gentle rise. It didn't look as homey as a wigwam, but she was becoming accustomed to it.

For a while, Fawn had been disturbed by an unsettling feeling that came over her when she watched Nathan secretly. She had attributed the odd sensation to the fact that he was so much larger and paler than any man she had known, but now his appearance was familiar, and she had to admit to herself that she found him very attractive. His deep voice reminded her of thunder resounding in the valley, and his great strength was obvious. He was a man of which she could be proud. And she experienced an odd thrill whenever their hands met or when he smiled at her unexpectedly. She had never known these emotions before, but she recognized them as the beginnings of love. Did he feel them also? She had no way to tell.

Slowly she swam back to shore and washed the remaining soap from her hair. She waded out of the river and sat on the warm rock to dry. Her thick hair streamed like wet fur behind her and sent rivulets of water coursing down the rock. With deliberate strokes, Fawn pressed the excess water from her hair and started running her fingers through it to remove the tangles. As happened several times a day, she wished for the pretty comb Storm Dancer had carved for her. It had been so much more effective than her fingers.

Castles of clouds were piling up on the horizon, and the sky was growing hazy above her. She smiled. The moon had not lied, there would be rain by nightfall.

The warmth of the sun and wind dried her body quickly, and already her hair was starting to dry as well. Fawn stood up and stretched as gracefully as a puma.

It was at this minute that Nathan came around the corner of the house. She was silhouetted against the sparkling grey water and pewter clouds, her arms stretched over her head. Her cape of hair hung well below her slender waist and billowed sensuously in the breeze. The sun kissed her rounded breasts and lay silver curves over her hips. Her long, shapely legs were slightly spread to balance her on the rock. She could have been a goddess or an angel caught in an earthbound moment.

Nathan stopped as if he had been turned to stone.

She turned slightly to let the wind blow her hair from her face and he could see the twin peaks of her breasts, as rosy as coral against her pale skin. Her stomach was flat and firm, her waist supple. He felt a stirring within his loins that he had difficulty ignoring. She was even more beautiful than he had remembered, for her loose dress did much to conceal her figure. How long could he live under the same roof with her and not touch her, not possess her as he wished he could at this moment?

He caught his thoughts up short. There was no question about it, he had to find somewhere else for her to live. No man could fight such a temptation forever. Nor was Nathan the sort of man who could ravish a woman and walk away from her. This was not one of Prairie Belle's fast women, but a lady, whatever her upbringing had been. Using all his willpower, he went into the house and firmly shut the door.

Fawn felt her hair and found it to be dry. She dressed, then braided it into a large twist over one shoulder. Humming a tune, she picked up the soap and went back to the cabin.

Nathan was already there, whittling furiously at the wooden bowl. He was frowning darkly.

"Hello, Nathan," Fawn said cheerfully. "Are you hungry?"

"Yes," he answered shortly. He had almost quelled his desires, but the sight of her had sent his heart pounding again.

Fawn's forehead puckered in her concern. What could be troubling him? He had been as cheerful as ever an hour ago. "Is something bothering you?"

"No!"

She took the bowl of corn she had ground earlier and began mixing it with salted water to make patties to fry in the skillet. "I went for a swim," she said brightly. "The water is still cold, but it was nice. I feel much better now that I'm clean." She sniffed the air unobtrusively. Nathan carried with him the odor of the tanning shed. "There is time for you to bathe before supper is ready."

To go to the river and take his clothes off was more than he could bear. "I'll sponge off in the other room," he said shortly.

She shrugged. Bathing was a pleasurable experience for her, but she had heard that whites felt differently. For his kind, Nathan was probably considered to be cleaner than most. Certainly he was cleaner than Charley Three Toes, who was the white man with whom she was most familiar.

Nathan was gone a long time, and when he came back, the smell of the shed was gone. He ran his fingers through his hair, then brushed it with the brush he kept on the washstand. Next he smoothed his close-cropped beard.

"Does that not hurt you?" she couldn't keep from asking.

"What?"

"All that hair on your face. I think it would hurt my skin if it were growing out of me."

"No, you can't feel it any more than the hair growing out of your head."

Fawn turned the bread with a long handled fork and said, "Is it soft or prickly? I have never seen anything like it."

"Feel," he offered, lowering himself to crouch down beside her.

She tentatively put her hand on his beard. It was soft but coarse and curled around her fingers. "It doesn't hurt," she reported. "It feels nice." Her eyes lifted to his and she felt her breath catch in her throat. He was so near she could see the silver glints in his deep blue eyes as well as a tiny reflection of the firelight.

The moment spun out long as Nathan lowered his head toward her. There was a need in his eyes and a tenderness she had not seen before. She felt her lips part and she tilted her head up to meet his. Only a breath separated them when he stopped abruptly. His expression closed and he moved away as if he had just realized what he had been about to do.

Confusion swept over Fawn and she quickly turned back to the bread. As she poked at it ineffectually with the fork, she wondered at the way her heart was hammering in her chest.

Nathan moved away and put the length of the cabin between them. How could she be so cool and collected about it all? His blood was roaring in his veins, and she was merely cooking supper. But wasn't that exactly the way he wanted it?

"I'll be back," he snapped as he strode out the door.

"Supper is nearly ready," she said in a strained voice as she stirred the simmering red beans.

Nathan hurried out and halted in the yard. He inhaled deeply and drew the cooling air into his lungs. What would Fawn have done if he had kissed her? Did Indians kiss? Would she have understood the gesture? He recalled the way her green eyes had softened to the color of woodland moss and the way her warm lips had parted so invitingly. He wished he had kissed her. He wanted nothing so badly as to go back in, sweep her up in his arms, and love her all night while supper turned to charcoal and ashes.

But what of tomorrow?

He gazed down at the river. The rock where she had stood was empty and silvering in the shades of dusk. Overhead the sky was leaden and heavy and the promise of rain hung almost visibly in the air. She had been right about her forecast, he thought with a tender smile. There would indeed be rain tonight.

Slowly he walked to the bench and sat down with his back against the tree. He crossed his arms over his deep chest and lowered his head to think. It was a good thing he had stopped himself, he decided. By tomorrow he surely wouldn't be as foolish as he had been tonight.

Nathan went to the tanning shed and got a mink pelt he had started working on. It would give him something to do after supper in the long hours before bedtime. As he started back to the house the first large drops began to fall.

Fawn was putting supper on the table as he came in. He leaned the skin in the stretching frame against the wall and went to the table and sat down. She looked at the hide and wrinkled her nose. Nathan glanced at the green hide. Mink did have an unpleasant odor, not much better than skunk, but he was used to it and it no longer bothered him.

"Supper looks good," he said with forced cheerfulness. "What do you call these corn patties?"

"Corn patties." She wrinkled her nose again, "Why is that mink pelt in here?"

He glanced back at it. "I thought I would work on it after supper. It's an extra fine one and I can get more for it if I take the time and finish it right."

Fawn sat across from him. "A mink is cousin to a skunk," she said carefully. "Only the stripe is missing."

Nathan glared at her. "There's a big difference between skunks and mink."

"Not in the smell," she said bluntly, dropping all efforts at tactfulness. "This woman will not eat in the same room as that hide."

Nathan studied her, trying to understand why she was being so edgy when he was the one who was still on fire for her. "I'm a trapper, Elizabeth. I have to work with hides."

"If you call me that name I will not answer you. But the hide must go."

"The hide stays."

Fawn stood up and grabbed back the plate of beans that Nathan was about to eat. "The hide goes or the supper goes."

"I said it stays!" His voice dropped to an angry growl.

With a flick of her wrist, Fawn tossed the beans into the fire. There was a loud hiss as ill-smelling smoke rose up the chimney.

Nathan glared at her and tossed her own beans in the fire.

Fawn stared at her supper as it scorched in the coals. She couldn't blame him, she could scarcely believe she had done such a thing herself. Nevertheless, she said frostily, "Will you take out the hide?"

"No!"

"You will stay in here and smell air made foul by a mink pelt?" she demanded. "Have you no sense of cleanliness?"

"After living with the Indians, you ought to be used to it!" he bellowed.

All the color rushed from her face and she stared at him with huge eyes. Without another word, she ran from the cabin.

"Damn!" Nathan growled. He kicked the heavy table and glared at the door as he ran his hand over his hair in an angry gesture. She must have gotten her feelings hurt!

Ignoring the rain, Fawn ran to the river. Tears were streaming down her cheeks, mixing with the rain. How could he say such a thing! She sat on the wet rock and hugged her knees to her chest miserably. Just as she had been about to apologize for her rash disposal of supper! He was insufferable! Raindrops splashed steadily into the water as if the sky were in sympathy with her pain. She shoved the tears angrily from her cheeks and glared at the river. Behind her she could hear Nathan calling, but she ignored him.

"Fawn, are you coming in out of the rain, or not?" he demanded.

"I am not!"

In the silence that followed she knew he had returned to the cabin, and it made her even more hurt and angry that he would leave her to be rained on with no more argument than that. When he sat down beside her, she jumped.

"I'm sorry," he said, handing her a corn patty.

She looked up at him and slowly raised her hand to accept the rain-splattered bread. He met her gaze for a moment, then turned to the water and leaned his elbows on his knees as he fished another patty from his shirt pocket. He munched on it as casually as if this were the usual way of serving a meal.

"The river's real pretty tonight, isn't it?" he said conversationally. "The rain looks like little stars falling in the water."

Fawn stared at him and slowly began to eat the bread. "Yes, it is. I've always thought the river was soothing."

He nodded. "Pine trees do that for me. Before I became a trapper I was a prospector. Did you know that? Yep, it's true. I panned this river for gold for a long time. Never found much." He wiped the rain from his face and took two more patties from his pocket. Giving her one, he continued, "I came across this cabin about two, three years ago. I reckon whoever built it had tried homesteading and gave it up and moved on. I added the extra room and fixed it up a bit. Lived here ever since." He shook the water off the last bite of bread and ate it.

"I'm sorry for throwing your supper in the fire," Fawn said cautiously. "It was wrong of me, and you should beat me for it."

Nathan looked down at her and after a minute he brushed the rain from her face. "You know I'm not going to beat you."

"He Whose Name I Will Not Say beat me for much less."

Knowing he was not using good sense, Nathan bent and kissed her lightly on the cheek. "I never tasted salty rain before," he said gruffly.

"Perhaps this woman is crying," she replied in an emotion-choked voice. "She is sometimes foolish."

"She is never foolish," he said as he gently caressed her cheek. "But she is very wet. Come on." He got off the rock and held out his hand to her. "We are going inside now."

With only a moment's hesitation, Fawn took his hand and walked with him to the cabin.

The first thing she saw when she went inside was that Nathan had removed the hide and frame from the cabin. She looked up at him and smiled tremulously, but was wise enough not to mention that she had noticed. "I will make more supper," she said quietly.

"I'll help you," he replied.

Chapter Six

NATHAN RODE INTO THE YARD AND HAILED FAWN AS he dismounted. For the past three days he had been trading his pelts at Fire Bluff and his two mules were heavily laden with fresh supplies. "Fawn! I'm home!"

She came to the door and stood there as breathlessly as if she had run to open it. Although she had only known him these few short weeks, she had missed him very much.

Nathan felt an ease of the emptiness he had known while he was gone. "I'm back," he said needlessly.

"I welcome you," she replied. She remained motionless, as if she were drinking in the sight of him. "Was your trading pleasant?" She knew this was the wrong word, but she didn't know the English version of "profitable" and she was trying hard to use as much of his language as possible.

"Yes, it was." He went to one of the seal-brown mules and unstrapped a bundle. "I brought you a gift."

Her eyes lit with pleasure. Quickly her fingers released the twine and she tossed him a dimpled smile as she unwrapped the heavy, brown paper. She withdrew two dresses from the package. One was of yellow calico with pale green flowers strewn among twining leaves of a darker green. The other was robin's egg blue with narrow ecru lace at the neck and cuffs. There were also undergarments trimmed with pink ribbons and a cotton petticoat, as well as two hair ribbons that matched the dresses.

"Oh," she gasped as she stroked the fabric of the blue one. "Never have I felt cloth so fine."

"I hope they fit. The wife of one of the owners of the trading post was about your size and she said they would fit her."

"Thank you, Nathan!"

"Go try them on while I put the animals in the barn."

Fawn caught the bundle to her and hurried into the house. Nathan chuckled and rubbed his horse's ears. "See, Horse? I knew she'd like them."

The animal flicked his tail and laid back his ears.

Taking the mules' lead rope, Nathan started to

the barn with the buckskin horse following him like a dog. "Come on, Stewart, Shirley. Let's go get some chow."

By the time he had unharnessed the mules and Horse and fed them, Fawn had put on the blue dress. She came shyly into the front room when she heard him enter the cabin.

He looked at her and caught his breath. The dress molded her graceful figure as if it had been made to her measure. Her full breasts were outlined by the thin fabric, and he saw that her waist was small enough for his hands to span. Had he made a big mistake, he wondered, in giving her a garment far more revealing than her Indian dress?

"Is it not right?" she asked in concern.

"It's beautiful," he reassured her quickly.

She moved doubtfully into the room. "I don't know, Nathan. It doesn't seem quite proper." She ran her hand over her waist and peered down at her skirt. "There are no leggings. Did you forget them? And the skirt is so long it will touch the ground."

"Leggings aren't worn with this kind of dress. Just a petticoat and the undergarments."

She looked up at him. "Those are worn beneath the dress? But they won't show."

"They aren't supposed to." Her words gradually sunk in. "Aren't you wearing them now?"

"Why, no. Only the dress."

Nathan drew a careful breath. "When you wear one of these dresses, put on the bloomers, then the chemise, then the petticoat, then the dress."

"Surely you are joking," she laughed. "With so many layers I will smother. Also I cannot fasten these buttons." She turned her back to him and he saw a great deal more of her than he had expected. "Will you fasten them, Nathan?" she asked innocently.

Numbly Nathan came to her and began to button the dress. Her back was satiny and warm and he couldn't avoid touching her as he fastened the opening. By the time he had secured the last button he was sweating.

Fawn smiled at him and twirled to show her bare feet and a good bit of her leg. "The skirt feels so nice, Nathan. Much like the fringe feels on my other dress. But even if I had on the petticoat my legs would still be bare. Are you certain this is proper?"

"Stop spinning around," Nathan said as her skirt lifted higher. "I have something else for you."

"Another gift?"

He reached in his pocket and brought out a comb and a small mirror. "It's not much. I just thought you'd like it."

Almost reverently Fawn took the comb and mirror and ran her hands over them. The comb was pale ivory with garlands of flowers carved on its handle. The mirror matched it and was just large enough to reflect her face.

Fawn touched her cheek as if to be sure it was her in the glass, then turned to Nathan with happiness shining in her eyes. "Never, never have I owned such a grand gift," she exclaimed. "You have honored me!"

"I hoped you would like them. There's a Chinese man at Fire Bluff who carves them to sell."

"The comb is even more lovely than the one Storm Dancer made for me," she said with awe. Quickly she unfastened her braids and ran the comb through her hair. It fell in shimmering strands of dark flame over her back and shoulders.

Nathan felt an almost irresistible urge to touch her, to run his fingers through her marvelous hair. The knowledge that she wore only the thin dress kept him at a distance. "I'd better get to work on those hides," he said hurriedly.

"Wait. I have a gift for you as well."

"You do?" he asked in surprise. "Where did you get it?"

"I made it while you were gone." She went to the table and handed him her offering.

Nathan unfolded it and held up a leather shirt. It was as soft as the doeskin of her dress and sewn with leather thongs. The neck was slit almost to the waist and laced up with another thong. Short fringe decorated the sleeves and trailed across the shoulders. He was deeply touched.

"It's beautiful, Fawn," he said after examining it carefully.

"I made it from the deer skins you gave me."

"How did you make it so soft?"

"I worked it through these rings I made of branches. See?" She showed him three rings of decreasing size. "By the time it will pass through the smallest ring, it is very soft and will stay that way if you always take it off before you swim. Do you really like it? Try it on."

Nathan unbuttoned his shirt and slipped it off. The hard muscles of his chest and his ridged stomach flexed as he pulled on the shirt. He laced the front opening and held out his arms to show that it fit.

"You have hair growing on your chest!" Fawn gasped. "You do!"

Nathan glanced down at his exposed chest as if he had never seen it before. "I know I do."

"I never saw anything like that!" she stated. "Do all white men grow so much hair?"

"Not all," he said testily.

She regained her composure. "It is very strange," she told him. "Much like a grizzly bear."

"I think I had better go see to the provisions," he said to change the subject.

"All right, Nathan." Fawn gave him another smile. "I am very glad you've come home."

Fawn and Nathan sat atop a large outcropping of rocks, their backs to one another. Around them curved a crescent-shaped pond which was fed by one of Wolf Creek's many tributaries. Spear-like cattails waved lazily in the sun and flat water plants floated on the smooth surface. Warm weather had brought wild flowers and the ground under their feet was dotted with blossoms as yellow as Fawn's dress. Although Nathan had been fishing longer than Fawn, she had three brown trout on her string and he had none. Behind them, Horse grazed on the weeds that grew along the bank and occasionally switched his tail at a fly.

"This wasn't such a good spot after all," Nathan grumbled as he put a new worm on his hook.

Fawn glanced at him over her shoulder and smiled. They had ridden some distance to this pond at Nathan's insistence, yet she had caught all the fish. "It is your fish pole," she told him. "The fish are Indian fish and they don't know what to do with it."

"I'm telling you all the big ones are out in the middle," he said stubbornly. "You can't reach them using just a string."

"Yes, Nathan," she agreed as she felt another tug on her line. She pulled in a fat perch, its scales gleaming gold and green in the sunlight.

"Don't gloat," he threatened her as she added it to her string.

"What is 'gloat'?"

"You know what I mean. Just don't do it."

She flicked her baited hook back into the water. "Why have you not named your horse but you named your mules?" she asked as she watched Horse chomp the grasses.

"The mules have more sense. Horse is too ornery to deserve a name."

"Why did you name the mules Stewart and Shirley?"

"They remind me of one of my aunts and her husband. Something about their eyes." He jerked his fishing pole experimentally. "You have to be careful what you name animals. I knew a man once that named his dog Tiger. The blamed dog tried to bite him every time he saw him."

Fawn laughed, a low throaty sound that Nathan found very appealing.

"I have been thinking," Fawn said after a while. "You should take the bedroom."

"Why? That's where the bed is."

"Exactly. I don't use it and you would."

"You don't use it? Where have you been sleeping?" he asked, turning to face her.

"On the bearskin in front of the fire. It's much warmer and doesn't rattle like the mattress."

"It makes noise because it's stuffed with corn husks."

"The bearskin is better. Also softer."

Nathan lifted his head and looked back at the woods. "Did you hear something?"

"No."

He turned back to his pole and pulled the hook out of the water. "All these damned fish just eat the worms and leave the hook," he complained. "I think you ought to sleep on the bed," he returned to their conversation. "It's not healthy to sleep on the floor."

"Why not? It's clean. All my life I have slept on furs on the ground."

He jerked his head back toward the woods. "I *know* I heard it that time."

"Nonsense, Nathan," she scoffed. "If something was there, would I not hear it before you? Indians are closely attuned to nature."

"Who ever heard of an Indian with red hair and green eyes?" he teased her as he surreptitiously studied the woods.

"My hair is not red," she protested. "Red is like a cardinal. My hair is more the color of a chestnut pony."

"Right," he said uneasily. "Just slide off the rock and stay behind me."

"What?" She looked around but saw nothing.

"Don't sit there asking questions, just do as I say!" Every muscle in Nathan's large frame was tensed as he pulled her from the rock.

Fawn suddenly saw what Nathan had seen. Walking Tall and a band of warriors were creeping through the underbrush. She gave a startled cry and the Indians began running, their battle cries renting the air.

Horse lifted his head inquisitively and munched the mouthful of grass.

Nathan whistled sharply. "When Horse comes, I'll pull you up behind me," he told her tersely. "Be ready."

Huge hooves flying, Horse laid back his ears and ran straight toward Nathan. The large man crouched, gauging the distance to the broad back, his hands ready to knot in Horse's mane. At the last minute Horse swerved, kicked at Nathan, and ran hell bent for home.

"You damned horse!" Nathan yelled after him. "Run, Fawn! Run!"

She stood rooted in terror as the Indians swarmed over Nathan. Then they were upon her and she saw flashes as one struck her hard in the jaw.

Nathan saw Fawn go down and a red haze of battle smoldered in his eyes. With a growl he swung at the nearest Indian, his huge fist bowling the brave over. With the prowess that made him feared in Bancroft bars, Nathan went after another. Suddenly two braves jumped on his back. Just as he sent one flying over his shoulders, the other brought him down with a blow from his war club.

Chapter Seven

NATHAN GROANED AND TRIED TO FEEL HIS LEGS beneath him. Sparks were flashing behind his eyelids, and he felt a wave of nausea.

"Nathan?" Fawn murmured. "You're alive? I was so worried." In her panic she spoke in Arapaho.

"Speak English, damn it," he moaned. As he shook his head to clear it, the pain worsened.

"It's Walking Tall, the son of my husband," she whispered. "He has been waiting for you to come awake." She tried to touch him, but her arms were wrapped around a tree, lashed together with a rawhide rope.

Nathan moved and found that he was tied in the

same way. His thoughts cleared immediately. "Are you all right?" he asked in a low voice.

"Yes. They are going to take us back to my village."

He raised his head and narrowed his eyes speculatively. From where he lay he counted seven braves, all in the prime of life. No wonder they had taken him. He looked over at Fawn.

She was not far away and he could see a dark bruise marring her cheek. "You're hurt!" he growled angrily and yanked at his bindings.

"They are going to kill us," she whispered. "A bruise is of little note."

"Some damned Indian you turned out to be," he complained to hide his worry. "And when I catch Horse I'm going to kill him!"

A tall brave heard him speak and started walking toward them. Fawn made a sound almost like a sob. "I knew a man once," he said in a conversational tone, "that said if you ever get caught by Indians, you should pick out the biggest one and spit in his eye. He'll kill you, but it'll be quick. Trouble is, if I did that now, it wouldn't help *you* any."

"He is my stepbrother, Storm Dancer," Fawn said in a choked voice. "I had not thought I would see him here!"

The Indian squatted a few feet from them and ran his unfriendly eyes over Nathan. "This is your man?" he asked Fawn in their language.

She nodded helplessly. "I have love for him, Storm Dancer. Please help him," she pleaded.

Storm Dancer scowled at her and didn't answer. Then he untied them from the tree, rebound their hands in front of them, and motioned for them both to stand up. Nathan got up and held out his bound hands to help Fawn. Storm Dancer's eyes flicked from one to the other and he motioned for them to go to the horses.

Nathan and Fawn were led on foot behind the mounted riders. His long legs had no trouble keeping the pace, but he swore angrily when he saw Fawn stumble. She regained her feet, however, and made no sound. Nathan felt his heart go out to her. He knew few men who would show that much bravery.

"Fawn, there's something that's been on my mind for a bit," he called over to her. "I think I'm in love with you."

She managed a wan smile. "You have picked a bad time to tell me that, Nathan." In spite of their dire predicament, she felt a surge of happiness at his words. He loved her! If only he had told her sooner.

"I just wanted you to know."

Her burst of elation sent her into even deeper despondency. She had so much to live for now! And now it seemed to be too late.

The hunting party paused once to water their horses in a stream, then pressed onward. By the time they reached the Indian village, Nathan was tired and Fawn's eyes were glassy from exhaustion.

Without a word, Walking Tall and another brave

tied them to separate trees, arms behind them. Walking Tall spit on the ground at Fawn's feet and then left them alone.

"Now what?" Nathan asked reluctantly.

Fawn swallowed, though her mouth felt cotton dry. "They will not speak to us. I am considered to be dead since they have buried my spirit with my husband. You are white and therefore beneath notice. They will feast and dance, and tonight when they are full of the Spirit, they will kill us."

Nathan bunched his muscles and pulled at the rawhide that bound him. It remained as tight as ever and a trickle of blood ran down his hand.

"Nathan, I want you to know. I have love for you, too."

He leaned his head back so he could see her. "If we ever get out of this, we're going to do something about that."

The dancing started and Nathan glared at the leaping, chanting Indians. They were whirling and gesturing angrily, working up a lather of sweat over their bodies. No children or young women were present, but several old crones sat to one side of the fire and brandished knives to spur their men to greater frenzy.

After what seemed to be several hours, a light footstep sounded nearby and Nathan pulled back to look at Fawn. Storm Dancer stood beside her, the thick underbrush obscuring him from the dancers. Wordlessly he sawed apart the leather thong that bound Fawn, then the one that held Nathan.

Storm Dancer's black gaze bored into Nathan's blue eyes. "Take care of her. She is my sister," he said in Arapaho.

Nathan nodded as he caught the meaning, if not the actual words. Storm Dancer silently stared at Fawn, then faded back into the bushes.

"Nathan, run up that path to my right," Fawn said. "I know a way we can escape."

"Let's go!" He grabbed her hand and they bolted toward the path.

The dancing and chanting stopped abruptly. For a stunned moment, the Indians only stared, then gave cry and raced after them. Fawn ran in front of Nathan and crouched low to avoid the limbs that would slow her. Her long legs carried her almost as quickly as he could have run alone but the Indians were right behind them.

The ground sloped downward, and soon they crossed a hollow, splashed through a stream, and started uphill.

"Faster!" Fawn hissed as she saw Walking Tall burst out of the underbrush brandishing his scalping knife.

Nathan needed no urging. He put his arm around Fawn's waist and charged uphill. They fought their way through the underbrush and ran out onto a rocky ledge. Fifty feet below, Wolf Creek rolled in a swollen current. By the slow movement he knew it was deep here. Maybe as deep as the spot by his cabin. On their right was a chalky cliff streaked with red and white rubble.

"Oh, my God!" he gasped. But Fawn grabbed his hand and dragged him on.

There was no escape back the way they had come, and less than twenty feet ahead the path dwindled to nothing, leaving only a sharp cliff. Suddenly, Nathan realized what Fawn intended to do.

"Jump!" she commanded in English. "Swim underwater and trust me."

He gaped at her and at the sheer drop. His lips moved but no sound came out.

"Jump!" she shouted.

"I can't! You don't understand!"

The Indians had cleared the underbrush and were hurtling toward them. Fawn shoved Nathan as hard as she could. She saw him fall just before she jumped after him. Walking Tall's hand grabbed the air where she had been and she heard a whistle of wind from his war club.

"I can't swim!" Nathan yelled as he plummeted downward.

They fell in a sweeping arc that carried them away from the deadly rocks of the cliff. Nathan hit the water a split second before she did.

Fawn felt the shock of the cold river as her body hit the surface. She sank far underwater where the light was dim and no sound penetrated. The pressure on her ears told her she had gone quite deep. Silver bubbles drifted upward as the air pockets in her clothing were released. Looking around frantically, Fawn located Nathan. She swam to his side and caught him deftly from behind. Her hand closed over his nose and mouth and she towed him underwater toward the cliff. He struggled futilely as she swam toward the rocky barrier ahead. She went lower and pulled him under.

Within seconds she passed beneath the submerged rocks and kicked upward, dragging him with her. Her lungs were burning and she could hardly refrain from giving in to the impulse to inhale. She prayed that Nathan could hold out, too. Just as she felt herself weakening, her head came out of the water. She gasped at the air and hauled Nathan up to breathe.

"Be still!" she ordered sharply as he fought the water. She looped her arm around him and pulled him through the water in the darkness. Soon her feet touched the sandy bottom and she felt Nathan struggle to stand.

"Where in the hell are we," he wheezed as he staggered to the bank and looked around at the massive grey walls that surrounded them.

Fawn pulled herself out of the water and rolled onto a rocky ledge. "It is an underground cave," she said between gasps. "I found it when I used to swim here."

"You used to jump off that cliff for fun?" he demanded. "Are you crazy?"

"I never jumped off until today. I thought we might make it though. Why didn't you tell me before you couldn't swim?"

"How was I to know you would take it into your

head to push me off a cliff! I can't fly either, if it ever comes to that!"

She sat up and smiled at him weakly.

"Are you hurt?" he asked, though he could see she wasn't.

"No. Just out of breath."

Nathan looked around. They were in a large cave that sloped into the water. An opening like a smoke hole far above them gave light and air but was inaccessible from where they stood. A broad ledge of rock stretched along one wall and a mass of stalactites and stalagmites encircled the rest of the cave. The silence was broken only by the steady drip of an underground spring.

"How do we get out?" he asked in a voice that echoed hollowly.

"Not that way," she answered gesturing at the hole in the roof of the cave.

Nathan pointed toward the inky water and raised his eyebrows.

She nodded.

"Oh, no! Not me. I'm not going back in that water!"

"We will talk about it later," Fawn placated him. She stood and wrung the water from her gingham skirt. "This dress is no good for swimming," she commented. "It is a wonder we didn't drown."

Nathan sat on the ledge and stared longingly up at the hole. "I sure wish we could fly." Night was falling and the small patch of sky was disappearing into the solid blackness of the cave. "How much longer do you think we should stay here?" he asked after a while.

"We can leave now, I think. They will have had time to decide we are dead." She unbuttoned the front placket of her dress and slipped it off. The cave's dank air was pressing around her and she was more afraid than she wanted Nathan to know. "Stand up," she said. She reached over to him in the darkness and knotted the dress around his waist into as small a roll as she could wind it.

"What are you doing?"

"I will not leave your gift behind. Here. Wrap my braid around your hand and don't dare let go. Can you do that?"

"Why would I want to do that?" he asked cautiously.

"I don't want to lose you and I need both my arms to swim."

"Fawn," he croaked. "I can't even see the water!"

"And the sentries will not be able to see us. Come." She caught his arm and led him firmly into the shallows. "Here it begins to get deep. Do you have me tight? Take three long breaths as deep as you can. Hold the third one and dive."

Together they filled and emptied their lungs. On the third breath, they jumped forward. Fawn felt a strong tug on her hair as the water closed over her and she struck out with as long a stroke as she could pull. In the darkness she felt disoriented but she swam in the direction she remembered the submerged mouth of the cave to be. When she was sure she must be past the rocks, she paddled upward. Even though Nathan was buoyant, his bulk was difficult to pull, and she had to fight hard to surface. She prayed to the Water Spirit that she had gone past the rocks. If they came up under them they were as good as drowned.

Her head bobbed up into the air and she drew Nathan up beside her. As she caught her breath she treaded water and searched the bank.

"Sssh," she whispered in Nathan's ear. "Over there by the rock."

He looked where Fawn indicated and saw the motionless figure of Storm Dancer. The Indian was gazing sadly at the river but he gave no signs of having seen them.

"Kick your feet well under the water," she whispered, "and let me carry you." She pulled him against her and they floated into the current.

With aching slowness they drifted downstream. When they drew level with Storm Dancer, Fawn held her breath. If he saw them, would he allow them to escape a second time? She couldn't hurry their progress. Their escape depended on them looking like a drift of wood in the moonlight.

As they passed her stepbrother, Fawn thought she saw him raise his right hand in a sign of peaceful farewell. She lifted her hand just above the water and imitated the gesture in case she was not mistaken. She knew she might never see Storm Dancer again. The current carried them beyond a curve and out of sight.

"Can you keep going a while longer?" she asked

in a low voice. "There may be other sentries about."

He nodded. "I'm almost beginning to enjoy this." Her breasts were soft against him and her sensuous body lay close to his as the current carried them on.

"You can kick your legs harder now," she instructed. "We are past the village. There are rapids not far ahead so we must swim toward shore." She made a sweeping motion with her arm and they started drifting toward the bank.

As soon as Nathan's feet touched the rocky river bed, he grew more confident. Even as a child he had mistrusted water but on land he felt invincible. He led Fawn to a nearby thicket of aspen and untied her dress from around his waist. Wringing the water from it, he gave it to her. The moon silvered her body and she looked almost ethereal. He wanted to take her in his arms, to caress her, but he knew reaching safety was far more urgent.

Fawn dressed hurriedly, glancing back in the direction from which they had come. Crickets sang loudly in the grass and occasionally she heard the faraway hoot of an owl, but there was no sound of pursuers.

When she was clothed, Nathan motioned for Fawn to follow him. He kept to the heart of the woods where no stray moonbeam would illuminate them. They forded the stream not far from the log that had hidden Fawn when she had first escaped. As before, the bushy pines surrounded them. Nathan knew the mountain well and chose to follow a shorter path, rather than the natural lay of the land which would have led them to sheer cliffs where they could be cornered. They soon left the pines and were swallowed by an alder grove.

"Are you tired?" Nathan asked as he held back a branch for her to pass.

"No," she lied.

"There's a ledge not far from here where we can spend the night."

"A ledge?" she asked doubtfully.

"It's not safe for us to go back to the cabin right now. If Walking Tall thinks we're still alive he may be there waiting for us. We'll be safe on the ledge. Indians avoid the place."

By the time they reached the chasm, Fawn was too tired to care why her people would shun the cliff. Nathan eased his body between two halves of a large boulder that a tree root had cracked neatly in half. He held out his hand and Fawn let him help her down the narrow, winding path. She couldn't see the valley in the darkness—she could barely follow the path—but she could tell by the deep stillness and the constant breeze that she was climbing beside a gorge.

The ground beneath her feet leveled off and the path widened into a spacious ledge. The moon came out from behind a cloud and revealed a towering cliff into which had been carved a series of box-like rooms with gaping doors and windows. Fawn caught her breath in surprise.

"Where are we?" she asked. "Is there anyone here?"

"No, this place was abandoned long ago. Nobody knows why, but the tribe that lived here just moved away one day."

"Tribe? These are not like any Indian dwelling I have ever seen." She approached one and gingerly touched the adobe wall.

"There are several of these all along this gorge. Some of them are smaller than this one, others much larger."

The wind shifted and a low moan seemed to come from the doors and windows. Fawn jumped and moved closer to Nathan. He laughed and put his arm around her.

"That's why I know the Indians won't happen upon us here. It's supposed to be haunted. Relax, it's only the wind. Haven't you ever blown on a reed flute?" When she nodded doubtfully, he said, "The wind is using the houses as its flute. Come on in out of the breeze."

She hung back as he strode into the nearest doorway. "Are you sure my people will not come here looking for us?"

"From what I've heard, there hasn't been an Indian up here in a hundred years. I'm sure we'll be safe."

"Well, could we not sleep outside?"

"No, inside is better. By the way, don't back up. You're not far from the edge."

Fawn hurriedly followed Nathan inside. There was not enough moonlight to see anything, and she found Nathan by running into him. He bent, and she heard him pick something up.

"I left this blanket up here last winter," he explained as he spread it on the ground. "Sometimes I trap in the woods behind us and I stay here rather than sleep out in the open."

"Why?" she asked nervously.

She heard him chuckle in the darkness. "Wait until tomorrow morning and you'll see."

He sat on the blanket and pulled her down beside him. "It would be more comfortable if we had a bedroll, but this will be all right." He lay down and guided her head to his shoulder. "Tomorrow morning we will go home and try to figure out what to do next. Tonight we must rest."

Fawn lay rigidly in his arms and listened for the ghostly sounds. Had a specter appeared she would not have been more frightened.

"Relax, Fawn. You're wound tight as a clock spring. Nothing's going to get you."

She made an effort to appear more relaxed, but her mind stayed painfully alert. She noted every shift of the wind and the musty smell of ancient earth.

"I trusted you in the underwater cave," he reminded her.

Taking a deep breath, she forced herself to release the tension from her muscles. "Are you sure this is safe?"

"Positive. I've been coming here for years and I've never seen one thing to be afraid of. As long as you stay away from the edge of the cliff," he added. "It's a long way down."

Her eyes were becoming adjusted to the dark,

and she could make out a rectangular smudge of deep blue that indicated the open door and a smaller square that must be the window. Surely, she decided, if there was anything to fear, it would have attacked by now. Somehow the thought was reassuring.

Nathan's shoulder felt very comforting, and his muscular arms circled her protectively. She lay her cheek against his chest and felt the steady rise and fall of his breathing and the calm rhythm of his heartbeat. Now that she was losing her fear, she became aware of a strange stirring within her.

For weeks her friendship with this man had grown and more recently she had begun to realize she loved him. To be held in his arms and feel the great length of his body against her was making her heart pound as if she were still running. She was tormentingly aware of every minute movement he made. As a widow she was free to choose another man. And now that she was an outcast, no one would stop her even if she chose one of the enemy. But Nathan no longer seemed to fit that category.

"Nathan?" she said as the silence grew taut and long. "Are you still awake?"

"Yes."

"Did you . . . That is, did you really mean what you said this afternoon?"

He was quiet for a long time, and Fawn began to dread his answer.

"You mean the part about me loving you?" he asked at last. "Yes, I meant it."

Her pulse was a roar in her veins and she

swallowed dryly. "I meant it, too," she ventured. "I have loved you for weeks."

There was a rustle as he rolled toward her and she felt his large hand cup her face. "Fawn, I still don't want to get married. A man like me would make a terrible husband. I'm always off hunting and I don't want to be tamed by anybody." His thumb was stroking the planes of her cheek and confusing her thoughts.

"I could hunt with you. I don't want to cage you."

"A woman needs more than that." He was so close she could feel his warm breath against her forehead.

"I do not need more. Besides, I have not asked that you marry me."

Again the silence lengthened, and Fawn wondered if she had said something wrong. "I have been married and didn't like it. Never again will I let someone own me. I love you and I want to lie with you and share that love. Do your people not feel this way?"

"Yes, of course they do." His voice was deep and husky with emotion. "I just don't want you to do something you will regret."

"How can I regret showing you love? Only anger or some other emotion that kills a person's soul is regrettable. Love is good and gives only happiness. I would not be sorry if we love."

Nathan's face lowered and she raised her lips for his kiss. At first his beard scratched her, but as she became acquainted with its texture, she found she didn't mind it as much as she had expected. His lips were gentle at first and she kissed him in the wonder of new love. Then his growing passion made him pull her to him, and his kisses seared her soul as she responded.

Fawn ran her hand over his chest and felt the hard muscles beneath the soft leather of his shirt. She explored his body and marveled at the way he was built. In spite of his size, Nathan was rock-hard beneath her fingertips. His waist was lean and his hips were narrow. His buttocks swelled firmly as she stroked them.

"Are you sure, Fawn?" he asked. "A man can only hold back just so long."

"Love me, Nathan," she whispered. "I want to be your woman and for you to be my man."

This time when he kissed her, he drank deeply of her passion. He had loved this woman almost from the first moment he saw her. She lay willingly— even eagerly—in his arms and she was returning his kisses with a hunger he had never known a real lady could muster. Nathan freed her braids and ran his fingers through her thick hair, letting the masses enmesh his fingers. Since the day he had seen her drying her hair on the river rock, he had wondered what it would be like to touch it. He had been tormented by the memories of her lithe body. And now she was coming to him and, miracle of all miracles, she actually loved him!

His hand stroked her face and he taught her to meet his exploring tongue as he tasted the sweetness of her mouth. Her hands upon his body were turning his blood to flames, and he pulled her tightly against him. He released her long enough to remove his shirt and lay propped up on one elbow as he rubbed her glossy hair against her cheek.

"I just wish I could see you," he whispered.

"We could go out into the moonlight," she suggested. "I want to see you, too."

He stood, pulled her to her feet, and took up the blanket. Hand in hand they went out onto the broad ledge. The years had worn smooth the rocky surface and a fine dust softened its harshness. Nathan spread the blanket. The moon glinted off his mighty torso and made the blond hair that covered his chest look as soft as fur. Fawn lifted her hand and reached out to touch his chest and experience the thick texture of the hair.

Nathan stood still and watched the love that shone in her face. Her eyes were a dark gray-green in the night and her hair streamed in umber masses down her back. Slowly, savoring the moments, Nathan began to unbutton her dress. Her skin was pale as silver in the moonlight and the revealed globes of her breasts were tipped with dusky coral. He refused to hurry, although he could see her breath coming quickly and he knew she was as anxious as he was.

When the last button was released, he stepped closer and eased the fabric from her shoulders. Her breasts were bared and the cool night wind teased the twin peaks to hardness. Nathan let the dress drop to her feet. She stood unashamedly before him like an exquisite statue. He gently ran his fingers along the underside of her breasts and touched her proud nipples.

After he had looked his fill, Fawn smiled. "You see, Nathan? I told you all those undergarments would just be in the way."

He could only nod as his eyes and hands feasted on her perfection. "When we get home we'll burn them."

She loosened the buttons that held his pants and let them drop. He impatiently kicked them to one side of the blanket. "Oh, Nathan," she murmured as she gazed at his naked body. "I never knew a man could be so handsome." Slowly she grazed his arm with her fingertips and their eyes met. The night deepened his eyes to a darkness that she found less awesome than their natural blue. Hesitantly she stepped nearer and they embraced.

The tips of her breasts traced fire across his chest and his eager manhood burned against her flat stomach. Magic seemed to be woven about them as he lowered his head to kiss the sensuous curve of her lips. She pressed more tightly against him, her skin cool to his touch, yet setting his body aflame. Nathan marveled at her slenderness as he enfolded her in his arms.

Nathan drew away reluctantly, and pulled Fawn down to lie with him on the blanket. For a moment the wool scratched her skin, but Nathan was caressing her breasts and Fawn soon forgot her surroundings. Only she and Nathan existed in all the universe and their only need was to become as one.

He rolled her nipple between his thumb and forefinger as he kissed the slender column of her neck and Fawn responded by arching her back against him. She knotted her fingers in his hair as her pleasure brought a murmur to her lips. Never had she felt desire like this, never had she dreamed she might. Nathan seemed intent on driving her to the brink of madness with his passionate kisses, his knowing fingers.

Nathan lowered his head to her breast and ran his tongue over the luscious curves. When he reached the summit, he flicked her nipple with the tip of his tongue until she cried out in ecstasy. He covered her with his mouth and drove her to ever higher excitement.

When she could bear to wait no longer, Nathan knelt between her thighs and guided himself gently into her depths. Fawn lifted her hips to meet him and gasped at the sensation of their merging. He lowered his body until he lay upon her, his arms supporting most of his weight. Slowly, deeply, he moved inside her and Fawn met his thrusts in love's own rhythm. Her passion took even greater fire. Before she was aware what was about to happen, a pleasure such as she had never known sent her flying as waves of indescribable ecstasy flowed through her again and again. Fawn held Nathan close in amazement as the pleasure that was so great as to be near pain gradually subsided.

"What," she said at last, "what happened to me?"

"Do you mean you have never felt that before?" he asked in surprise.

"Never!"

A smile tilted his lips. "You see? We white men know a thing or two."

Again he began the deep thrusting movements and his fingers sent shivers of flame through her breasts. Miraculously, she felt the fires begin to build again within her, even more quickly this time. It was as if a volcano had burst inside her and sent white-hot lava into her veins. She cried out, enraptured, and Nathan tightened his arms around her as they rode the waves of love together.

When their breathing slowed he rolled from her, never letting his arms loosen their embrace. She lay on her side, her leg draped comfortably over his thigh, and touched his face. Her face was alight with love and wonder as she tried to read what lay in his eyes.

"How is it that I have never known such pleasure before?" she asked.

"I suspect you were never loved before. There is a great difference between coupling and loving."

She nodded, awe still upon her glowing face. "I can see that."

"Fawn," he said hesitantly. "I know I have no right to ask you this, but . . ."

She put her fingers to his lips to save him the words. "The Man Who Has Died was an old, old man. If he ever knew tenderness he buried it years ago. He never loved me; he wanted only for me to

106

bear him sons. With him, it was degrading and painful. With you it is like becoming alive."

A smile crossed his handsome face, and he pulled her head down to his shoulder. "I'll never ask you that again."

"He was never alive in my heart and now even his body is burned to ashes. There is no reason for you to ever feel jealousy over him." She lay still, her hand caressing his chest. "Nathan," she said at last, "have you ever had a wife?"

"No, I never fell in love before I saw you."

"Do you suppose marriage is always so bad?" she asked drowsily. "I would not like to give up the feeling I have for you."

"Neither would I," he said thoughtfully. "I never knew a man and woman to be so well matched as we are. Except for my friend, Jesse Keenan, and his wife, Darcy. They are a lot like us."

"She is Indian?"

"No, but neither are you."

She sighed. "I am in my heart, Nathan. And I think perhaps you are, too. Why else would you be here on this mountain?"

He lay his head against the soft cloud of her hair and stroked her until he felt her breathing become slow and even in sleep.

High above him the half moon did little to dim the millions of stars, and Nathan studied their familiar faces as he had on countless other nights. He no longer felt insignificant as he pondered the vastness of the heavens, and now the ache of loneliness was erased by the woman who cuddled against him. Perhaps, he thought as he caressed her arm, he had been too set in his ways regarding marriage. Fawn would never be happy living in civilization, but neither would he. He had no desire to live anywhere but in his cabin. He had given up his lifelong dream of seeing San Francisco and the Pacific Ocean when he gave up prospecting for trapping. No, he was content to stay on the mountain. He smiled as she snuggled even closer to him. What was there to prevent him from marrying Fawn? He had no doubts that she loved him, and it was almost frightening to realize how much he loved her. They would be a good match. But, until they were sure that the Indians believed them to be dead, there was no time to think of anything else except their defense.

Chapter Eight

FAWN AWOKE JUST AS THE DEEP AMETHYST SKY WAS fading to shell pink. She stretched languorously and instinctively snuggled closer to the warm body at her side. The unexpected contact brought her wide awake, and she opened her eyes to see Nathan smiling down at her.

"You looked happy in your sleep," he said as he stroked her hair. "What were you dreaming?"

Before she answered, Fawn intertwined her fingers in his thick golden hair and kissed him. His beard tickled her, but she found that pleasant. "I dreamed of you. We were building a wigwam from hides marked with marriage signs in the middle of a huge forest. Deer were watching us and fish were jumping in the lake. You were an Indian. It

109

was such a perfect dream that I did not want to wake up. But I did," she smiled tenderly and kissed him again, "and I find reality is even better than my dream."

"I love you," he said in his gentle growl. "You're a good woman."

Fawn let her fingers glide over his ear and down the curve of his strongly formed jaw. "What do you look like underneath here?" she teased. "I cannot even see your face."

"It's pretty much like any other face, I guess."

"No, I'm certain it is far more handsome than that. Even hidden behind a beard you are more well-favored than any man I have seen."

He let his eyes drink in her beauty, then he looked down at the canyon. "Look, Fawn. This is what I wanted you to see."

She sat up and pulled the edges of the blanket around them. He sat behind her and cuddled her back against his warm chest.

A sliver of red-gold sun was climbing over the far horizon and, as it rose, the land came alive. First the mountain peaks with their eternal patches of snow became blue, then rose, as the fingers of light gave them color. Gradually the hues spread down the tremendous slopes, giving life to deep green pines and firs, paler aspen and cottonwood, to sweeping fields of wild flowers. Finally the sun's rays touched the chasm at their feet. The air turned from mauve to a dusky rose, then to pale gold as the warm sun melted away the night mists. Enormous cliffs and boulders lined the walls of the valley far below, and a strip of water cut like quicksilver in its depths.

Fawn looked at Nathan in awe, then back at the lovely view. He held her comfortably in his arms, his cheek resting against her hair. "It's the most beautiful sight I have ever seen," she said at last.

"This is my special place. I come here when I need to think or when I get lonely," Nathan said quietly. "When I first came here as a prospector, I had never been away from people before. I grew up in a large family and there were always folks around to talk to. That was the hardest part of learning to live in the wilderness—not having anybody to talk to."

Fawn turned until she lay against his chest, then took his face in her hands. "You will never be lonely again, Nathan. I will be by your side for as long as you want me."

He tightened his embrace. "Do you mean that? I don't have much to offer you."

"You are all I want. I have more than I need already, and my heart sings when I hear your voice."

"My heart sings for you, too," he told her in their odd mixture of Ute and English. "Don't leave me, Fawn."

"I will never leave you unless you want me to go."

"That will be never," he assured her.

She lifted her head and kissed him gently, exploringly. As he returned her kisses with growing ardor, Fawn felt the quickening of her pulse. He had done no more than embrace her and caress her lips, yet already her body cried out for his. Fawn ran her hand over the smooth muscles of his back and marveled at the power she could sense beneath her palms. Yet he was a gentle lover and the most sensitive man she had ever known.

Nathan lay Fawn back on the blanket and matched his body to hers. He ran his large hand down the graceful curve of her hip, reaching back to cup her rounded buttock in his palm. Next to him Fawn seemed almost petite. He easily slid her beneath him and then gazed down at her.

The sun was higher now and had lit deep russet fires in Fawn's auburn hair. He threaded his fingers through its masses and watched the silken strands cascade over his hand. Returning his gaze to her face, he touched the creamy gold of her tanned skin.

"Your eyes are like wood ponds reflecting the trees above. I can see flecks of gold in them. And your lips look as if they were made to be kissed."

Fawn smiled, her dimples appearing magically in her cheeks. "Your soul is beautiful, Nathan."

He blushed. "I didn't mean to go on like that."

"No." She caught his arm as he moved away in embarrassment. "I like for you to say such words to me. They are the sounds of your heart singing. I meant only that you must have the spirit of an Indian." She smiled up at him and teasingly dared him to take offense at her words.

"Indian, hell," he muttered as he silenced her

with a kiss. He pulled the blanket closer and looked down at her. "You aren't cold are you?"

"No, I am very warm." She traced a trail of fiery kisses down his neck and let her caressing fingers explore his hard body. "And you, Nathan? Are you cold?"

He laughed and kissed her again. She parted her lips and felt a tingle of desire as his tongue tasted the warm softness of her mouth. Experimentally she ran her own tongue over his lips and laughed at the texture of his beard.

Wrinkling her nose, she declared, "I have given you a proper name. One with a meaning you can be proud of. I will call you Bear Who Talks."

"And I will call you 'Elizabeth,'" he promised her, tickling her sensitive neck with his beard.

"Enough, enough!" she laughed as she squirmed under his onslaught.

"What's my name!" he demanded with pretended ferociousness.

"Nathan!" she gasped gleefully. "Nathan Stoddard!"

He raised his head and grinned down at her. Her thick hair made a cape behind her and cushioned her head. Her eyes were dark emerald jewels in her oval face, and laughter made her appear to glow with health. "You're so beautiful," he said softly. "It's hard to believe you really love me."

The laughter in her eyes mellowed to deep emotion and she answered, "I am honored to share love with you."

He smiled. "Fawn, I sure do wish you'd learn more English." He stood and helped her to her feet.

"Why, did you not understand me?" she countered as she started to dress.

"I understand you, all right, but what if we have company? How will you talk to them?"

"Perhaps they will speak Arapaho," she replied saucily. "In which case you should be improving your own vocabulary."

Nathan snorted, but his eyes were smiling as he put on his pants. He went to the adobe building to get his shirt as Fawn braided her hair into a thick plait.

The sunlight had turned the abandoned cubicles into a faded gold that matched the ledge from which they were hewn. It would indeed be difficult to see this place from across the chasm, probably impossible from the upper cliffs or from the valley.

With Nathan's assurance that they couldn't be seen if anyone had been trying to find them, Fawn relaxed. She wandered into one of the small rooms and looked around with interest. It was no larger than the floor of a wigwam and the flat ceiling was not much taller than her head. The door was so low, she had to duck to go into the adjoining room, and the windows were made to the same scale. A shelf that could have been a bed or a bench was part of one wall. Other than this, the room was identical to the first. Opposite from where she entered a doorway led to yet another similar room.

Fawn concluded the former inhabitants were decidedly short of stature and not overly fond of privacy.

Near the end of the row of cubicles, and dug into the outer ledge, was a hole several feet in width and deeper than a man's height. Fawn went to the edge and looked in, but aside from rubble and debris from storms, she saw nothing of interest.

"Don't fall in there," Nathan cautioned as he came out of the cubicle. "I don't want you to break a leg and have to be carried."

"I have no intention of falling in," Fawn informed him. "Why is this hole here?"

"I have no idea." He carelessly folded the blanket and tossed it to the dryest corner of the adobe room. "We need to get back on the trail. I won't feel comfortable until I get back to the cabin and see that everything is all right."

Fawn followed him up the torturous path that led back to the woods and away from the cliff. "Had I seen this path you would never have made me walk it," she complained as she looked over the sheer drop on her left.

"It's a good thing we came at night then, or you would have missed the sunrise."

"I'd have missed more than that," she answered as she recalled the hours they had spent in each other's arms.

He glanced back over his shoulder at her and held out his hand to help her over a difficult place. "No, you wouldn't. Wherever we were, the loving would have happened."

Their eyes met and when their fingers touched, Fawn felt a spark of excitement tingle through her.

They neared the cabin within the hour, and Nathan dropped low in the bushes to study the clearing around it. Nothing broke the cadence of the ordinary forest sounds, and Horse stood docilely in the front yard nibbling at the tufts of grass that had managed to sprout through the pine needles. He still wore his saddle and bridle, but one rein was broken off near his bit and as he grazed he stepped on the remaining one.

"Is something wrong?" Fawn asked in a low voice.

"No," Nathan said cautiously. "Everything seems to be all right." He stood, his muscles tensed for battle. Horse merely looked at him and continued chewing rhythmically.

After a few moments, Nathan relaxed somewhat and motioned for Fawn to come out of hiding. "I was afraid Storm Dancer might have had second thoughts about his loyalty to you, or that one of the other braves had seen us as well. Everything seems to be as it should. I guess they think we're dead."

Fawn slipped her hand into his and looked around. "If my people had come they would have taken Horse and the mules."

"They would have burned the cabin, too. Looks like we're safe." He led Fawn onto the lawn where the huge pines towered like the pillars of a pagan temple.

"I think we may be safer here than you realize," Fawn said reassuringly. "When one of our people dies, all his belongings are shunned lest his spirit covet them. Usually they are burned along with the body. My people may believe this place to be haunted, and they will avoid it."

"Could be," Nathan agreed. "But we must be very cautious for a time. And we should stick close to the cabin so we don't run into any Indians by accident—when we're unprepared."

Horse ambled over to Nathan and drooped his head over the man's shoulder to be petted. Nathan absentmindedly stroked the velvety muzzle before pushing the horse away.

"Don't you come over here and try to make up with me," he scolded the animal. "Thanks to you we could have been dead by now!"

Horse shoved him roughly with his large head and refused to look downcast.

"Damned horse," Nathan grumbled as he removed the bedraggled bridle. "It's a good thing he didn't decide to roll or he could have ruined my good saddle. Just look at his bridle!"

Fawn patted the animal's neck. "I can mend it, Nathan."

"Well, I can too, but it's the principle of the matter."

She smiled at him, understanding his tone if not all his words. The deep dimples flashed in her cheeks and his eyes softened. Shyly Nathan reached up and caressed her cheek.

"If anything had happened to you, I might as

well be dead, too," he told her. "It's amazing how much I've come to love you in such a short time."

She placed her hand over his to hold it to her cheek. "I will feed Horse and unsaddle him," she volunteered. "Then I will make you some breakfast." She smiled at him again, then started toward the barn with Horse at her heels.

She pulled off his saddle and blanket and put the animal in his stall, then poured a measure of grain for him and the other animals. Of all the white man's strange living habits, Fawn liked the barn best of all. The golden haze of sunlight on dust, the musty smell of grain and hay, and the sounds of the animals as they ate all evoked some long-forgotten memory. Had she once known a similar barn and gone there with her unknown father or her mother? The memory was too dim to recall, but its pleasant aura lingered on.

Climbing to the loft, Fawn cut the ropes that bound a bale of hay and kicked some into each of the hayricks. A door at the far end of the loft was open, and a sudden movement near the edge of the forest caught her eye. She knelt quickly in the loose hay and peered through the doorway at the two people below. Her eyes narrowed and a coldness knotted her stomach. Even from that distance she could recognize Charley Three Toes and his Ute wife, Pale Moon.

Fawn eased back into the shadows of the barn, her thoughts racing. Her first impulse was to kill him and avenge her father's death, but reason overtook her. If she showed herself to Charley and failed to kill him, he might tell Walking Tall that she still lived.

From the noise below she knew Nathan had entered the barn. She retreated further into the loft and scanned the stalls below. "Nathan!" she hissed.

At her second whisper, he found her in the loft.

"What are you doing up there?" he grinned. "A man could starve while you lay around in the hay."

She frantically motioned him to silence. Behind him she could see Charley's moccasins and only the dimness of the barn hid her. Once more she cautioned Nathan to be quiet, and drew back from the stairs.

Nathan frowned at her odd behavior and was about to demand an explanation when he heard the footsteps behind him. Whirling, he saw the couple coming toward the barn and he relaxed. It was only his old buddy, Charley, and Pale Moon. Grinning, Nathan went out to meet them.

Chapter Nine

"CHARLEY!" NATHAN BOOMED IN HIS DEEP VOICE. "It's good to see you. It's been months since the last time you were here. Hello, Pale Moon. Have you been keeping him out of trouble?"

The Indian woman blinked and glanced from Nathan to Charley, then back again, but she didn't answer. Nathan had not expected that she would. As far as he knew, Pale Moon spoke little English and was slow-witted as well.

"Hello, Nathan," Charley greeted the huge man. "You look real well." Next to Nathan, Charley seemed small. His wiry frame was encased in greasy buckskins that had taken on the appearance of a second skin. They were grimy and worn slick in places, as was the battered felt hat he wore jammed low on his head. With his swarthy skin and dark hair braided in two strands over his shoulders, Charley looked as much an Indian as Pale Moon. Only a closer inspection revealed the light blue-gray of his eyes.

Pale Moon looked like a female replica of her mate, except that she was as round as he was thin and her eyes were as expressionless as black agates. She wore an even shabbier felt hat and her dress and leggings were embellished with gaudy beads from the trading post at Fire Bluff.

"You're not looking bad yourself," Nathan said heartily as he shook Charley's hand. "Have you been down to Bancroft lately?" At the same time his mind was trying to unravel Fawn's strange actions. Was she all that shy with strangers? Then Nathan recalled Charley's alliance with the Arapahos. Without breaking his stride, Nathan spun Charley around and headed him toward the cabin. "I just put some coffee on to heat," he said jovially. "You go on in and make yourself at home. I've got to look in on my horse but I'll be there in a minute."

Charley nodded and motioned for the woman to follow him. She tied their horses within reach of the watering trough and waddled after him.

Nathan nonchalantly went back into the barn, glanced over his shoulder to make sure he was alone, then hurried up the ladder to the loft.

"What is it, Fawn," he demanded. "Do you know Charley?"

"Yes!" she snapped, her eyes flashing hotly. "He is the snake who shot my father!"

"Charley? Are you sure?"

"Would this woman be mistaken about such a thing?" she demanded. "I'm positive! Not only that, he knows me! If he sees me here, he will tell Walking Tall." She decided it was more prudent, in view of Nathan's friendship with the snake, not to tell him just yet that she still intended to have her revenge by killing Charley.

Nathan frowned. "That's not too good. Charley's my friend and all, but he's Walking Tall's friend as well, and he might let your name drop."

"He is not to be trusted, Nathan!"

"I never said I trusted him. Just that he's my friend. Charley's mean as a rattler. There aren't that many men around here, for me to be choosy." He bit his lip as he puzzled over his newest problem. "It's best if they don't see you, then I won't have to trust him. You stay out here in the loft until I can get him to leave."

Fawn nodded, her almond shaped eyes large in her face. "You won't give me away, will you, Nathan? I mean, you are both of the same people."

He held her face in his hands and kissed her gently. "You don't know much about being in love, do you? Of course I won't tell him you're here."

She studied his face anxiously. She had never heard anyone say that a white man's word could be trusted, but he loved her as she loved him. Perhaps that would make a difference. Besides, she had no other choice. Not unless she wanted to strike off on her own and that seemed unthinkable now. "I will trust you," she stated.

Nathan sighed and shook his head. "It took you long enough to decide. Sometimes you're enough to drive a man crazy. Stay here now and I'll get some food out to you as soon as I can. Charley will probably stay until midafternoon and then be on his way."

Fawn nodded. "You must leave now before he comes looking for you. Never mind the food. I'll eat after they leave."

Once more Nathan kissed her soft lips and looked deeply into her worried eyes. Then he climbed back down the ladder and crossed the yard to the cabin.

"I was about to give you up," Charley said as Nathan came into the house. "Something ailing your horse? I'd be glad to help you with him."

"Nope, Horse is fine. I was just in the middle of feeding when you rode up. How about some breakfast?"

"Don't mind if I do. Pale Moon cooked, of course, but she don't know how to cook anything other than Indian grub. I've tried teaching her, but it just don't take." He swatted the woman's enormous buttocks and she grinned at him.

Nathan turned to the fire and poured himself a cup of coffee. He didn't especially like Pale Moon, but he was offended at Charley's treatment of her. He showed her no more respect than he would a dog and less than he did his scrawny pinto pony. "One of these days Pale Moon's going to learn enough English to understand you, and she'll put a knife through your ribs," Nathan warned.

"Not her! She hasn't got that much gumption, let alone brains. If she can't learn English in the five years I've had her, she can't learn it at all."

"Does she speak any Arapaho?" Nathan asked casually as he put bacon in a skillet.

"Not much. One or two words, near as I can tell. She's Ute, you know."

"Yeah, I remember."

"You ought to buy you a woman," Charley counseled. "I gave her daddy a bundle of hides and a brown mare for her. Of course she's ugly as sin, but she serves her purpose." He grinned over at the woman.

Pale Moon sat stoically gazing at the fire. If she had even heard his words, she gave no sign. Her black eyes were as emotionless as ever and no change of expression crossed her broad face.

"Cut it out, Charley," Nathan said gruffly.

"Why? She can't understand me."

"No, but I can. You want some grits?"

Charley grimaced. "Lord no. That's no better than Indian food."

Nathan spooned the white meal into a small pot of boiling water that sat on a low, iron spider in the coals. "Did you just come from Bancroft?"

"Yeah, there's a passel of folks settling in down there. They've already put up a new boarding house, and there's talk of erecting a church over where the Silver Betty mine used to be. Before long it'll be so civilized, it'll be more crowded than it was in the mining days. People everywhere. When that day comes, I'm moving on."

"But you're the go-between for the Arapahos and us. You won't just clear out and leave us in the lurch, will you?"

Charley shrugged. "Old Many Rivers won't bother you. Why your ways are nearly as Indian as his are—no offense intended. If he wipes out Bancroft, who will care? The place is a blight. Always has been."

Nathan stirred the grits and kept his face averted. So Charley didn't know yet that Many Rivers had died. That meant he didn't know the tribe had been looking for Fawn. Nathan let out his pent up breath. Charley was a superb tracker, and if Walking Tall had sent him to find her, he probably would have. "I'm going to take it that you're joking about that," Nathan said smoothly. "There's a lot of lives at stake in Bancroft with settlers moving in. I can't believe you're the sort to let them be butchered."

"You know me too well, don't you," Charley grinned. Yet his voice was unconvincing.

As Nathan ladled the grits into a bowl, he scrutinized his friend. As a drinking and brawling buddy, Charley had his merits, but he sure wasn't trustworthy. Nathan had no doubts at all that Charley was capable of shooting Fawn's father. He shifted the conversation to trapping and hoped Charley and Pale Moon would soon be on their way.

* * *

Fawn lay on the hay and tried to ignore her growling stomach. The sun was low in the darkening sky and heavy clouds wiped all color from the sunset. The scent of rain hung palpably in the air, and she knew a storm was imminent. Still Charley and Pale Moon lingered in the cabin.

After their escape from Walking Tall, Fawn was exhausted and wanted to lie by the fire and eat a hot meal. Though the days were quite warm now, the nights were still cold and she was too tired to be stoic. And she desired to be near Nathan. His love for her was like a miracle, and she wanted to explore further the wonders of that love. She closed her eyes and again felt his touch. His large hands had been so gentle and had enflamed her to such passion. As tired as she was, she longed to lie with him again. If only Charley would leave!

But what of her revenge? Her feelings of love for Nathan seemed to dispel for the moment her hatred toward her father's killer. She rolled to her side and watched the first raindrops plop down on the bare boards of the loft just inside the open door. The block and tackle used to hoist the hay was swinging in the growing wind and made a lonesome creaking. The treetops of the aspen behind the barn bowed before the sovereign storm like the loyal subjects they were. Their leaves, gray in the approaching night, had turned upside down in supplication for rain, the pale undersides looking ghostly in the dusk.

As the rain increased, the tin roof over her head

rattled loudly. In the distance she heard the low growl of thunder. Fawn sighed dismally. She had always liked rain as long as her bedding stayed dry, but now she was hungry and lonesome. Besides, Charley and Pale Moon were not likely to leave until the storm passed, maybe not until the next morning since it was near dark already.

The sound of the barn door opening below startled Fawn, and she quickly rolled over to face the square hole in the floor. If Charley came up the ladder, what would she do? It was a long way to the ground from the open loft door behind her, but Fawn decided she would take her chances if necessary. She might not survive the jump, but if she broke her neck, at least Walking Tall wouldn't get her.

"Fawn?" she heard Nathan's rumbling whisper. "It's me!"

She edged nearer as Nathan came up the steps. "They have gone?"

"No, I'm afraid not. The rain is keeping them here overnight. Here. I brought you some food." He pulled a bag made of a gunny sack out from under his shirt. "It's some venison and a bit of bread. Not much, I know, but it's all I could slip out. There are some horse blankets in the tack room if you get cold."

She stared at him, incredulously. "You mean I am to sleep out here all night?"

"What else can I do? Charley doesn't even know yet that Many Rivers has died. You're safe as long as you stay out of sight. He let their horses out into the pasture, so he has no reason to come in the barn. Just lie low. I'm sure they'll leave tomorrow."

Fawn grimaced and sighed. "I don't like sleeping in the barn, Nathan. I want to be beside you."

He raised his hand and stroked her face. "I know, Fawn. I want that too, but it can't be helped. I've got to get back inside before they wonder what's keeping me so long." He kissed her, intending the caress to be short, but her softly parting lips held him captive. He drew her to him and kissed her with all the love in his heart. Her yielding body and eager passion made his blood pound with desire. Reluctantly he forced himself to release her. "Tomorrow," he said hoarsely. "They will be gone tomorrow."

Fawn's eyes followed him miserably as he backed down the stairs. She could still taste the raindrops that had clung to his lips and beard, and her dress was damp from his wet shirt. "When you get inside, put on dry clothes," she whispered after him. "I would not want you to get sick."

He grinned up at her, his teeth flashing whitely in the barn's shadows. "I will. You stay dry, and if you get cold, the blankets are in there." He gestured toward the door behind him. Then he was gone.

Fawn flopped back on the straw and frowned at the tin roof as she ate her supper. The last vestiges of light were fading fast and soon the loft would be as dark as the stalls below. A gust of wind hammered rain against her shelter and she shivered. The calico dress wasn't as warm as her Indian clothing, and she wondered why a woman should choose such inconvenient apparel.

Before dark could settle in earnest, Fawn went down the steep stairs and into the tack room. She could make out the mounds that were saddles, feed bins, and other equipment. Feeling around, she discovered several blankets and draped them over her arm. The aroma of horse was strong upon them and she wrinkled her sensitive nose.

She pulled shut the tack room door behind her and felt her way back up the steps to the loft. She knelt on the loose hay from a broken bale and fluffed it into a bed, laying one blanket over the hay and spreading another at her feet.

The worst of the storm had passed, and the rain splattered musically on the roof. Occasionally a flash of yellow lightning illuminated the loft, but the receding thunder held no threat in its voice.

Fawn eased her tired body down onto the blanket. The damp air made its gamey aroma more noticeable, and horse hairs prickled her. She got up and turned the blanket over. For a while she contemplated undressing—the tightly fitted bodice was uncomfortable to sleep in—but the thought of her bare skin on the scratchy horse blanket stopped her. She decided to sleep in her clothing.

Slowly she stretched out, willing herself to sleep. As she drew the top blanket over her, it reached as

far as her elbows before uncovering her toes, but
when she pulled it up to cover her shoulders, her
legs were bare to the knee. Fawn frowned and
kicked the blanket lower. Now her shoulders were
cold again.

She lay on her back and wondered what she had
ever done to deserve such foul treatment from her
totem. True, she was safe to some extent, but she
was far from comfortable. Dampness seeped in
from the gaping loft door and gusts of wet air
penetrated every crack and crevice in the barn
siding. She was aware of a bothersome draft from
below. Her nose tickled from the close proximity of
the horse blankets and she felt an almost over-
whelming urge to sneeze.

Fawn sat up and glared at the bed. Perhaps
Nathan could be content with such meager comfort, but she could not.

She worked her way back down the steps and
threw the offensive blankets into the tack room. It
was warmer down here with the barn door shut and
the body heat of the horses and mules. Perhaps she
could sleep in one of the empty stalls.

She groped her way down the lane between the
stalls, but before she had found the one she knew
to be clean and empty, she heard Horse stamp his
feet warily.

"Quiet, Horse," she whispered. "It is only
Fawn."

Horse had formed a liking for her and he whickered softly at her voice.

"Sssh!" she pleaded.

Again he nickered, this time more loudly. She rarely came to him without a treat in her pocket and he was always ready for a handout.

Fawn made an exasperated noise and backed away. Horse would have them all out here if she stayed there. Cautiously she opened the door and peered out.

The cabin was almost invisible in the night. The pines made an umbrella through which the rain dripped gently, and the thick carpet of needles soaked up the puddles. All the lights were out, as she had expected.

Silently Fawn let herself out of the barn and made her way from tree to tree to the cabin. Her heart was thudding at her daring, as she crept to the window and looked in.

Charley and Pale Moon lay in front of the dying fire, the woman a mound under the blankets, dwarfing Charley's thin form. There was no movement except for the steady rise and fall of their breathing. Fawn smiled.

Being careful to make no noise, she went around the cabin to the bedroom window. In spite of the darkness, she stealthily raised the window and swung her long legs over the sill. It was even darker inside as Nathan had not bothered to make a fire for himself.

Moving barely an inch at a time, she pulled off her damp dress and let it fall to the floor. Pulling her moccasins from her feet, she felt for the bed.

Her fingertips brushed it and she discovered Nathan's form beneath the blanket.

Carefully she eased onto the bed and relaxed happily as the clean, warm sheets enfolded her. Suddenly she was grabbed by two enormous hands and she nearly cried out in surprise.

"Fawn?" Nathan hissed. "Fawn! It *is* you! What in the hell are you doing in here!"

"The barn is cold and wet and smells of animals. I came in here to sleep!" she answered in a low whisper.

"I told you to cover up with the horse blankets!"

"I am longer than a horse blanket, Nathan, and they *smell.*"

"But damn it, Fawn, if Charley hears you . . ."

"He will not hear me if you will not be so loud! I was very quiet and even you didn't hear me come in. Is this not true?"

"What if he's not asleep yet?"

"He is. I looked in the window. Trust me, Nathan. We Indians know how to do these things."

He scowled at her in the darkness. "Do you remember how much trouble we got in the last time you said something like that?"

"If you want me to leave, say so," she retorted. She slid closer to him and let her body brush against his. She heard him draw in his breath sharply and she knew she had won.

"You aren't wearing any clothes!" he observed.

"I never sleep in clothes, Nathan. Is it the custom of your people's women to sleep in their clothes? It seems to be a silly custom to me. The dresses are too tight for one to breathe properly." She put her hand on his chest and entwined her fingers in the thick curling hair. Slowly she nuzzled in the warm curve of his neck and traced a fiery trail with the tip of her tongue. "Must I go back to the barn, Nathan?" she asked innocently.

"No," he answered hoarsely as he pulled her to him.

Their lips met in the velvety darkness and Fawn felt her world spin as he kissed her thoroughly, expertly. With maddening slowness he ran his hand over her back, bringing her skin to flame, stroking her rounded arm, then cupping her breast. Fawn felt her nipple tighten against his palm and she arched her back to make greater contact with him.

Nathan stroked her satiny skin, teasing the peak to throbbing eagerness. He let his knowing fingers caress the sensitive swell of her straining breast, then travel lower to rest on the flat plane of her stomach as he lowered his lips to encompass her nipple. It was all Fawn could do to remain silent as he took her breast in his mouth. The hotness of his tongue brought her to even greater heights. He flicked her tender nipple with the tip of his tongue and she bit her lip to keep from moaning aloud.

His manhood was hot and erect against her thigh and she rubbed her body against him sensuously. As her hand found him, she heard him smother his own moan of desire.

Gently he eased her legs apart and entered her.

Fawn buried her face against his shoulder to prevent herself from crying out as he began to move deeply, slowly, urging her to an eager response. She met and matched his rhythm and before she knew what was happening, she seemed to burst in a golden ecstasy that sent waves of sheer delight pounding through her. As she gripped him in her passion, he gave a low murmur and she felt him reach his own release.

They floated in the dreamy haze of afterlove, sharing gentle kisses, loving caresses. The night shrouded them, wrapped them in a protective cloak. Still nestled securely in Nathan's embrace, Fawn lay her head on his shoulder and began to drift into sleep.

Before dawn Nathan awoke her with soft kisses. She smiled and snuggled deeper into his arms.

"Wake up," he murmured in her ear. "Pale Moon will start moving around soon and you have to go back to the barn."

Remembrance flooded over her and Fawn sighed. "Will they leave today?"

"Yes. Charley told me he is on his way to the Arapahos with furs for Chief Many Rivers. He's late making his rounds this year and he plans to leave early this morning."

She narrowed her eyes angrily. "I will wait for him beside the trail and kill him to avenge my father's death."

"No, you won't. In the first place, I'm not going

to let you get hurt. If you try anything like that, Charley will finish whatever you start. In the second place, if Charley doesn't show up, Walking Tall may send scouts looking for him. Those furs he's delivering are yearly payment from some of the settlers around here."

Gracefully, Fawn rolled from the bed and found her doeskin garments in the dark. Silently she dressed and pushed the dress she had worn the day before under the bed.

"You heard me, Fawn," Nathan whispered warningly. "Let Charley go in peace. Do you hear me?"

"This woman has perfect hearing," she snapped as she slipped on her moccasins. As silently as she had entered, Fawn raised the window and climbed out, closing it behind her. For a moment she was silhouetted against the graying sky, then she merged with the deeper shadows and was gone.

Fawn made her way cautiously back to the barn, but she was seething with rebellion. All her troubles stemmed from Charley murdering her father. Had Elk Tooth lived, he would have counseled her not to marry Many Rivers. She wouldn't be a castaway now if it weren't for Charley's bullet. Besides, a blood oath was not to be taken lightly, and she had sworn revenge. Already she had weakened her oath by deciding to spare other whites—but how could she let Charley go free?

She looked in the front window where Charley still sprawled beside the Ute woman. If they were

135

anywhere else, she could stab him in his sleep. Of course that was cowardly. And Pale Moon might attack her in retribution. Fawn drew back and grimaced. It was out of the question to do anything to Charley in Nathan's cabin. Charley's spirit would never leave them alone, and Nathan would certainly never agree to burn down his house to get rid of the ghost. She thought with exasperation of one more way that a wigwam was superior to a cabin—it could be replaced much more easily.

Fawn went across the yard to the barn, her feet leaving no mark on the thick pine needles. The sky was lightening to pewter in the east, and already the stars had hidden from their enemy, the sun. Fawn glared balefully at the cabin as she went into the barn.

When she reached the safety of the hayloft, Fawn lay back on the straw and watched the sky grow paler. There was only one logical path for Charley and Pale Moon to take up the mountain with their laden horses and the travois. She sat up, her moss-green eyes alert and thoughtful. If she left now she could reach a certain thicket before anyone else was fully awake.

Fawn hurried down the steps and skirted the barn, keeping the building between her and the cabin. Trotting steadily uphill, she found the point she sought. A wall of red rocks jutted from the mountainside and split to form a tiny canyon. The opening was wide enough to allow the passage of one rider at a time, but not broad enough for maneuvering room. Fawn hid herself in the bushes above and held her knife in a clenched fist.

After nearly an hour, she heard the muffled clopping of horse's hooves and the low sound of conversation. She tensed. If she handled this right, she could throw her knife into Charley and be gone before Pale Moon saw her. She would have only one chance, but she felt confident she could do it. With muscles quivering from tension, Fawn leaned forward and balanced the weapon in her fingers.

They were close enough now that she could see Charley's rangy pinto heading into the rock crevasse. Behind him trailed a dun colored buckskin with a distinctive blaze face. Fawn drew back abruptly. Nathan! Nathan was riding close behind Charley with Pale Moon bringing up the rear.

Her plan was ruined! Nathan might see her, and even if he didn't, he would recognize her knife. Fawn was overcome with disappointment and she sent a mental apology to Elk Tooth in case his spirit hovered nearby and knew of her plan.

Nathan was carrying most of the conversation, with Charley infrequently adding a word or two. He seemed blithely unaware of the spoiled ambush as he joked with the smaller man. Fawn let herself smile at the white man's naivety.

At the end of the crevasse, Nathan bid Charley good-bye and nodded a farewell to Pale Moon, who ignored him as always. "Next time you're down this way, drop by," he said jovially.

Charley shot him an appraising look and narrowed his eyes. "For a man that was so glad to get back to his trapping, you sure are wasting a lot of time."

"I don't know what you're talking about, Charley. I told you I left those traps up on the ridge there. It's time to check them."

"Something just don't feel right. Like those hide hoops I saw. I never knew you to soften hides like that. The only people I ever saw use those kinds of hoops were Arapahos." Charley grinned slyly and poked at Nathan with his elbow. "You wouldn't have you a little squaw hid out around here, would you?"

"Of course not!" Nathan stated emphatically. "But what if I did?"

"Why, it'd be funny if you had one. After all your talk about not needing a woman around and all, it'd be a real joke to find out you'd turned into a squaw man, at that."

Nathan frowned. "That's mighty peculiar talk coming from you."

Charley grinned back at the expressionless Pale Moon. "The difference is that I don't care." Still laughing, Charley kicked his horse and went on up the trail with the woman following behind.

Nathan grimaced. If he and Fawn got married, this was only a sample of the ridicule they would have to bear. Still scowling, he guided Horse back into the crevasse. "Come on, Fawn," he called out. "I know you're there. Let's go home."

She jumped at his unexpected remark and without showing herself said, "How did you know I was here?"

He glanced up at her hiding place. "The bush in front of you is the only one that isn't waving in the breeze. Besides, it's the place I would have picked for an ambush, too. Come get on behind me and I'll give you a ride."

Glumly she climbed out of the bushes and down the low rocks to jump onto Horse's broad rump. "You see, Nathan," she said respectfully, "in your heart you are Arapaho."

He rode quietly, enjoying the feel of her hands on his waist. "I told you to leave Charley alone," he reminded her gruffly. "You can't go around killing people. It's not right."

"Even if he killed my father? Surely even whites have a system of justice."

"Sure we do, but we don't go around ambushing people."

"He shot my father in the back."

Nathan took a deep breath and let it out slowly. "How can you be so sure it was Charley?"

"I was there and I saw it. I had become separated from the other women and was tired of picking berries, so I went for a walk. My father had killed a doe and was skinning her when Charley rode up. Charley demanded that my father give the deer to him, and when my father refused, he shot him."

"That seems pretty unlikely. The woods are full of game, and Charley's a good hunter."

"This is what Storm Dancer said, too. But I heard all that went between them. Charley said, 'I have come for her and I want you to give her to me.' My father looked very angry and told him, 'Never will I do this!' Then Charley said, 'Then I will take her anyway!' and when my father turned to walk away, Charley shot him. I backed away quietly, then ran to the village. Later, when Storm Dancer questioned Charley, he claimed he had been hunting with my father and shot him accidentally, thinking he was a deer. No one believed me. I was young and unmarried and could not sit in council." Her voice had been carefully modulated throughout her story, but now it quavered in painful recollection.

Nathan pulled her hands around him so that her cheek was on his back and he covered both her hands with one of his. "I believe you, Fawn."

"You do?"

"Yes, but I don't think it was the deer they were discussing. I think it was you."

"Me!"

"And that's all the more reason to stay out of Charley's way. I don't want him around you even if I thought he wouldn't tell Walking Tall where you are."

Fawn rode silently for a while, her cheek feeling the rippling muscles of Nathan's back as Horse walked along. "That does make more sense, doesn't it!" she said at last. "Charley must have been bargaining for me!"

"You're safe with me," Nathan said tersely. "He probably won't be back this way for another six months."

Chapter Ten

FAWN WANDERED BESIDE ONE OF THE STREAMS THAT fed Wolf Creek. The crystal clear water threaded its way over and around mossy logs and large, rounded stones as it hurried down the steep incline. At the bottom of the hill the woods ended and the tiny stream widened into a high meadow where tall grasses furred the meandering banks. Fawn saw no sign of life but knew by the series of dams and mounded sticks that she stood beside a large beaver colony. The creatures were notoriously shy and, not expecting to catch even a glimpse of one, she made no effort to be silent. She picked up a stick that had been stripped of its bark. Both ends were chiseled where the beavers had cut it to their measure. Fawn idly poked around in the long grasses, enjoying the warmth of the sun on her back.

Beyond the meadow, the craggy mountain reared high above the trees. Its wind-battered tundra was covered with a plant that clung like fur to its surface and was broken only by the slate gray of granite sheets. In the deep ruts of the upper slopes lay milky white snow that never thawed, even during the hottest summers. Four small dots moved beside one of the glaciers. Fawn squinted to improve her vision and recognized a family of mountain goats.

Intently watching the goats, she was suddenly startled when iron jaws grabbed the stick and jerked it out of her grasp. Trembling all over, Fawn stared down at the trap that had nearly severed the end of the stick. Were there others nearby? She looked around quickly, unsure of the way she had come, but her path was marked by the bent grass beside the stream.

Sudden anger flared within her. It was wrong to trap animals! It was grossly unfair! At least in a hunt the animals had a chance to outmaneuver the hunter!

Using the end of the mangled stick, Fawn dug out the metal pin that held the trap in place. Holding it by the chain, she whirled the trap around her head once then let it go. It arched high over the grasses and landed squarely in the middle of the beaver pond.

Methodically, Fawn searched until she had found ten more traps. She tripped the jaws and threw them all into the pond. With each one she felt a strength flow into her spirit and she knew her totem was pleased. No more metal traps would ensnare the shy beavers.

Fawn sat on a knoll beneath a maple tree, regarding the beaver pond. She knew she had done the right thing, but what would Nathan say? He depended upon his traps for the furs that he traded for their necessities. She knew it would be futile to tell Nathan that many of the items he considered necessary were really luxuries. Besides, Fawn was beginning to enjoy these luxuries as well.

From her childhood a thought came to her. As a boy, Storm Dancer had taught her to make rabbit snares out of limber branches and leather thongs. Later he had shown her how to build a live trap. But at this point in her training, Elk Tooth had caught his son demonstrating these tricks and up-braided him severely. Women had no need of such knowledge, and Fawn would be wanting to know next about forbidden things like warrior rituals. The lessons had stopped—but Fawn remembered.

Using her knife, she cut an armload of tender saplings from around the pond. On the way home, she hummed a lullaby from her half-forgotten childhood.

Later that day, Nathan sat whittling on the bowl he was carving for the baby of friends down the mountain. He was contented after the delicious meal Fawn had prepared, and his cabin was spotless and comfortable as it had rarely been before she had come. Fawn sat on a bear rug in front of the fire, completely oblivious to his scrutiny. The golden blaze silhouetted her patrician features and the graceful curve of her neck. A thick braid hung over each shoulder and glowed dark red in the firelight. Bronze highlights played upon her sensuous lips and high forehead, and her well-molded cheeks were planes of gold.

For a long time Nathan watched her and drank in her beauty. He had not realized what a lonely life he led before he met Fawn. She made him wonder if he had been wrong about marriage all along.

"What are you making?" he asked in order to hear her voice.

She glanced up at him and smiled, her deep dimples appearing enticingly. "I am making traps. See? The animal goes in this hole here into the cage after food. But the sticks of the opening point toward the cage so he cannot get out again." She held the trap up for his inspection and her teeth gleamed whitely in the firelight as her sparkling eyes enslaved his heart. "Is this not a good idea, Nathan?"

"Yes, it's a very good idea. But Fawn, I have all the traps I need."

"No, you do not, Nathan. Not anymore."

He laughed down at her, enjoying the sound of her lilting, oddly phrased words and her fleeting smile. "Sure I do. I have nearly a dozen up at the beaver pond."

She shook her head. "I threw them all into the water today. Look, Nathan, do you think I have made the door large enough?"

"What?" he said, still grinning. "I must have missed that first part. Say it in English."

She repeated her words. "I threw all your traps into the pond. Now I am making new ones that are kinder to the animals." She tossed him another angelic smile and firmly knotted the thong that held the cage together.

For a few moments Nathan sat there, the grin slowly fading from his face. "You threw the traps into the pond? Is that what you said, Fawn?"

She nodded. "These are so much better. Every night I will make two and soon you will have all you need."

His roar startled her. She jumped as he leaped from his chair and towered over her. "You threw my good metal traps in the *water?*" he bellowed. "Damn it, woman, have you lost your mind?"

"No, Nathan! There is nothing wrong with me. Did you not hear me say I was making you more to replace them?"

"Why in the hell did you decide to do such a damn fool thing? Those traps cost every cent I had saved from all my years as a prospector! Without traps we'll never make it!"

"We will use live traps," she said staunchly as she stood to face him. "We will catch more pelts than ever and the animals' spirits will not be angry at us."

"Don't talk to me about spirits! I'm not interested in any Indian mumbo jumbo."

"I do not understand that word," she snapped as her own temper flared, "but I hear your meaning! I have been insulted!" She jerked her head up regally and her eyes became daggers of flint.

"Don't you take that high and mighty attitude with me! You're the one at fault here!"

"This woman cannot hear you!" Fawn turned her back stiffly and crossed her arms in a stance that spelled stubborn withdrawal.

Her attitude infuriated Nathan even further. "Turn around here and talk to me!" he growled low in his throat.

Fawn glared at him over her shoulder. "This woman cannot understand your words." She looked back at the fire. "If she *could* understand you, she would say she threw the traps away because one of them attacked her."

"Attacked . . ." Nathan tried to sort out her meaning. "Fawn! Did you step in one of those traps?" He pulled her around and held her at arms length. "You aren't hurt, are you?"

"No, Nathan," she said coldly, her arms still crossed. "I was not hurt, but I might have been."

Relief brought back his anger. "Then why in the hell did you do it! In one afternoon you threw away my entire livelihood!"

"Again this woman cannot hear you." She compressed her lips into a firm line and glared at him. "My way is best! An Indian knows these things!"

"You're not an Indian! Your name is Elizabeth!" He shoved up her sleeve and pointed at her pale skin. "You're as white as I am! Look at these braids! Red as fire! And your eyes are *green,* not black!"

Tears welled in her large eyes. "You need not insult me! Never have I done this to you—even though you have yellow hair on your face and your eyes are light and not dark as eyes are meant to be! Why do you insult a helpless woman!"

"Helpless! Hah!" He glared down at her. "You're the least helpless person I ever met! *Elizabeth!*"

"I'm glad I threw your wicked traps in the water! I wish I had thrown you in as well!"

"Talk English, damn it!"

"I said I wish I had thrown you into the river too!" she shouted back at him.

Nathan frowned down at her. She didn't seem the least bit intimidated by his angry bluster. Not many men had ever come back at him like that. The sight of her face so pale with righteous anger made him realize the uselessness of their battle. "You've already thrown me in the river, once. Remember the cliff by the Indian village?" The tone of his words had not changed, but his angry expression had softened.

Fawn looked puzzled as she tried to understand the incongruity. Then she realized that teasing had replaced his anger, and she relaxed somewhat. "I apologize for throwing away your traps," she ventured cautiously, ready to back up and attack again if necessary. "It was, perhaps, presumptuous."

He nodded wryly. "Perhaps." He made a move to take her in his arms, but she planted her hand firmly on his chest.

"Now you!" she said unequivocably.

"What?"

"You said I was not of the People."

"But you aren't!"

She tossed her head. "When you are ready to apologize, I will hear you." She turned to go.

"Wait, Fawn. Don't go." Nathan pulled her into his embrace and nuzzled her hair. "I'm sorry I hurt your feelings. Forgive me?"

"Yes," she said reluctantly, "I will forgive you."

He kissed the tender skin behind her ear, sending sparks of desire racing through her. She murmured gentle sounds of love and put her arms around him to pull him closer. His soft beard tickled her neck, but it felt sensuous rather than irritating. She ran the tip of her tongue over the curve of his ear and laughed when he shivered.

"I'm glad I forgave you," she told him as she ran her fingers through his thick hair.

"Let's talk about it in bed," he suggested as he caressed her supple back and ran his hand over the curve of her breast.

With a smile, Fawn took his hand and led him through the bedroom door.

"Put one there, near the packed grass," Fawn instructed as Nathan sat the trap on the ground.

"This is where the otters have been using the bank as a slide."

"I know," he said with thinning patience.

"Here. Put this dried fish in the bottom. A little further inside."

Nathan sighed and looked up at her testily. "How many more of these do we have?"

"Maybe half a dozen," she replied looking at the string of wooden traps.

"That means we've already set out eight?"

"Yes, Nathan."

"Well, I think I've got the hang of it. You've been a lot of help, Fawn, but I'm able to do it on my own now."

"You put the fish too close to the opening. The otter can get it without going all the way into the cage," she pointed out helpfully. "See? If I put it in this corner, he has to come all the way inside and the ends of the sticks keep him from getting out again."

"I know how it works, Fawn."

"Nathan! You are angry with me," she accused in a hurt voice.

He stood and put his hand caressingly on her glowing auburn hair. "I'm not angry. But you must have other things to do and I don't want to inconvenience you."

She gazed up at him uncertainly. "There is nothing I need to do right away." Her expression brightened and she smiled. "Next we will go upstream to the rocky shoal. I saw raccoon tracks there yesterday." She picked up the string of traps and hung it over her shoulder.

"Wait a minute," Nathan caught her arm. "You know, this is giving me a big appetite, what with us working so hard and all. A few days ago I was up on the ridge behind the cabin and I noticed the first of the raspberries are ripe. What I would really like for supper is a raspberry pie."

"Pie?" she said doubtfully.

"I'll show you how. First though, we need some raspberries. Would you mind picking some?"

"Of course not, Nathan, but I promised you I would help you set the traps."

He smiled and took the string from her. "I know, Fawn, and I can't tell you how much help you've been, but I can handle it from here." He bent and kissed her. "I'll see you in a couple of hours, and between the two of us we will turn out the best raspberry pie this mountain has ever seen."

Reluctantly she turned to go. Glancing back over her shoulder, she said, "You're sure you don't need me any more?"

He waved her on. "Just get the berries, Fawn. A syrup bucket full will be about right."

"Be sure to put a trap at the shoal," she called out as she left, "and don't forget to tell the trap's spirit that you are Indian or it won't work as well for you."

"Right."

Fawn went back to the work shed and got the tin bucket she used for berrying. A gallon sounded like too many berries, but she decided she could dry whatever they didn't use. It was a beautiful day with skies the color of Nathan's eyes, and as she walked up the ridge she swung the bucket by the wire bale and hummed a tune. Far away in the woods she could hear a quail calling for its mate. The female answered in a plaintive tone. Fawn smiled. All of nature seemed to be as much in love as she was. She listened to their whistles as the quails made their way to each other.

The ridge was covered with bushes and the ripening berries were clustered thick upon them. She knelt and started picking. They made a satisfactory thumping sound when they hit the metal bottom of the bucket. The sun was warm on her back and a breeze cooled her face. The day was perfect.

In the woods beyond, another male quail called out. The female answered and veered in his direction. The first male whistled imperatively. As Fawn munched on one of the juicy berries, she wondered which male would win the fickle attention of the hen.

The contest made her think about Nathan. She had never asked him if he had been seeing another woman before she came onto the scene. He had told her once that he never intended to marry, but she put very little stock in his speech. Storm Dancer had used almost the same words only weeks before he took a wife. So had Many Rivers. It was clear to her that all men said such things and that it meant nothing.

Fawn pushed the leaves aside to find more of the hidden berries. She tried to imagine what sort of woman Nathan would have chosen. Probably one with hair as yellow as his own, she decided. Had he remained unmarried because there were no women? Settlers had only recently moved into the former mining town of Bancroft. She frowned slightly. Nathan went to Bancroft and Fire Bluff fairly often. Did he see a woman while he was there? Fawn wished this thought had never occurred to her, but the notion lodged firmly in her mind.

For weeks now they had lived together as husband and wife. She cooked his meals, mended his clothes, and cleaned their home. At night she lay in his strong arms and loved him. He had said that he wanted to be with her forever, but marriage was not a subject for discussion. Fawn threw a handful of plump berries into the bucket. Was this not a strange way for him to treat her? He said he loved her, but what did that mean? Words were easy to come by and Nathan was a talkative man. Was he telling her the truth?

The quails whistled again and Fawn noticed the female was again angling toward the first suitor. The second male called in vain as her voice grew fainter in the distance.

Was that the way it would be with her, she wondered. Would she only touch Nathan's life for a short time and then watch him leave her for some woman with yellow hair who always wore gingham skirts?

Fawn frowned down at her blue cotton dress. She wore it because Nathan had given it to her and it pleased him. Did he like it because it reminded him of someone else? It was time, she decided, to sew herself another doeskin dress. If Nathan wanted her, he must take her as she was—and that would not be in calico that caught on every bramble and was too snug to allow a breeze to touch her skin.

Fawn felt considerably better after her decision. She regained some of her former bounce as she planned the beadwork she would sew on the new dress.

Nathan shouldered aside the lower branches of a sapling and put the trap on the brown mud of the river bank. He glanced around and saw that Fawn was right about the location. Raccoon tracks dotted the mud by the water's edge. A long shoal of pebbles jutted out into the water and made a perfect place for a raccoon to fish.

He pushed the trap under a low juniper so that the wooden bars appeared to be juniper limbs. Then he put dried fish well inside and used a branch of leaves to dust away his tracks. Few animals were as crafty as raccoons but he knew most of their tricks. Fawn's words about spirits came back to him but he ignored them. Nathan Stoddard wasn't about to talk to a wooden trap, not even to catch prime pelts.

Shouldering the rest of the traps, he strode off through the woods. It was a beautiful day and the leaves reminded him of Fawn's eyes. When she faced into the sunlight her eyes looked almost emerald green, like river moss, with gold flecks in their depths. In the shade they were the color of pine needles, darker and more mysterious.

Nathan was so engrossed in his thoughts that he was almost into the tiny meadow before a movement caught his attention. He halted abruptly and looked again at the tall grasses. Something just didn't seem right. A breeze uniformly flattened the tips of the silky grasses, except at the far side of the meadow.

Nathan melted silently against the heavily furrowed trunk of a huge box elder and let its shadow hide him while he surveyed the area. In a few moments, he heard the faint rustle of dry twigs at the edge of the forest to his left. Seconds later, a large elk stepped cautiously into the meadow. Nathan glanced back at the still grass and his eyes narrowed.

The elk took another hesitant step and lifted his nose to scent the air. Suddenly there was a twanging sound followed by a dull thud. The elk dropped to the ground.

An Indian stood up and motioned to his two companions. Nathan's heart pounded as he watched the three men approach and begin to dress out their kill. Nathan didn't move a muscle, knowing he could easily be discovered. The Indians worked very swiftly over the animal and soon had the elk carcass slung onto a tree limb and were carrying it away between them.

Nathan remained still until they were too far away to hear him. He slowly let out his pent up breath and made his way back into the thick forest. Only sheer luck and a hunter's instinct had saved him. He had to be careful, he reprimanded himself. If the Indians had so much as seen him, they would know he and Fawn were still alive. Nathan shuddered. He and Fawn would never be able to lead a normal life together until the Indian danger was past.

Chapter Eleven

"I'VE NEVER KNOWN THEM TO HUNT SO FAR DOWN THE mountain," Nathan worried aloud to Fawn. "It's a miracle they didn't see me."

She remained silent, but a frown puckered her forehead as she stirred the dying fire back to life.

"If they ever see me, they'll know we escaped. I don't think they have a quarrel with me, but they'll never rest until they see you dead." Worry tinged his voice. Fawn caught his hand and pulled him down beside her on the bearskin rug. "We have to do something, but I'm blamed if I know what." He eased her back into his arms so that she lay against his chest. He rubbed his cheek on her soft hair and they gazed into the fire as if awaiting an answer.

Absently, Fawn picked one of the large pine

cones from the basket in which she had gathered them and tossed it into the fire. The flames quickly transformed it into a glowing red-gold fire flower.

"If only they were sure I was dead," she said at last, "they would leave you alone."

Nathan watched the pine cone disintegrate and fall to ashes. "Maybe we could make them think you are."

She turned her head to look up at him. "How can we do that?"

Nathan's sharp blue eyes studied the fire carefully before he spoke. "We could rig it up to look as if you died. If we leave your yellow dress—you remember you were wearing it that day—where they will find it, they'll assume you drowned."

"And the river washed away my dress? No, Nathan, they will never believe that."

"They will if they find your body in it."

She tried to sit up, but he pulled her back.

"Hear me out, Fawn. The skeleton of a bear's paw looks enough like a human hand to fool anybody. If a man found a few bones wrapped up in a calico dress and a skeleton hand wearing that beaded bracelet of yours, what else could he think but that it's you?"

"My medicine bracelet?" she said covering her wrist. "If you use my charm, I will fall sick!"

"Oh, shoot, Fawn. We can make another one. Think about it."

She frowned and looked back at the fire. "They might believe it. Maybe."

"Of course they would," he said with growing excitement. "The river has a shallow stretch not far below the Indian village. I know they use it as a ford because I've seen their tracks."

Fawn fingered the intricate beadwork of her bracelet. It was the best one she had ever made, but she knew Nathan was right. The spirits might be offended, but they had not been overly protective of her since her father's death anyway. Resolutely, she slipped the bracelet from her hand and gave it to Nathan. "We will try it," she decided firmly.

Fawn remained at the edge of the woods while Nathan hurried upstream carrying his grisly burden. He kept to the swift, shallow water so there would be no tracks in the mud or grass. Just beyond the ford, the water deepened and flowed around several large boulders. He waded out knee deep and submerged the dress in the river. Quickly, he secured the material in a crack in the rock so the current couldn't snatch it away. It streamed just below the surface like a billowing yellow flag.

Giving one last look toward the calico dress, Nathan hurried back to Fawn. "They can't miss it," he whispered.

She looked around nervously. "Let's go, Nathan. This is much too close to the village. The braves may ride by at any moment."

"Crouch down low in this gully and let's wait a bit longer. I want to be sure the dress won't work loose and float away before they have time to find it."

Fawn lowered herself to the ground so that only her eyes were visible over the small brush-strewn hillock. Nathan's amber hair and leather shirt blended invisibly into their surroundings. She prayed that she was equally well covered.

After what seemed to be an eternity, Nathan nodded in satisfaction. "It's going to stay there," he whispered. "Let's . . ."

Fawn's fingers bit into his arm, warning him to silence. She nodded almost imperceptibly at the wooded path beyond the creek.

Walking Tall and half a dozen braves were riding toward them. By the game they carried tied to their horses, Fawn saw they had been hunting. So close to their village, they were riding carelessly and talking to one another. A short, squat Indian made a joke and the men laughed. Fawn's heart felt as if it would burst with her fear. Incongruously, she recalled how often she had heard that same man joke, how many times he had made her laugh with some humorous remark. And now she was hiding from him with fear in her heart that he would surely kill her if he saw her. Fawn closed her eyes and wished she and Nathan were safely back at the cabin.

The first horses had splashed into the stream before anyone noticed the bright yellow garment waving beneath the rushing water. One of the older men exclaimed and pointed toward it. A young brave whom Fawn had helped nurse through an illness two winters before waded out and gingerly retrieved the tattered dress.

All the Indians dismounted and Walking Tall bent to inspect the dress. When he held it up, the carefully concealed bones dropped out, one of them wearing Fawn's medicine bracelet.

With a startled exclamation, the young chief jumped back. The braves moved away uneasily. It was the very worst of luck to touch the belongings of a dead tribal member, much less the decomposed remains, and the younger brave wiped his hands nervously on his leggings.

The Indians held a short conference of rapid words and gestures. The youngest brave was all for leaving the dress and bones where they were. The older ones insisted that as the remains of the dead chief's wife, they should be properly cremated. Walking Tall reluctantly agreed but he had the younger brave gather the bones into the dress rather than touch them himself.

The Indians mounted their horses, the unfortunate younger brave carrying the yellow dress and its contents. With a glance back at the river, Walking Tall signaled them toward the path that led to the village.

Fawn lay her cheek on the rough ground and breathed for the first time in several seconds.

"They went for it!" Nathan whispered excitedly. "By gum, they believe it was you!"

Fawn raised her head and threw him a withering

look. "You had better hope they burn those bear bones right away. They didn't look very convincing to me." She slowly sat up and looked up and down the trail. "Let's leave here, Nathan. I don't feel safe so close to the village."

He got up and held out his hand to pull her to her feet. Silently they went back to their horses. She jumped onto the broad back of the white mare that Nathan had brought her from Fire Bluff on his last visit and swung her leg over its round rump. As Nathan got on Horse, the big buckskin snapped at him, his long yellowed teeth making an audible click in the air beside Nathan's knee.

Nathan pulled the horse's head around and motioned for Fawn to move out ahead of him. As they rode away, he glanced back from time to time, but there was no sign of anyone following them.

"We got away with it," he said exuberantly as they neared the cabin.

"I am only glad my brother was not in the hunting party," Fawn replied. "It will make him very sad to think I am drowned."

"Better him sad than us dead," Nathan reminded her. "We just did what we had to do."

"I know." Fawn nudged her horse to a trot that made further conversation impossible. It was as if part of her had indeed died, and she felt a severing of her spirit from the tribe. No longer would her name be spoken, and in the hearts of her former friends and family she would be dead. Storm Dancer and her mother, Clouds Passing, would mourn. But their show of grief would be muted because she had brought them disgrace not only by refusing to follow Many Rivers into the next world, but also by becoming a white man's woman afterward. Fawn urged her horse to a faster gait to hide the tears in her eyes.

Chapter Twelve

A WARM BREEZE TOSSED HER UNBOUND HAIR AS Fawn gathered wild green onions and broad poke leaves. Nathan had been gone several days on another trading trip to Bancroft and Fire Bluff, and she had decided to surprise him with a white man's supper upon his return. She carried a pointed stick to dislodge the onions and any other tasty roots she might find. The summer had been plentiful due to an abundant rainfall and the plants were verdant and lush.

Nathan had packed several bales of pelts to trade and told her it would take him only three days to visit both trading posts. Still she was lonesome. She disliked being left behind, but in spite of all her arguments Nathan refused to let her go with him. It was better this way, he had said, but she wondered for whom. The cabin seemed to echo without Nathan and the nights were as endless as the days. Besides, now that she no longer feared him or his kind, she was curious to see how his people lived.

Fawn had wandered farther afield than usual and she looked up at the sun to gauge how many hours she had before sundown. The fiery ball hung midway down in the sky, casting shadows as long as the trees were tall. She decided to start back.

As she entered the woods, the trees arched like a cathedral above her and the leaves, deep green with summer health, made the sunlight seem cool, as if she were viewing it from under water. At intervals she passed clumps of woods flowers that bloomed only in the shade, their foliage too tender to bear sunlight and their blooms a waxy white like frozen flames.

Fawn crossed a narrow creek by walking across a fallen tree trunk. Judging by the dying leaves that still withered on its scaly branches, she guessed the tree must have toppled in a recent storm. She jumped off the log and felt the ground moist and springy beneath her feet. Near the stream she caught sight of a cluster of spear shaped leaves.

Fawn smiled. Some ramps would be good with the poke greens. They were stronger than onions and would give their strength to Nathan, who would be tired after his trip. Fawn knelt in the shade of the fallen tree and used her stick to pry the short, thick bulbs from the soil. They grew in a large knot of entwined roots, so when one came up the others followed.

As she pulled off as many as she wanted, Fawn glanced at the hole again. She lay the ramps, dirt and all, in her basket and prodded in the hole with her stick.

First one gleaming gold nugget broke loose from the soil, then another. There seemed to be many more beyond those, all shining in the brown mud.

Fawn sat back on her heels. Nathan had told her of the years he had spent searching for gold. But he had never said why. It was pretty, but it was too soft to use for arrow tips and it wouldn't strike fire like flint. All in all, it was rather useless except for its beauty. Besides, Nathan was no longer a prospector, he was a trapper.

Fawn shrugged, covering the gold with the surplus ramps and patting the earth back around the bulbs. They would continue to grow in the log's shadow and never know their roots had seen daylight. She knocked the excess dirt from the other ramps and put them into her basket.

As she walked briskly homeward, she thought about Nathan and his trips down the mountain. Was he indeed seeing another woman? She could think of no other reason for his steadfast refusal to take her with him.

By the time she reached the cabin the sky over the river was golden in the sunset. Fingers of brilliant pink and vermilion marked the heavens, and the arching dome shaded from deep purple overhead to the darkest of blues behind her. Fawn glanced in the feed lot and her spirits rose as she saw Horse, a few tendrils of hay clinging to his lips.

She ran into the house and tossed her basket upon the table. Nathan was kneeling beside the fire, but when he saw her he stood up and caught her in his arms. Hugging her close, he spun her around so that her feet left the floor.

"I missed you, Fawn," he said, burying his face in her billowing hair. "God, I missed you."

"I missed you, too," she murmured happily as she clung to him. "You were gone too long."

Slowly he let her slide down his body until her feet touched the ground. "I think you got prettier while I was gone," he teased her lovingly, "and you were already beautiful."

A dimpled blush appeared in her cheeks as she smiled. He bent his head slightly and Fawn met his kiss with parted lips, matching his own. As the tip of his tongue traced the inside of her lips, Fawn's head began to swim and she pulled him closer to steady her weakening knees. Nathan drank longly and deeply of her passion before easing her back so he could see her face. "I can't decide which I'd rather do, kiss you or look at you."

Fawn blushed again before asking, "Are you hungry? I picked some poke salad and some ramps as well as those little green onions you like. I didn't expect to be so late getting back to the cabin, but I found . . ."

"I'm not that hungry," Nathan lied. He had skipped dinner in order to get home sooner.

"Well, it will not take long to start the greens cooking anyway." As she started to turn away to get the black pot, he caught her arm.

"You're not going anywhere. Not yet." He pulled her closer and bent his head to kiss her again.

"When you look at me like that your eyes grow darker, like the evening sky," she said softly as she threaded her fingers through his hair. "You smell good. Like pine trees."

His lips touched hers and she felt a spark ignite her. He drew back for a moment and studied her face. Then he claimed her lips hungrily. Fawn returned his passion and pressed her body against his, wanting him, loving him, aching to become one with him. She pushed the discovery of the bright colored nuggets from her mind.

When Nathan again raised his head, his breath was quick, as if he had run a long distance. He lifted her easily, and Fawn circled her arms around his neck and kissed him, letting her tongue tease the softness inside his lips.

"I'm glad you are such a large man," she said as he carried her to the bedroom, "because I am too tall and have always been shy about it."

"Shy? You don't have a shy bone in your body," he laughed as he sat her on the bed. "And you're not too tall. You're damn near perfect."

"Only for you," she laughed at him as she kicked off her moccasins.

"That's all that matters." He unlaced the thong that secured the front of her dress and ran his

168

fingers down the curve of her warm breast. "You're wearing a new dress," he observed. "I like it. Especially with the laces unfastened."

She laughed and pulled his leather shirt off over his head. "You would have me go about the woods half naked if you had your way."

"No, ma'am. There wouldn't be any half way about it," he grinned.

Fawn ran her fingers across his gold furred chest. Beneath her hand she could feel his immense strength and the steady beat of his heart. Yet he was always so gentle with her. Lovingly she stroked his lean belly and ran her hands over his hard muscled ribs. "You are like a puma," she marveled. "All golden and smooth of muscle."

"I thought your name for me was Bear Who Talks," he teased.

"You are that, too." She caught his bearded face between her palms and pretended to have to aim carefully to find his lips.

Nathan pulled up her shift and ran his hands over her silken skin. "You feel so good," he said hoarsely.

She raised her graceful arms so he could remove the shift and lay back, clad only in her doeskin pants that clung low on her hips. Nathan gazed down at her as if he could never get enough of her beauty. Almost reverently he caressed her flat stomach and the full swell of her breasts. Already her nipples were erect and eager for him, inviting his kiss.

Nathan obliged with a trail of kisses from one

breast to the other, then let his tongue linger on the throbbing peak. Teasingly he flicked his tongue over her taut nipple until she arched beneath him. Only then did he take the prize more fully into his mouth. Fawn murmured in ecstasy as he kissed her body into greater desire.

Molten lava seemed to run through her veins as he toyed with first one breast, then the other. Fawn moved eagerly beneath him and felt his large hands lift her and bring her closer still.

After what seemed an eternity of bliss, Fawn felt him loosen the thong that held her pants and start to undo the lacing. He moved slowly, deliberately, sending shivers over her. When he ran his fingers inside the waist and touched her creamy skin, Fawn softly spoke words of encouragement to him in lyrical Arapaho. Words he could not understand, but whose meaning was apparent. Slowly, tauntingly, he pulled away her soft leather pants and ran his hand over the curve of her hips and down her long legs.

Nathan pulled off his boots and socks and stood to remove his pants. Fawn lay breathlessly eager and watched as he removed the last of his clothing. His body was tanned and hard, and the gold hair on his chest tapered to a vee just below his ribs. But her gaze was drawn to his erect manhood and she smiled.

"Come lie with me," she said, holding out her hand to him. "I can not bear to be away from you any longer."

Nathan lowered his body to lie beside her, their

flesh tingling with each contact. Her rosy nipples traced twin trails of desire across his chest and her hair made a soft cape for them to lie upon. Slowly he caressed her, touching her face, her lips, her breast, running his hand over her firm buttocks and up her slender back.

"I never knew a woman could be as beautiful as you," he said as his gaze followed the path of his hand. "Sometimes I can't believe you could ever love a man like me."

Fawn stopped his words with her fingertips. "A man like you? I find you perfect, Nathan. Your voice excites me even from across the room. I see the sunlight in your hair and my heart pauses. You touch me and my soul sings."

Their eyes met and she felt her spirit touch his. Gently they kissed, and then more passionately. He pulled her to him so that their bodies kissed as well. Fawn slid her leg over his thigh to draw him closer and she caught her breath when she felt him merge with her. Kissing him deeply, she moved in rhythm with him as her body quickened and her ardor became an aching need.

Nathan brought her to a dazzling, shimmering height and held her there until she felt she would burst, then he gave her the release she sought. Fawn held to him tightly as wave after wave of pleasure pounded through her.

He stroked her breast, gently rolling her nipple between his thumb and his forefinger as he moved again deep within her. Fawn moaned and ran the tip of her tongue over his shoulder and across the

171

hollow of his neck. Nathan held her firmly and rolled to his back, carrying her with him.

Fawn placed her outspread hands on his hard chest and sat up as her hips continued the swaying undulations of love. Her long hair spread over her shoulders and trailed across his chest as she looked down at him. He raised his hand and pushed her auburn tresses aside, allowing him a better view of her proud breasts. As she gave him pleasure he stroked her breasts, urging the nipples to even greater hardness until she cried out in passion. Fawn tossed her hair back to give him a better view as his hungry eyes drank in her loveliness.

With a low moan, Nathan pulled her down to his chest and rolled over so that she lay beneath him. Their eyes caught and held as he skillfully brought her to another and then another peak of ecstasy. This time he rode with her in the soaring pleasure that made them one.

Still holding her, possessing her, he rolled to one side so that her cheek lay comfortably on his shoulder. Gently he stroked her hair as the warmth of afterlove flowed soothingly over them. "I love you so very much," he said gently.

She looked up at him, her face glowing and her eyes like jewels. "I love you, too. With all my heart."

They lay there, their eyes speaking words that only souls can voice, their hands caressing one another in agreement with those words.

"Your supper will be very late," Fawn whispered, a contented smile on her lips.

"I'm glad." He traced the line of her chin and trailed his finger down the slender column of her neck where her pulse still beat rapidly.

"I had such lovely poke greens, too," she pretended to fret. "And those little onions. I even found some ramps."

"That's wonderful," said Nathan who hated the taste of ramps.

"If I get up now I can have it ready before too long," she said reluctantly. She didn't want to leave the warm circle of his arms.

Nathan kissed her temple and nuzzled her soft hair. "Now which would you rather do, Fawn, go cook poke greens and ramps, or lie here with me?"

"I'm not all that hungry if you aren't," she said with a smile as she snuggled closer to him.

"That's just the way I see it, too," he grinned as he rolled over to kiss her.

A memory of something she had meant to tell him crossed her mind, something to do with those ramps she had found. But Nathan's lips caressed hers and the memory faded again as she gave herself over to his loving.

Chapter Thirteen

"COME ON, FAWN, THE DAY WILL BE HALF GONE," Nathan complained as he held open the door for her.

"I'm coming," she called out from the bedroom. "I cannot find the ribbon for my braid."

"Just let it hang loose. I like it better like that anyway."

Fawn hurried through the door and across the room. "All right, Nathan. I'm ready. But I cannot understand why you want to go to the ruins just to eat dinner."

"It'll be fun. You're going to enjoy it." He nudged her out the door and shut it behind them.

"This woman cannot understand why we must hurry to eat food on a cliff."

Nathan sighed and picked up the sack that contained their noonday meal. "It's a long walk to the cliff and I want to have time to stay there a while before we have to come back."

Fawn had already witnessed a number of his unusual customs. She felt odd doing some of these strange things, but she enjoyed humoring him. Besides, it would be pleasant to sit on the sun-warmed adobe and watch the eagles drift in the deep valley below.

They left the park-like lawn and entered the closeness of the forest. Nathan held aside a branch to let her pass and a small moth, startled from its hiding place, fluttered to a tree trunk and blended invisibly into the scaly bark. Overhead a chickadee fluttered in the concealing leaves and far away a dove called mournfully.

"I like the woods," Nathan said happily. "Everything is so peaceful here. Not like a city at all."

"A city?" she asked as she dodged a leafy outcropping.

"It's like a bunch of tribes all gathered in one spot, all with houses and buggies, and roads with wagon traffic."

"Why would they want to live like that? So many tribes must have many battles among themselves and game would soon grow scarce. Besides, so many cabins as large as ours must take up much space."

Nathan laughed and his strong white teeth gleamed. "Most people live in houses much grander than our little cabin."

"Why? Do all the married children and their families remain with their parents? I should think that would be unpleasant to have so many under one roof."

"No, no. Each family has its own house usually, but there are several rooms."

"Why?"

"Well, there's a room for sleeping and one for eating, another to sit in, another to cook food in . . ."

Fawn laughed. "Nathan, you are teasing me again. I thought you were serious!"

"I am!"

She laughed and glanced back at him over her shoulder. "Do not tease me, Bear Who Talks. I am on to your game now." She straightened and a slight frown puckered her forehead. "Did you remember to pull the water pot away from the fire?"

"No, you said you were going to do that."

"Not I, Nathan. I thought you did." She looked back the way they had come. "I cannot leave it over the hot coals all day, it may boil dry and ruin the pot."

Nathan sighed in resignation. "You're right. I'll go back and tend to it."

"That you will not. I will go," Fawn said firmly. "Wait here." She melted into the underbrush to take the shortcut back to the cabin.

Nathan sat on a log and enjoyed watching her lithe form as she hurried away toward the cabin. Even in her concealing doeskin dress, her movements gave him pleasure. Perhaps, he thought comfortably, they should get married. Certainly he had no interest in seeing another woman, nor would anyone else be as perfectly suited to him as Fawn. Besides, he loved her with a depth that sometimes took his breath away. Still, there was no rush. She also loved him and would never leave. A scrap of paper and a few words from a stranger would not make them more married than they were now. There was plenty of time to see to the details.

A rustle behind him startled Nathan and his hand automatically found the handle of his hunting knife. The sound seemed different from the other forest noises. His eyes narrowed to flinty blue strips.

A lean man stepped out of the dense undergrowth and grinned up at Nathan.

"You shouldn't sneak up on a man like that, Charley," Nathan said warily. How long had Charley been there? "Where's Pale Moon?"

"I left her holding the horses down by the creek." Charley looked around. "As I was walking up, I could have sworn I heard voices."

"It was just me talking to myself," Nathan countered. "You know how lonesome it gets up here."

"Yeah, I know," Charley answered, peering up the path toward the cabin. "Still though, I was sure I heard somebody answer you."

Nathan's eyes regarded the smaller man speculatively. "Well, now, how can that be, Charley? You can see I'm all by myself."

Charley grinned and showed his tobacco-stained teeth. "It sure looks that way, don't it."

Nathan sat back down on the log and crossed his arms as if he planned to stay there all day. "Where are you headed, up the mountain or down to Bancroft?"

"Bancroft. Prairie Belle's been run out of town, but she's set her girls up in a foreman's house over by the old Lucky Lady mine. I hear she's got some new girls from back East and I want to check them out. How about coming along with me?"

Nathan frowned. "Charley, you know I don't go for stuff like that."

"Well, most of those settlers have good-looking wives and daughters. You make your tracks and I'll make mine."

Where he once might have agreed, Nathan now felt no urge. "No, thanks, Charley. I'm going to pass this time."

Charley leaned against a maple tree and broke off a twig to pick his teeth. "That sure don't sound like you, Nathan. You aren't ailing, are you?"

"No, I feel fine." Nathan glanced down the trail that led to the cabin. Fawn had had time to take the kettle from the fire and start back. Keeping his voice nonchalant, he said, "Well, it's been good talking to you, but I won't keep you. I know you want to get on down to town before dark, and Pale Moon must be wondering where you are."

Charley looked back in the direction where he had left Pale Moon. "It won't hurt her to wait a mite longer. By the way, I just came from the

Arapaho village and old Chief Many Rivers has died."

"Oh?" Nathan asked carefully.

"Yep. Just dropped dead, they say. That makes Walking Tall the chief. He's not as smart as his old man was, but he's young yet."

"Never met him," Nathan said tersely.

"It's a funny thing," Charley continued, "but the old chief had just taken him a young wife. The thing is, she wasn't really Indian, but was a white girl they caught with her ma years ago. I seen her often when she was growing up. She was a real beauty! I even tried once to buy her for myself but the man that owned her wouldn't let her go."

"Is that a fact?" Nathan choked down his anger and the acrid taste Charley's words were leaving in his mouth.

With a barking laugh, Charley tossed the twig aside and scratched his nose. "That man's dead now, but before I could claim her, Many Rivers took her as his wife. The tribe must have been real stirred up about that! Her being white and all, but she'd lived with them Indians so many years, you could hardly tell it, except for her coloring. Green eyes and reddish hair, she had."

"Why are you telling me all this," Nathan asked in a low voice.

"I was just coming to that. After Many Rivers died, she ran away rather than killing herself like a good wife of a chief is supposed to do. Managed to outfox the whole war party! Well, a month or so later, they're out hunting and come upon her and some white man by that moon-shaped pond up in the hills yonder. Captured them both. And be damned if she don't get away again! But then her and that man got trapped at the cliff and jumped off! Killed the both of them."

Nathan felt as if Charley must surely see him trembling, but he forced himself to say casually, "Killed them, you say?"

"Yep. Most of her washed up a few weeks later. Never did find him."

"That's a real interesting story, Charley. So Walking Tall is chief now."

"That's right. He's not the man his pa was. It seems he thinks the mountain ought to belong just to the Arapahos. Bancroft is safe enough, but I'm warning all the trappers and prospectors to keep an eye out."

"Thanks for the warning, Charley. I appreciate it." Nathan listened intently for sounds that would indicate Fawn's return. He prayed she wouldn't come running blithely down the path.

Charley tugged at the greasy brim of his hat and walked a few feet toward the thicker woods. "Just don't let your guard down for a while. You're sure now you don't want to go to Prairie Belle's?"

"Not this time." Nathan made himself smile naturally and stood up as if he, too, were about to leave.

Charley waved and ducked back into the underbrush.

Slowly Nathan sat back down on the log. The

Indians had believed the hoax about Fawn's death! But if Walking Tall was out to chase the whites from the mountain, it was only a matter of time before they would be on his doorstep. Nathan stroked his beard and studied the leaf-strewn ground.

Within minutes, Fawn returned. "It was a good thing I went back," she admonished cheerfully as she held up a stoppered crock. "You forgot our water. We would have been very thirsty after eating the venison, and there is no creek near there." She saw the expression on his face, and her words died away. Looking around, she said, "What is wrong, Nathan? Something has upset you."

Quickly he told her how narrowly she had missed being seen by Charley and what Charley had said.

Fawn paled at his words and moved to him. "We are not safe here! What if Charley Three Toes should come back?"

"He's gone. There's no reason for him to come back this way, and the woods are too thick for him to ride by accidentally. No, we need only be concerned about the Indians."

Fawn put her hand on Nathan's chest and looked up at him, worry clear in her eyes. When he gathered her into his protecting embrace, she clung to him tightly.

Several yards away, Charley squatted beneath a thick bush and bared his teeth in a wolfish grin. So that was it! Not only did Nathan have him a squaw hidden up there, but it was none other than the "dead" Fawn! Charley waited until Nathan took her hand and led her away before he stood up. Nathan Stoddard was playing a very dangerous game by sheltering Fawn. Slowly Charley made his way back to Pale Moon and the horses as he wondered how he could best profit from this knowledge.

Nathan sat on the granite boulder, hanging his feet over the edge. Hundreds of feet of emptiness yawned between him and the verdant plumage of the trees along the valley floor. He was as relaxed as if he sat on his own hearth, but Fawn crouched nervously behind him. He tossed a pebble and watched it soar in a downward arch before it hit the lower rocks and bounced out of sight into the valley. Fawn closed her eyes and tried to calm the flutter in her stomach.

"I sure wish I knew what to do," Nathan grumbled. "Walking Tall could ride into our yard any day. If it was just me, I could talk him into a trade like I did the old chief. But once he sees you, we're both dead." He swung his feet and viewed the faraway river between his boots.

Fawn caught his shirt tail and gripped it firmly even though she knew it would be of no help if he fell off the boulder. She, too, enjoyed the view from the ruins, but this was closer to the edge of the cliff than she preferred to be.

Nathan gazed off in the distance where an array of blue-gray mountains were piled in muddled confusion on the horizon. "I guess we could move on, but damn it, this is our home! I've been on this mountain a dozen years and I don't want to leave it now."

"Twelve years?" she laughed in spite of her trepidation. "You must have come here more than once, for I have heard you say it was six years."

"Six, twelve, what's the difference. The point is, I don't want to leave. And we're sure not going to go running down to Bancroft and live in that rabbit warren of a town. Settlers or no settlers, the place is a blight! The miners should have burned it to the ground when they moved on." He threw a handful of rocks to clatter down the cliff.

"Nathan!" Fawn burst out. "Will you come away from the edge?"

He looked at her in surprise. "What for? This boulder has been here as long as the mountain. It's not going anywhere."

"Please! It's a long way down, and this woman doesn't want to have to search for you if you fall off."

For a minute he stared down at the valley and then back at her. "Are you scared of heights?"

"No! Now come away, please!" She eased off the boulder and walked toward the security of the level ground in front of the adobe ruins.

Nathan came to join her. "I didn't mean to scare you. I never knew heights bothered you."

"I am not frightened by the height, only by falling off it," she informed him. "And I don't want *you* to fall off, either." She ducked and went into one of the tiny cubicles. From inside, the view was beautiful and not threatening at all. "You once agreed with me that Walking Tall would probably shun our cabin because of our 'deaths.' Is this not true?"

"Who knows?" he shrugged as he followed her through a doorway. "I thought so once, but according to Charley, Walking Tall wants the mountain back. It wouldn't take much observation to see that our cabin is occupied. I think we can count on trouble unless we do something to prevent it."

"But what can we do?"

"How should I know? You're the Indian—you tell me. What will keep them away?"

Fawn bridged a knee-high step and ducked into the next room. "Maybe we could convince them that my spirit haunts the cabin. Walking Tall would fear that." She sat on a broad window ledge and looked out at the mountains beyond.

"How can we do that?" he asked eagerly. "Do you have an idea?"

"No."

Nathan sighed and leaned his head back to study the centuries' deposit of grime on the ceiling. "I had hoped you did."

Restlessly, Fawn left the window and paced the narrow confines of the room. "Surely we can do something."

"I hope so. I don't want to leave our home, but you know I will if it's a matter of your safety." He caught her wrist and pulled her to him. "I won't let anything happen to you, Fawn. You can count on that."

She smiled wanly and lay her hand on his bearded cheek. "Nor will I let Walking Tall hurt you," she promised.

Chapter Fourteen

"YOU'LL LIKE THEM, FAWN," NATHAN REASSURED her as they neared the cabin.

Fawn met his eyes doubtfully. "You have told me so, many times now," she reminded him.

Nathan smiled and nodded absentmindedly. The nearer they came to Jesse and Darcy's cabin, the more nervous he was becoming. With Walking Tall posing such a threat, he wanted Fawn to know the way to their nearest neighbors. He hadn't told her that this was the motivation for their visit, but he knew Fawn would never forget the trail once she had seen it.

The problem in Nathan's mind, however, was what his friends' reaction might be. He knew what

Darcy thought of Charley and Pale Moon, and it wasn't favorable. True, Pale Moon was slovenly and stupid, while Fawn was clearly the opposite, but his relationship with Fawn was no more sanctified by marriage than was Charley's with Pale Moon. Nathan recalled uneasily how shocked Darcy had been when she learned that Charley had bought Pale Moon and was living with her in what Darcy had termed "open sin." His relationship with Fawn might seem no better to Darcy's eastern way of thinking.

And there was the matter of her Indian appearance. He knew many people who were prejudiced against Indians, especially now that Walking Tall was causing trouble. Would Darcy and Jesse feel that way about Fawn? Nathan was certain they would like her when they got to know her, but what would their first reactions be? He glanced at Fawn and tried to smile casually when she looked back at him. Yes, despite her auburn hair, she carried herself like an Indian. There were no two ways about it.

What if they didn't get along with her? Fawn would be terribly hurt, and Nathan would have trouble being friends with anyone who could or would hurt Fawn. Even if it was Jesse, who had been his best friend for years, and Darcy, who held a special, sisterly place in his heart. Nathan hoped with all his might that the meeting would go well.

They rode through a tiny meadow where a waterfall splashed into a serene pool. It was a beautiful spot, quiet and unruffled in spite of the wooden scaffolding that seemed to have sprouted from the rocky falls.

Nathan looked curiously at the square-hewn timbers. "Now I wonder what Jesse is building up there," he mused to himself. "It looks like some sort of mining equipment, but I never knew Jesse to do anything but pan for gold."

Fawn shrugged. She was growing more and more uneasy. What if Nathan's friends didn't like her? What if she didn't like them?

After staring at the scaffolding a bit longer, Nathan nudged his horse forward. They passed through the meadow and up a well-worn path. As he rode, Nathan whistled, something Fawn had rarely known him to do. She cocked her head inquisitively to one side and raised her brows.

He grinned. "I'm sure Jesse's heard about Walking Tall's threat by now. He's never been one to shoot first and ask questions later, but I don't know about Miss Darcy."

"Why? Has she shot at people often?" Fawn asked with alarm. "She sounds frightening."

"No, no. I was only joking." Nathan held aside a branch for her to ride under. The language would be a problem, too, he suddenly realized. Fawn knew some English, of course, but the two of them talked in a vernacular of their own that contained not only English, but Ute and Arapaho. It occurred to Nathan that this difficulty would be a large obstacle for Fawn in getting acquainted with his friends. "Try to speak English as much as you can," he told her. "I'll translate whatever else you want to say, but try to stick with English."

Fawn hid her grimace. Since they had started down the mountain, Nathan had given her a dozen instructions and at least that many topics that she should avoid. She looked at his broad shoulders as he rode ahead of her. If he was so uneasy about her conversation, why had he wanted her to meet his friends in the first place? She found she was quite prepared to dislike both Darcy and Jesse on sight.

They left the trees and moved out into a long clearing that sloped down to the river. At the far end of the clearing, Fawn saw a cabin with a wispy finger of smoke rising from the chimney. A strikingly handsome man with dark hair knelt in the yard, playing with a small child. He looked up as Nathan called out a greeting, and a woman, with her rich brown hair coiled neatly in a bun, came out of the door and shaded her eyes against the sun to see him.

"Hello there, Miss Darcy, Jesse," Nathan bellowed jovially. "Where's that baby I've come all this way to see?"

The toddler laughed and ran shakily to meet him, her arms held up confidently. Nathan dismounted and swooped her up in a bear hug. The little girl shrieked with delight and hugged him as if she would never let go.

"Nathan! How good it is to see you!" the woman said affectionately as she cast curious glances at Fawn. "I should have known you wouldn't let the summer go by without coming to visit."

Jesse shook Nathan's hand vigorously and clapped him soundly on the shoulder. "You're looking good for a trapper," he teased. "Giving up prospecting must have agreed with you!"

Nathan grinned sheepishly. "It wasn't trapping, Jesse. I want you to meet . . . Elizabeth." He nodded toward the woman who was riding silently behind him. Nathan didn't miss the surprise that kindled in Fawn's eyes, but he had had the sudden inspiration that her English name might mellow her exotic appearance.

Darcy was already trying not to stare at the other woman who sat with regal grace astride the white horse. She wore a fringed doeskin dress trimmed in elaborate beadwork and her hair was braided in thick plaits, yet her coloring didn't appear to be that of an Indian. "Elizabeth, did you say?" she asked doubtfully. "My name is Darcy Keenan," she said, holding out her hand.

Fawn looked at the woman's empty palm. What was she expected to give her? Fawn also held out her hand to show that it, too, was empty. "I am Fawn," she replied in English.

Nathan quickly explained, "She prefers to be called Fawn. She grew up with the Arapahos and she only speaks a little English."

"Then how do you talk to each other?" Jesse asked. "I thought you only knew Ute?"

"She speaks a bit of Ute as well as the English I've taught her, and I've learned some Arapaho." He motioned for Fawn to dismount.

She hesitated, then slid from her horse's bare back, and landed with catlike grace. Because of Fawn's unusual height and proud carriage, she towered over Darcy and could almost look eye to eye with Jesse. This made her feel even more awkward. Nathan's extraordinary size had dulled the shyness she had always felt about her height, but now it all rushed back to her.

The tense silence was broken by the baby's babbling half-speech and Nathan reached in his saddle bag to get the bowl he had carved.

Darcy took the gift in both her hands and she and Jesse admired the carving that decorated the outside. Nathan frowned a little when he noticed how large the bowl looked in Darcy's hands. "Kathleen will grow to it," he told her reassuringly.

"It's a lovely gift, Nathan, and I'm sure she will be very proud of it," Darcy told him with a smile. "Here, let me have her and I'll go see about supper."

"She's just fine where she is," Nathan said in his rumbling voice. "I'll look after her for you."

Darcy smiled at Fawn and said, "Come with me. I know you must be tired after riding so far."

Fawn nodded. She had understood most of Darcy's words, though her accent was different from Nathan's. She followed Darcy inside.

The cabin was small and dark, as there was only one window placed high beside the door. Opposite the fireplace a doorway led to another room which was obviously an addition. The newer room had a pine floor but the one in which they stood was hard packed earth.

"Jesse is going to build us a new floor in here as well," Darcy chatted as she added more water to the simmering pot of stew. "We just finished building Kathleen's room. She has only slept in it for a week or so." Darcy glanced at her silent guest. "Jesse tells me Nathan has a two room cabin, too."

Fawn nodded slowly. Darcy seemed to be telling her about the floor of the cabin, but Fawn had no idea why. She wished she had paid more attention when Nathan had tried to teach her English. "Our floor is wood, too," she ventured.

Darcy looked puzzled, then smiled. "How nice."

Politely, Fawn refrained from staring around the room and tried to keep her features calm and her eyes on her hostess. But for some reason this seemed to make Darcy uncomfortable. "Will I help you?" Fawn said in broken English. "I can cut up the dried meat." Her melodious voice made the words sound pleasant, if not meaningful.

For a moment Darcy looked at her blankly. Then she said kindly, "Here, you take this meat and slice it for me. Small strips. Do you understand?" She made slicing motions and handed Fawn a knife.

Fawn nodded and took the knife. It felt strange in her hand, however, so as soon as Darcy turned, Fawn put it down and used the knife that she always wore at her side. For some reason this seemed to bother Darcy, but Fawn decided to ignore it. Her blade was sharper and she knew her own utensil was clean. Whatever was bothering the other woman would have to remain a mystery. She smiled and after a moment, Darcy smiled, too. Fawn felt relief wash over her. Perhaps this wouldn't be so bad after all.

Covertly she looked around the cabin as she worked. The white woman was neat—even though she had not expected company, the room was clean and looked quite cozy. Fawn liked that. Even Clouds Passing would be pleased with Darcy's housekeeping abilities. Fawn felt the other woman's eyes upon her so she looked up and smiled again to put Darcy at her ease.

Outside on the doorstep, Jesse turned to Nathan. "Where did you come across her? I've been to Bancroft often and I've never seen her. Lord knows I couldn't have missed her! Not only is she beautiful, but she carries herself like a queen."

Nathan felt a stirring of jealousy mixed with pride at his friend's open admiration of Fawn. "She's not from Bancroft. Never been there in her life as near as I can tell. And in a way she is royalty. She's Many Rivers' widow."

Jesse looked at him in surprise. "Are you serious? How can that be? I heard in Bancroft that his widow drowned!"

"The Indians think that, but it's not so. That's her, all right." He pulled his knife from its sheath and looked around for something to whittle. "That's one reason I'm here. If Walking Tall finds out Fawn is still alive, it's going to be hard on all of us. Charley says he already wants the whites off the mountain. Harboring the old chief's widow will give him a good excuse. Not that he's likely to be looking for one."

Jesse whistled low. "What do you plan to do?"

"I don't know." Nathan sat on the step and scraped the edge of a stick as he watched a strip of thin wood curl over the blade of his knife. "I wanted you to meet her and I wanted to be sure she knows how to find you. If anything should happen." He looked up at his friend and there was no need to explain further.

"If she ever shows up here, we'll take care of her," Jesse said quietly. "Don't worry about that."

"I've been giving a lot of thought to this trouble with Walking Tall," Nathan said with studied casualness. He nodded toward Jesse's barn. "I figure that shed of yours would be a good place to hold them off if there's an attack. Not only is it built into that shallow cave so we have fewer walls to protect, but the window opens onto the gully. If the Indians set fire to the barn to burn us out, we can climb down on a rope and get away. I think."

Jesse narrowed his eyes and regarded his barn as a possible fortress. "You're right. In the house we could get cut off and burned out. We don't have enough windows in it."

"Now, you know my place has a window on each wall, but it's closer to the village. I figure they're more likely to hit it first and work their way down here."

"That's the way I see it, too," Jesse said. "I'll

194

stock the barn with blankets, lanterns, food, and of course some extra bullets. Then if we need to go there fast, we won't waste any time."

Nathan nodded. "I think that's a good idea. If this blows over, you can always bring it all back to the house. But this way you're sure."

"You know it's a dangerous thing you're doing, keeping Fawn at your cabin. That makes you a prime target."

"It would if the Indians knew she was there," Nathan agreed, "but so far they still think she's dead. Let's just hope it stays that way. Besides, could you send Miss Darcy away just because it would be safer? Of course not."

"No, I couldn't. Have you thought about moving closer to town?"

"Nope. I couldn't stand that and neither could she. Fawn is as much an Indian as Walking Tall himself. Bancroft would drive her crazy."

Jesse grinned. "You sure sound like a husband all of a sudden. I thought you were the one that said you never would get married. That you didn't want any woman tying you down."

"I guess I did say that," Nathan admitted sheepishly.

"When did you two get married? It must have been recently. Why didn't you let me know?"

Nathan whittled with great concentration. "Well, now, we haven't exactly gotten married yet. Way up on the mountain like that, it's easy to put things off. We've been so busy trying to keep Walking Tall off our doorstep, we haven't gotten around to the legalities yet." He raised his piercing blue eyes to Jesse's. "Does that bother you?"

"Nope. I figure that's your business."

"We are going to get married though. I just don't know when. The longer we keep quiet about Fawn being alive, the better it'll be."

"If you show up in either Bancroft or Fire Bluff with someone who looks like Fawn, there's going to be a lot of questions raised. I think you're right about not rushing down to the preacher."

Nathan nodded. "I've thought about that. It's best not to jump into it."

"Supper is ready now."

Nathan turned and saw Fawn standing in the doorway. By the strained expression on her face, he could tell she had heard just enough to get the wrong impression. "Fawn, I didn't mean . . ."

"Come and eat now. The food will grow cold." She turned abruptly and went back into the house.

Nathan started to call her back, but he stopped. This was no time to air their differences. He would explain later.

The men followed her inside and washed up at the tin basin. They talked freely with Darcy, but Fawn remained aloof. Occasionally Nathan tried to draw her into the conversation, or to translate for her, but she found it difficult to follow most of what was said. And she was still upset with what she'd overheard. The casual supper talk went on as if she wasn't there, and Fawn decided this was all right with her.

Darcy, however, was determined to make

friends with her and finally found a subject that she assumed would be of interest to all women. "Well," Darcy said cheerfully, "I didn't even know Nathan was planning to get married. I guess it took place in Bancroft? How long have you lived there, Fawn?"

"Nope," Nathan said with a glance at Fawn. "Fawn's never been to Bancroft."

"Pass the beans, Partner," Jesse said quickly.

Darcy gave him the bowl and smiled at Nathan. "Fire Bluff, then? You certainly went a long way to court, didn't you."

"She's never been to Fire Bluff, either. You know, Miss Darcy, this is the best cornbread I ever ate."

Darcy looked puzzled. "There aren't any other preachers around here, that I know of. Where else . . ." Her eyes grew round and a blush colored her cheeks.

"You got it," Jesse said amiably. "I told Nathan that it wouldn't matter to us. Right, Partner?"

"I'm sorry, Nathan, Fawn," Darcy stammered. "I didn't mean to . . ."

"Don't worry about it," Nathan quickly interjected. "It's just a technicality. Fawn and I are as married as any two people you'll ever see."

Fawn had sat quietly trying to follow the exchange. As the import sank in, she blushed furiously. The food—which she already thought strange— became tasteless in her mouth. Carefully she lay down her fork and clasped her trembling hands in her lap. Intense embarrassment continued to sweep over her as everyone tried to smooth over Darcy's unintentional blunder. Suddenly she stood. Keeping her eyes averted, she mumbled in Arapaho, "Your food has nourished this woman and she is grateful." Then she turned and hurried out into the night.

"What did she say?" Darcy asked as Fawn shut the door behind her.

"She said, 'Excuse me,'" he translated. "Maybe I'd better go talk to her."

"Nathan, I'm so sorry. I didn't mean to say the wrong thing."

"That's all right, Miss Darcy. You didn't know. Excuse me." He followed Fawn out into the night. As his eyes adjusted to the darkness, he quickened his pace to catch up with her.

"I am surprised to see you," she informed him curtly. "I thought you would stay inside with your white friends. The married ones."

"Fawn, you've misunderstood some things."

"Did you not tell Jesse that we are not married?"

"Yes, but . . ."

"Was Darcy not shocked when she found this out?"

"Maybe a little surprised, but . . ."

"I understand perfectly, Nathan. You have shown your friends you do not consider me worthy of marriage." Fawn kept her face resolutely turned forward and her voice was clipped.

He pulled her to a stop beside the river and made her face him. "Fawn, Fawn, how can you say this when you know we are married in our hearts? If we go to Bancroft and get married, how long do you think it would take for word to get to Charley and from him to Walking Tall?"

Reluctantly, she lifted her eyes. "I had not thought of that. This is why we are not married?"

"Yes."

She studied him in the moonlight and wondered if he were telling her the truth. Yet, this made sense. She had to admit that it would be foolhardy to take a chance on her tribe learning she still lived. "Perhaps I will believe you," she said slowly.

He put his arm around her and guided her along the river bank. "I love you, Fawn. I really do. You know I wouldn't tell you that if I didn't mean it. When two people love each other, they get married. It's just that we don't have the freedom to do that right now."

She walked silently beside him. With all her heart she longed to believe him, but still she worried. What had he told Jesse before she had walked in on the conversation? All she had really heard was them agreeing it was best for Nathan not to rush into marrying her. Was Walking Tall really the reason? "I want to believe you," she admitted at last.

"Good," Nathan said with relief. "I'm glad that's over! I sure don't like it when we argue." He led her over to a large flat rock that jutted out over the water and they sat down. "How do you like Miss Darcy and Jesse?"

"She is hard to understand. She speaks so much faster than you. I wish we could talk together, though. It's been so long since I talked to another woman. Jesse is easier to understand because he talks more as you do. I like the way they smile so often and I feel happiness in their home. Still, their language is a great problem."

"Soon you'll know enough English to carry on a conversation," he comforted her. "Look how much you've learned already." He engulfed her hand in one of his and kissed her palm.

The black and silver rapids of Wolf Creek swept by under the rock on which they sat and made a roaring sound that blotted out the night song of the crickets. Peace seemed to hang almost visibly about the place.

"Still, Darcy was shamed to have me at her table."

"No, she wasn't. Miss Darcy understands. Did I ever tell you about those two?"

She shook her head.

"Well, I had heard for months that Jesse was lonesome up here by himself. That's all he could talk about. One night when I was in Bancroft, Charley Three Toes slipped me some bad whiskey. Stood me on my ear, it did. Anyway, before I was sober enough to think straight, I had signed Jesse up to marry a strange woman. A mail-order bride, they call them. I even insisted on marrying her for him by proxy and put my mark by his name. Of course, once I got my head back together, I had forgotten all about it. The next time I remembered anything about that night was when Miss Darcy showed up believing she was married to Jesse. And she was. Only Jesse didn't know about it." He shook his head slowly. "It takes a good friendship to weather something like that. Jesse's a good man."

Fawn stared at him. "Are you saying you married Jesse to Darcy?"

"Something like that. She lived back East and wanted a new life, so she agreed to become a mail-order bride. She's the one who picked Jesse, but she only had a name to go on. He could have been anybody." He laughed. "Now you're the one who looks shocked."

Quickly she swept the expression from her face and said, "Certainly not, Nathan. That was a look of surprise."

"Anyway, you can see for yourself that Miss Darcy is a proper lady. She can see the same about you. Understand?"

"Yes," she admitted. "Now that I know this, I see it all differently. We should go back so I can help her with the dishes."

Fawn smiled to herself as they returned to the house. These friends of Nathan's were certainly more interesting than they had first appeared!

Chapter Fifteen

FAWN SAT BY THE FIRESIDE AND PLAYED HIDE THE Thimble with Kathleen. In the past two days, Fawn had become more accustomed to Darcy and Jesse's speech and now she could understand much more of what they said, though she still had trouble finding the proper words to express herself. From the corner of her eyes, she watched as Darcy washed the supper dishes. Instead of going to the river to do this, she was using a large tin bowl and hot water from the black kettle on the hearth. When she had cleaned the dishes in soapy water, she rinsed them in the kettle, then dried them and placed them on the shelf. This seemed so much more convenient, Fawn wondered why it had never occurred to her to do the same. In the winter, the river water was always very cold, if not frozen. She decided to ask Nathan to bring her a wash bowl next time he went to Bancroft.

Kathleen discovered the thimble in Fawn's left hand and crowed with delight. Fawn smiled down at the child. She longed to have Nathan's baby, but so far she had been unable to conceive. Perhaps, she thought, the spirits that brought Indian babies and the spirits that brought white babies were warring over which to give her. The idea made her sad—she seemed to belong nowhere.

Nathan and Jesse sat with their feet propped toward the fire, Nathan's arms crossed over his large chest, Jesse's thumbs looped carelessly in his pants pockets. The fire popped as a resin deposit burst and myriad gold sparks rose toward the sooty chimney.

"So you finally found it," Nathan said in a voice filled with wonder. "You struck gold."

"Yep. It's on top of the falls by the scaffolding. A big vein—as wide as Partner, there."

Nathan grinned at Darcy who shot a perturbed look at Jesse. "That's not real big, Jesse," he said gallantly.

"It is for a gold vein," Jesse blundered on happily. "Just when we had given up, we stumbled upon it."

"That's the best news I've heard in a long time. But the trouble is, when will all the others arrive?"

"The others?"

"Sure. You can't hit a mother lode like that and not have miners and prospectors crawling all over themselves to share it with you."

"You can if you don't tell anybody," Darcy smiled as she put away the last cup. "And you just keep it to yourself, you hear?"

"We take out what we need," Jesse explained. "The rest stays where it is. Like in a bank."

"Well, I'll be fiddled," Nathan said. "I guess that would work. But, Miss Darcy, don't you miss having all those doodads and fine clothes that all that gold could buy?"

"Not for a minute," she answered as she sat on a stool beside Fawn and took up her knitting. "We live comfortably and can buy supplies without having to fight Wolf Creek for every nugget. That's all we want."

"I sure wish that river had been so obliging to me. I wouldn't mind having my pockets lined with gold."

Fawn looked up surprised. What was all the excitement about gold? Certainly her people had no need for the pretty but useless metal. "Nathan, I found . . ."

"Kathleen! Give me that button!" Darcy broke in to scold her daughter. "Where did you find it?" She expertly fished the button from the child's stubbornly clenched mouth. Kathleen responded with a bellow.

"She's stubborn," Jesse observed with a wink at Nathan. "Takes after her mother."

Darcy playfully kicked his boots as she passed to put away the button.

"Would you keep trapping if you found gold?" Jesse asked his friend.

"I don't rightly know. That's hard to say, since I haven't found any. Of course, if I had, I wouldn't have started trapping in the first place. I have to admit, I would like to travel. See San Francisco and the ocean, maybe."

Fawn tried again. "Nathan, do you recall the night I picked those ramps? I also found . . ."

"Ramps? I dearly love them," Darcy exclaimed, "but they don't seem to grow around here. The next time you come down, could you bring me a starting of them?"

Jesse grinned. "Partner would just love to be a farmer. Give her something to plant and she's happy."

"He's teasing me again," she complained to Nathan, but she had a twinkle in her dark eyes. "You can look at that pitiful excuse for a garden and tell that."

"You mean that patch of high grass behind the cabin?" Nathan asked with deliberate seriousness.

"You're as bad as he is," Darcy retorted.

Fawn sighed. She would remember to tell Nathan later about the gold. She watched Darcy's clicking knitting needles in fascination. "Will you teach me to do that?" she asked hopefully.

Darcy smiled and nodded as she went to get another pair of needles and more yarn.

Jesse uncoiled his long frame and got up from the chair. He took the kettle of dishwater to the door and tossed it out into the night. "Darcy's not supposed to lift this heavy kettle," he explained. "Kathleen's going to have a brother next summer."

"Or a sister," Darcy called out from the back of the room.

"How nice," Fawn exclaimed. "Your totems must be very pleased to send you another baby so soon." In her enthusiasm, Fawn spoke in a combination of Ute and Arapaho.

"What?" Darcy asked.

"She said congratulations," Nathan translated.

Fawn frowned slightly. She wasn't at all sure her meaning had been conveyed in the English word even though it was impressively long. Taking care to speak in their language, she continued, "I will make a carrier for you. My mother, Clouds Passing, taught me to do this."

"I would be honored," Darcy replied as she returned with knitting materials for Fawn. "Here. Hold the needles like this and loop the yarn around, so."

Jesse watched the knitting lesson for a few minutes, then turned back to Nathan. "How is the trapping business?"

"Not too good," Nathan admitted. "Here it is late summer and fall approaching, and I'm low on furs. It's prime season, too."

"What seems to be the trouble?"

Nathan glanced at Fawn and chose his words carefully in order not to hurt her feelings. "The traps I'm using aren't catching as well as I'd hoped."

"Oh? They looked good to me. Did you get some faulty ones?"

"No, no. The ones you saw worked just fine. These are some others I'm using now." He looked over at Jesse and slowly shook his head. "It's a long story, Jesse. I'll tell it to you one of these days. Besides, with the threat from Walking Tall, I've been staying closer to the cabin."

Darcy looked up from the knitting needles and her hand strayed to Kathleen's silky dark curls. "Do you think there will really be trouble?"

"Oh, no, Miss Darcy," Nathan soothed hastily. "You needn't worry about that."

"The truth, Nathan," she said firmly.

He drew a long breath before answering. "Could be, Miss Darcy. Could be. Walking Tall never did agree very much with his papa. He's hotheaded and looking for a fight, from all I've heard."

Fawn looked up at the sound of Walking Tall's name, and made an effort to understand the difficult language.

"Charley Three Toes says Walking Tall wants to clear us off the mountain."

"Charley Three Toes! He's more their friend than ours," Darcy scoffed derisively.

"Still, he has ways of knowing, Partner," Jesse reminded her. "We might not like him, but he's in the position to know."

"You and Charley had a falling out?" Nathan asked.

"More than that," Jesse answered grimly. "He won't be back here."

Nathan glanced at Darcy's set face and nodded. "It's just as well, if you ask me. He's not a man to trust. I just wish we had someone else to act as our go-between with the Arapaho. I don't worry about the Utes. There's a mountain between us, and they have always been friendly. But Walking Tall's people are a wild bunch. I don't know what will happen there."

Fawn was following the conversation closely. She wanted to speak up and tell them that the Indians had a side to the issue as well. They argued that the whites were driving away the game and moving into their hunting preserves. But she couldn't justify defending the man who was determined to kill her, so she held her tongue.

As she listened to Nathan and Jesse discuss whether Walking Tall would try to move down the mountain, she felt torn by her allegiance to both people. Although Walking Tall was indisputably her enemy, most of his tribe were her friends—or at least had been. Some were her family. She couldn't turn her back on them, no matter what.

Yet Nathan's people were also her people and she was growing more and more accustomed to their language and their ways. Her future lay here, and she loved Nathan with all her heart. How could she ever choose one to the total exclusion of the other? And there was a further complication in her love for Nathan. Fawn had decided he was speaking the truth when he had explained why they couldn't marry just yet, but would she ever be right for him if she couldn't wholeheartedly shun his enemies? Perhaps she was wrong for him and should free him to find one of his own kind. She ached to consider this, but she loved him too deeply to think only of herself.

She gazed into the leaping fire in the hearth and tried to read an answer in the glowing embers. Shamen could do this, she knew. Silently she asked the spirit of the fire to give her a sign. Some way of knowing who she was and what she should do.

A resin knot exploded loudly and a handful of sparks flew up the chimney. Had this been a sign? She was no Shaman, so she didn't know.

Nathan gave Fawn a leg up onto the back of her horse, then mounted his large buckskin. The animal flattened his ears and bowed his back as if he were about to buck, then relaxed and placidly chewed at his bit.

"Come again soon," Darcy said again as she smiled up at them and slipped her arm around Jesse's waist.

"We will," Nathan assured her in his booming voice. "Jesse, you take care of these ladies now, you hear?" He reached down and tousled Kathleen's tumbled curls.

Darcy caught up her daughter who was bent on climbing Horse's legs. "Take it easy going home. And come back when you can. You have to go near here to get to Bancroft, so you can stop on the way." She smiled up at Fawn. "You see that he does it, all right? I'm going to piece a quilt and I'll wait for you to help me put it together."

Fawn smiled and nodded. She hadn't the heart to remind Darcy that she never accompanied Nathan to either Bancroft or Fire Bluff. Nathan nudged Horse forward and Fawn reined in behind him, waving at the small family until the forest separated them from her view.

"Nathan," she said after they had crossed the meadow beside the falls, "why do you never take me to Bancroft?"

He looked over at her and reached out to stroke her deep russet braid. "You're too pretty. I'd have to fight every man in town. Not that I'd mind, but it wouldn't leave me any time for trading."

"Tell me true," she insisted.

Nathan studied her lightly tanned face. In the sunlight her leaf-green eyes shone like jewels and her hair had the burnished red of fine mahogany. She moved with lithe grace and he knew well the luscious curves concealed by her dress. "Maybe I was telling the truth," he countered. "You're an uncommonly beautiful woman, Fawn."

"I am too tall," she disputed.

"Not for me, you aren't." He held aside a branch and they rode into the quiet shadows of the woods. "You and Miss Darcy got to be good friends, didn't you."

"Yes. I like her. She reminds me of my mother's younger sister, Gray Dove. She, too, is small and cheerful."

They rode in silence for a while. Then Nathan

asked casually, "Why is it that you rarely wear the blue gingham dress I brought you from Fire Bluff?"

"Why is it you introduced me as 'Elizabeth'?" she retorted.

"That's your name."

"I am Fawn, and I do wear the dress at times. This one is more comfortable and doesn't snag on every bramble as does the cotton one." She studied his broad shoulders as he rode first up a hill. "Why is it that you speak ill of all my people when it is Walking Tall that angers you?"

"Why do you insist on denying my people when you are as white as I am?" he asked with forced calmness.

She frowned and dodged a leafy branch that slapped back at her. "Are we having an argument?"

"Not yet," he snapped.

"Good!" she retorted.

Chapter Sixteen

"FAWN, WE HAVE TO DO SOMETHING TO PROTECT ourselves against Walking Tall," Nathan stated flatly. "You aren't going to like my plan, but I have an idea."

She looked up at him expectantly and put down the clothing she was washing. "An idea?"

"If we make him think Many Rivers is displeased, maybe he will leave us alone."

"Hush. You mustn't say his name. What if his spirit is near." She glanced around, even though the spirit of her dead husband was presumably invisible.

"You see? Even you are uneasy about it."

She went back to scrubbing the soapy shirt and

dousing it in the river. "Perhaps. What would make my people think such a thing?"

"What if they found Many Rivers' war vest on the trail to this cabin?"

Fawn looked up at him and squinted against the sun. "That is impossible. He was cremated in his vest. I myself dressed him and saw him on the funeral pyre."

"We could make another one just like it." He knelt beside her and his eyes were alight with his plan.

"We?" she asked doubtfully.

"I only saw him a few times and I don't know how to sew well enough for the workmanship to pass a close inspection."

"This woman will not do it," she replied firmly as she wrung the water from his shirt.

"Come on, Fawn. We have to try. What harm could it do?"

She stared at him, the drips from the shirt making a puddle at her feet. "What harm? All the harm in the world! What if Many . . . He Who Died's spirit is offended? What if Walking Tall sees it as a hoax? Then nothing will stop him from his vengeance." She frowned and snapped the shirt briskly in the air to shake out the larger wrinkles, then draped it over a bush to dry.

"But suppose he *does* believe it!"

Thoughtfully Fawn arranged the sleeves over the bush. "It might work. Walking Tall was always fearful of his father. Always they argued about driving the whites from the mountain. Many Rivers insisted they stay because they traded the tribe items of use, like iron pots and woolen blankets."

Nathan grinned and playfully tugged at one of her braids. "I thought you said my people were no use to your people."

"I was on the side of Walking Tall," she retorted as she reached for a dusty pair of trousers.

"Are you still?" he asked in an offended tone.

"No," she laughed. "Now I see some of your people are good." She smiled up at him mischievously and her dimples appeared. Kneeling by the water, she wet the pants and scrubbed them with the yellow cake of soap.

"Listen, Fawn," he said as he sat beside her. "This plan will work. We can sew a war vest just like the one Many Rivers always wore. Then we leave it on the trail where anyone passing will see it. Walking Tall will think it's an omen from his father and be warned away." He studied her impassive profile. "Well? Do you think it will work?"

"I am trying to decide if Walking Tall will understand if you are not there to explain your logic to him. Yes," she said after a pause, "I think he will see it that way. Whatever he believes, it will cause him some worry. But where am I to get the beads and colored porcupine quills?"

Nathan shifted uneasily and looked away as he tried to appear nonchalant. "Your ceremonial dress has a lot of beads on it."

"Nathan! You would cut up my best dress?" she

exclaimed and threw the wet trousers so hard into the water that they were both splashed.

"Not cut up, Fawn, just trimmed a little. Only the beads and some of the quill work. That's all, I promise."

"That's all there is but the doeskin!"

"And the fringe, Fawn. Don't forget that! That dress is just covered with fringe. You won't even miss the beads."

"I will miss them," she stated indignantly.

"When I go to Fire Bluff I'll bring you some more. All right?"

She tightened her lips firmly but said, "All right. But you see that there are plenty of red ones, just as I have now. Clouds Passing helped me make that design and I don't want to change it."

"All right, Fawn. It's a deal. Can we start on it now?"

"Now? I have more washing to do."

"I'll help you. After all, I did this alone for years before you came along," he reminded her.

He took his other shirt and doused it twice in the river, wrung it out and was about to hang it over a bush when Fawn grabbed it from him.

"I will do this. You go cut me a square of leather large enough to cover your chest." She smiled. "Make it smaller. That Man was not so large."

Nathan nodded and gave her a quick kiss before he went whistling on his way. Fawn shook her head as she watched him go. She wondered how he had ever survived without her help.

When all the clothes were laid out on the bushes

to dry, Fawn picked up the soap and went back to the cabin. Nathan had cut a leather square and had slit the corners where the thongs that were to hold it in place were to be inserted. Fawn examined it and nodded. She had given it much thought and decided Nathan had had a good idea.

"I will get my dress," she said.

"Here it is." He held it out to her.

Slowly she took it and held the soft leather in her hands. The beadwork was intricate, the design meticulous. In her mind she could see Clouds Passing and herself sewing the beads and weaving the colored quills into the fabric as they laughed and spun dreams of her future as wife to the chief. How different it had all turned out.

Tears gathered in Fawn's eyes and she turned away so Nathan wouldn't see them. "Here," she said quietly. "You cut them off while I find the needle."

Nathan caught her wrist as she started to move away. "We don't have to do this. Maybe there's a better way."

"Such as what?"

"I don't know."

"I'll get the needle. You cut off the beads."

The rest of the day and the next she sewed, and her skilled fingers developed a new pattern, one vibrant and hostile, to frighten enemies. More than once Fawn put the vest aside and vowed to do no more. If it was tempting disaster to speak the name of the dead, how much more terrible must it be to make a garment for one of them? But each time she balked she remembered Nathan and the imminent danger and she continued sewing.

"Are you certain you have the pattern right?" Nathan asked as she put the finishing touches to the vest.

"Of course I'm certain," she replied testily as she flexed her aching shoulders. "Have I not seen his war vest many times? I myself sewed beads upon it. This one is exact," she stated emphatically as she presented it for his inspection.

Nathan took the garment from her. It was stiff with beads and dyed porcupine quills. The brilliant colors would surely have been an easy target for enemy arrows, but the heavy ornamentation acted as a shield. "It's beautiful," he complimented her.

She shrugged. "The pattern was worked by his first wife. I merely copied it."

Taking it near the fire, Nathan held the leather in the smoke so that it blackened slightly as the cabin filled with the smell of burning wood.

"What are you doing!" Fawn exclaimed.

"You said he was cremated in it. I'm just making it look that way." Then he rubbed it in the ashes so that it looked as if it had been in a fire. "How does that look?" he asked critically.

"It frightens me," she whispered.

Nathan put it aside and took her into his arms. Cradling her head on his chest he smoothed her hair away from her face. "Don't be afraid," he reassured her in his deep voice. "I won't let anything hurt you."

Fawn held him tightly and tried to believe his

words, but still the fear persisted. "This may give us a few days, weeks even, but what will happen then? Eventually they must come."

"If we can stall, perhaps the older and wiser braves can convince Walking Tall to leave the whites alone. As long as we stay on the lower mountain there's no reason why we can't all live here peacefully."

Fawn closed her eyes and tried to shut out her thoughts. What if the new settlers decided to move up the slopes and into Walking Tall's hunting grounds? Not only that, there was the knowledge that if the Indians did attack, her brother would be in the war party—and this time he would be powerless to refrain from aiding his chief in killing Nathan and herself. "Hold me," she whispered against Nathan's shoulder. "Hold me close."

Knowing the turmoil that must be ripping through her, Nathan tightened his embrace. "You're safe with me, Fawn. We're in a ticklish situation, but we can handle it. And, if need be we can outrun them to Jesse's where we'd have a better chance of defending ourselves."

She forced a smile to her lips. "Since we visited Jesse and Darcy, you talk too much English. How can a woman understand such words?"

"A woman understands more than she pretends to. I saw you talking to Miss Darcy often enough to know that."

Fawn rubbed her cheek against the soft cotton of his shirt. "Where will you leave . . . it?"

"The vest? I thought I would put it near the

mouth of that little arroyo where you tried to ambush Charley. That's the best path down to our cabin and I think they will come that way, if they come at all."

She nodded. "It is a good place. You will be careful, won't you? If anyone sees you . . ."

"No one will see me. You worry too much."

She lifted her head and let her dark eyes search the depths of his blue ones. She saw worry, but confidence also. He believed the plan would work and so did she.

"Your eyes are like the reflection of still water under a noonday sky," she said wonderingly. "How could I ever have been afraid of you?"

"The same way I thought all Indian women were like Pale Moon. I was so wrong." He touched her cheek and ran his fingers over the petal softness of its curve. "I'm sorry I ever thought that."

"And I regret thinking all your people are savages," she answered. "Never has there been so gentle a lover nor so wonderful a protector as you. I give you my heart."

"I will keep it safe," he responded in Arapaho. "Who will win, Fawn? Will I turn you into a white, or will you make me over into an Indian?"

"As long as we are together, we will both win."

Nathan bent and kissed her with loving gentleness. Fawn sighed and molded her slender body to his as naturally as a reed to the wind. He loosened the thong that held her braids and ran his fingers through her hair to free it. When it cascaded in silken strands through his fingers, he wrapped it around his hand and directed her face upward for his kiss.

Fawn's lips parted and her tongue met his in its exploration of her lips. A tremor of delight ran through her as she felt the fires awaken in her body. She ran her hand over the firm expanse of his back and marveled at the breadth of his shoulders. Only the gods of her tribal legends were built so magnificently.

Nathan bent and scooped her up into his arms. "Not in here," he answered her unspoken question. "Not with that around." He nodded toward the war vest that still lay beside the hearth.

Fawn lay her face against his neck. Only then did she realize this was as difficult for him as it was for her. While the vest reminded her of an unpleasant marriage, it reminded him that she had been a wife to another man. "I understand," she replied.

He carried her to the bedroom and lay her carefully upon the bed, as if she might break. Not taking his eyes from her, he removed his clothing until he stood naked before her. "Now you," he said.

Fawn swung her legs over the edge of the bed and slowly removed her moccasins. Then she stood and began to pull on the thong that fastened her dress. It came free and she took her time in opening the laces, slowly revealing her creamy skin and the full curve of her breasts.

Nathan sat on the bed and watched her hungrily, his body showing her the effect her actions had upon him. Fawn smiled and leaned over to kiss him. When she did, her dress fell open allowing him a clear view of her coral tipped nipples.

Straightening, she pulled the dress over her head and shook her hair into auburn waves that draped over her shoulders. Her supple waist curved down into her rounded hips still covered by her leather pants, and her skin was the texture of an apricot as he touched her warm flesh. Letting his fingers travel upward, Nathan stroked the undercurve of her breasts and then cupped them in his hands as his thumbs and forefingers teased her nipples to greater hardness. Fawn rested her hands on his shoulders as he took first one, then the other nipple into his mouth and kissed them gently, then more passionately. Fawn moaned with pleasure and arched her back to encourage him to continue.

Nathan started to untie the waist of her pants, but Fawn stopped his hand. Stepping back, she loosened them herself and inch by inch, let them fall to the floor. He sat gazing at her and she let him look to his content as she in turn studied his powerful frame. At last she came to him again and sat on his lap, her arms entwined gracefully about him.

He tumbled her over onto the bed and rolled her onto her stomach. Gently his large hands massaged her tired shoulders, and she murmured happily. Nathan kneaded her soft back until he felt the tension slip from her and felt her relaxing under his hands. Slowly he smoothed her skin, feeling the velvety texture as he stroked her. He ran his hands over her back, down the valley of her waist, and over the twin mounds of her buttocks. Fawn sighed and he continued his caresses up her sides to the swell of her breasts. Fawn smiled and tried to turn over, but Nathan gently pushed her back down as he tantalized only the outer curve of her breasts. Bending, he ran the tip of his tongue over her sensitive shoulders and laughed when she trembled with delight. He nuzzled her back with his soft beard as he once more explored the curve of her buttocks, then slid his hand between her thighs. Teasingly, he stroked her and Fawn moved eagerly against his hand. Still he kept her on her stomach, insisting with his caresses that she merely accept and enjoy the pleasure he was giving her. Only when her breath came quickly and she moaned in ecstasy, did he allow her to turn toward him.

"Love me," she whispered. "Love me."

"I do love you," he answered. "I love you with all my heart. I love you as I never dreamed I could love anyone. You are my soul, my heart, my reason for being." The Arapaho words of love came easily to his tongue and he felt her response as she claimed his lips with her own.

He rolled over, carrying her with him in his embrace and her hair tumbled about their faces, making a veil against the outer world. She kissed him eagerly, her tongue tasting the warmth of his mouth, the softness of his lips. Her body lay on his in a long kiss of flesh that thrilled her even more. She felt the hardness of his manhood and moved against him seductively, urging him to the height of passion he had kindled in her.

Still holding her close, he rolled over so that she lay beneath him. Nathan smoothed the hair back from her face and traced her features with his fingertips as if he were memorizing them. Their eyes met and held for an eternity of moments.

"I love you," she whispered in English. "I have never loved anyone but you, nor will I ever."

He sealed her words with a kiss and shifted his body so that he lay between her thighs. Fawn pressed her hips against him, willing him to become one with her. Slowly he complied, taking her deeply, deliberately, with a skill that enflamed her as unbridled passion would not.

She moved with him as her hands explored his lean waist, the firm buttocks beyond, his muscled thighs. Placing her hands on his hips she pulled him to her and found even greater pleasure when he moved to her rhythm.

Lowering his head, he took her nipple into his mouth and teased it with his lips and tongue as he moved deeply within her. Fawn felt the passion build in her loins as he guided her to an ecstasy that was ever new. Suddenly she felt a tremendous surge that threatened to shake her soul and the universe seemed to explode in every cell of her body.

Nathan chuckled when she cried out in delight and clung tightly to him as the waves thundered through her again and again. "You were made to be loved," he said.

"Only by you," she whispered as the passion subsided. "No one else has ever kindled a fire within me. No one else ever could."

As he softly brushed her lips with his own, he began to move within her, arousing her again with his powerful body. Holding her close, he nibbled on her earlobe and neck as his sure movements built the passion between them. When he felt her gain her release, it triggered his own and they rode together on love's wave.

He held her securely as the warm satisfaction enveloped them. Fawn snuggled closer, unwilling to part from him even as sleep claimed her. Nathan cradled her in his arms as her breathing became slow and even. Only when she was completely relaxed in a deep sleep, did he move.

Being careful not to awaken her, he rolled to a sitting position and stood up. Silently he dressed, his eyes upon her. He had to put the war vest on the trail and it would be safer to do so at night and when he was alone. Touching her cheek gently, he slipped from the room.

Chapter Seventeen

THE NIGHT AIR WAS COOL ON HIS FACE AND THE darkness wrapped around him like a blanket. Nathan looked back at the cabin and thought of the woman who slept there. He worried about her almost constantly. She was given to taking long walks in the woods when he wasn't around, and that made her an easy target for Walking Tall. One day she might stumble upon a band of hunters as he almost had, and that would be the end of her. But he couldn't keep her prisoner.

Less dramatically, but even more certainly, loomed the prospect of a hard winter. With only the wooden live traps, he barely caught enough game to bother with tanning the pelts. His rifle still brought down elk and deer, but his main income came from fancy hides like mink, ermine and beaver, the ones he had always caught with his good metal traps. Soon he would have to buy winter provisions, and there were almost no pelts in the tanning shed to trade. He thought enviously of Jesse's gold vein and shook his head. He didn't wish he had it instead of Jesse, but he certainly wished he had one of his own.

The moon was just a few days away from extinction and cast only the faintest of lights. Using familiarity as his guide, he worked his way up the mountain. The enormous Ponderosa pines made an inky blot against the starry sky, and the night sounds seemed even louder in the darkness. In spite of his thoughts, Nathan paid sharp attention to all the forest's sounds.

He found the narrow draw and located a bush that grew close to the center of the path. It was as tall as he was, with blood-red berries and treacherous thorns. Nathan positioned the war vest at an appropriate height so that it would look as if it were being worn by a man as tall as Many Rivers, and stepped back to view his handiwork.

The vest seemed to hang in midair, and the breeze gave it a movement not unlike that of a man standing quietly but not motionless. In the darkness it was a fearsome sight. Even in the daylight it would appear startling. Nathan hoped the Indians' superstitious nature would make it seem even more awesome.

Nathan went into the woods and got a branch far

from the path and began meticulously sweeping away his footprints. When he was well below the draw he tossed the branch away and went home.

Fawn lay on her side, her arm curled under her head. Nathan looked lovingly down at her as he removed his clothing. She looked so young and helpless in her sleep. Carefully he got into bed beside her and snuggled against her back, his long body curving to fit hers. She moved closer in her sleep and pillowed her head on his shoulder.

The next few days passed uneventfully. Nathan often wondered if the war vest had been found, but he was too prudent to return and risk being seen. If it had been spotted, Walking Tall might have posted a guard nearby until he decided what course to take.

As he continued with his routine activities, he shot an elk and the traps yielded a squirrel pelt. Aside from numerous raccoon tracks, he saw little evidence of other game. To add to Nathan's worries, the nights were growing cooler and the days shorter. Over and over he counted the pelts in the tanning shed, but the number was always the same. He recalled the year before when he had so many fine pelts, he had to make two trips down the mountain. His tension was considerably heightened as he recalled that his good steel traps lay at the bottom of the beaver pond.

Fawn helped him tan the few pelts and took her turn at scraping hides from the elk and deer he brought down with his rifle. To her eyes he had an abundance of skins, but she was accustomed to a different sort of life altogether. Her attitude angered him unreasonably. In the space of a few months she had managed to turn his well-ordered existence topsy-turvy.

Nathan stretched the elk hide taut on the wooden frame and tested it with his fingertips. Fawn did good work, he had to admit. When it came to curing hides, she could turn out a finished leather faster than he could.

As the sun climbed higher in the sky, Fawn hummed and worked a doeskin through the cane hoop over and over. It was almost supple enough to be drawn through the smallest ring. There was no blemish on its buttery tan surface, and she was certain it would bring a top price. Proudly she looked over at Nathan and smiled. He was a good hunter, her Nathan. His gun brought down more elk than either her brother or father ever had with their bows, and they had been among the best hunters of her tribe. She wished Nathan had known Storm Dancer. They would have been friends, she was certain. They had so many traits and interests in common.

"Are you hungry?" she asked when Nathan paused in his scraping. "Our dinner must be done by now."

He nodded and leaned the stretcher against the shed. "I am for a fact."

She put down the doeskin and stood up. "I'll go set the table." Happily she crossed the golden lawn of pine needles. She was glad Nathan's cabin sat among tall pines. They gave the place a majestic serenity unlike any other tree.

Fawn pulled the cabin door shut behind her and went to the fire. A venison stew was bubbling in the black pot, and she hooked its bail with the poker and swung it toward her on the fire arm. The aroma reminded her how hungry she was, and she took two bowls from the shelf. As she lifted the ladle, a noise from outside caught her attention. She turned toward the window.

Charley Three Toes and Pale Moon were riding into the clearing.

Fawn froze for a moment, her mouth dropping open. Had she not come inside so quickly, they would have seen her! Could it be that he had seen her anyway? She hurried to the door and tried to hear what was being said.

Nathan called out a greeting loud enough to be heard in the back room of the cabin. "Hello, Charley! I sure didn't expect to see you today."

Fawn couldn't hear Charley's response, but Nathan boomed, "You're here for a few days, you say? Well, climb down off that horse. Are you coming up the mountain or going down?"

Whatever Charley had replied made no difference to her. The only important thing was to know he wasn't just passing by. Fawn looked around frantically. Nathan wouldn't bring him in until he was forced to, but there was no other way out except through the back window. Not only that, but there was evidence all over the room that Nathan no longer lived alone. Her tanning hoops for softening hides hung on the wall, her old moccasins stood behind the door, her dresses hung in the bedroom on pegs.

She rushed around the room, grabbing up all her belongings. With her arms full she looked frantically around the room. Had she forgotten anything? The men's voices still came to her from outside. Nathan was showing Charley a pelt.

As she tossed her belongings under the wide bed and kicked them out of sight, she remembered Charley's last visit. She had felt half starved by the time Nathan had been able to smuggle food to her. And the barn! She had almost forgotten the musty smell of the horse blankets and the dampness of the rainy night. A frown puckered her forehead. She didn't want to do that again, and it was dangerous besides. Either Charley or Pale Moon might find her at any time.

Quickly Fawn grabbed one of the clean feed sacks Nathan used to carry provisions. Keeping a cautious eye toward the window and the three people in the yard, Fawn scrambled around the kitchen, throwing in all the supplies she could reach. She was halfway to the bedroom when the front door suddenly opened and Nathan strode through.

"Fawn! Charley's here!" he hissed, holding the door shut behind him.

She jumped and nearly dropped her sack of food. "You scared me half to death!" she retorted in a loud whisper. "I know he's here!"

"You've got to get out and hide. I'll keep them

around front. Go out the back window and hide in the woods until dark. Then go to the hayloft like you did before."

"No. This woman is not going to stay in the hayloft again."

"What? You have to!"

"No, I don't. I have food," she held up the bag, "and I have hidden all my things under the bed. I will go to the Pueblo village until they leave."

"Nathan?" Charley's voice sounded just outside the door. "Are you talking to somebody?"

"Me? Of course not, Charley. Nobody's here but us." His eyes met Fawn's and their expression spoke of his love and concern.

She nodded as if he had said the words and waved to him as she swung her legs over the open window sill. Silently she lowered herself to the ground and ran noiselessly to the thick woods behind the cabin. Nathan still held the door shut, giving her all the time he could.

"Nathan, this damned door's stuck," Charley called out.

"Try it again," Nathan yelled as Fawn disappeared in the bushes. He released the latch strap and the door opened easily. "It's probably warped from the rain we had last week," he said guilelessly as Charley came in. Across the yard he could see Pale Moon turning their horses into the pasture. The cabin shielded Fawn's escape route from Pale Moon's vision. "Come on in, Charley. Dinner's on the fire."

Charley sauntered over to the pot and used the

ladle to poke at the stew. "I believe your cooking has improved," he said as he smelled the tempting aroma. His eyes wandered to the cabinet and he picked up a bowl. "But why are there two bowls out?"

"Did I leave that sitting out? I guess I'm getting absentminded. Just get another one down for Pale Moon and I'll lay out some spoons. So you're on your way to Bancroft, are you?"

"More or less." Charley wandered around the room. "Taking up sewing, are you? There's a needle here on the sideboard and what's this? A bead?"

Nathan kept his face impassive. "I was trading over at Fire Bluff not long ago. I guess that bead followed me home. As for the needle, I guess I can sew as well as any man can. What about it?"

Charley grinned up at the tall trapper. "Not a thing, Nathan. Not a thing in this world. You can sew beads all over if you want to. Won't matter a bit to me. I was just wondering, was all."

Pale Moon came inside and dropped their bed-rolls in a heap behind the door. Without a word, she went to the pot and began to ladle out the stew. While the men ate she fetched bread and coffee and more stew as the need arose.

"You know, Nathan," Charley said with satisfaction as he picked his teeth with his fingernail. "You really ought to get you a squaw. It's not right for a man to be alone so much of the time." Out of habit he swatted Pale Moon's broad rump as she passed.

The woman did no more than blink. "But you get yourself a pretty one while you're at it."

Nathan drank the last of his coffee, his eyes cold and calculating. "I'm happy just the way I am," he said firmly.

Charley grinned again and his teeth seemed to glint like a wild animal's. "I just bet you are, Nathan. I just bet you are."

Chapter Eighteen

"WOULD YOU LOOK AT WHAT I FOUND UPSTREAM,"
Charley said as he brandished one of Fawn's traps
in his swarthy hand. "Looks like those damned
Indians are getting in your territory."

Nathan glanced at the trap and looked back at
the bridle he was mending. He hoped he had
covered his alarm at seeing one of the traps so
unexpectedly. "Where did you get that, Charley?"

"It was in the high grasses by the beaver pond. I
looked around and found several others. I broke
them up but I wanted to show you this one so you'd
know what to be on the lookout for."

Nathan barely suppressed a moan. The traps at
the beaver pond were the best of the lot. "I sure

wish you hadn't done that," he said with a sigh. "Now the Indians that set it will wonder who tore up their traps."

Charley scratched his head and stared at the trap he held. "I never thought about that," he admitted. "I sure never did. Well, it's done now and there's no need to keep this one." He dropped it to the ground and smashed it with his boot.

A muscle knotted in Nathan's jaw, but he said nothing. His large hands worked at the stiff leather straps, threading the harness together with great dexterity.

Charley tossed the remnants of the trap toward the trash bin. "There's been trouble up the mountain."

"Oh?" Nathan put his hole punch on the leather and began working a series of holes down the strap. "What kind of trouble?"

"Walking Tall is all fired up. A few days ago one of his braves found a vest hanging on a bush north of here. Seems it was the spitting image of the one old Many Rivers had worn. The brave made a lot out of the fact that it was hanging as far off the ground as the old chief was tall. Singed, it was, like it had been in a fire."

"Singed?" Nathan asked carefully.

"Yeah, that bunch of Indians always burn up their dead instead of burying them proper like. So of course Many Rivers was burned up wearing his war vest along with all the rest of his belongings. Well, I can tell you that really shook up Walking

Tall. Turned as pale as I ever saw an Indian get. Took to the hills for two days, just him and the medicine man, to study over what the sign meant. See, he was sure it was a message from his papa."

Nathan ran the strap through the metal buckle and tested the tongue for a fit in the holes. "What did he decide it meant?"

"At first everybody said the old man was mad because Walking Tall has been hassling the whites. But by the time Walking Tall and the medicine man came back, Walking Tall had convinced hisself that Many Rivers was just telling him that he was on his side now. You see, it was his *war* vest he left as a sign."

"How's that?" Nathan said as he looked up, his blue eyes piercing.

"So now Walking Tall is stirring the others up to run the whites off the mountain."

"What about you?" Nathan said absently as his mind raced.

Charley chuckled. "Don't you worry about old Charley. Those Indians have plumb forgot I'm not one of them. I'm practically a member of the tribe. Besides, if it gets too risky, I'll go stay with Pale Moon's people until it blows over. She's Ute, you know, from the other side of the mountain."

"What about your people? You wouldn't just leave them to be surprised by a war party of Arapahos?"

"What do you think I'm doing? Going on a picnic? I'm warning you, ain't I?"

"You've been here three days. That's riding pretty slow to warn folks."

Charley shrugged. "I'll get around to them all sooner or later. I figure it will take a couple more weeks before Walking Tall convinces his braves' council. Those older warriors are getting too cautious to decide anything fast."

"Isn't there anything we can do to stop this?" Nathan stood and hung the repaired bridle on his saddle horn just inside the tack room.

"Well, now, I did think of one thing," Charley admitted in his nasal whine.

"What's that?" Nathan demanded.

"There's one thing those Indians would want real bad. Funny thing is, they think they already have it. I know better though." He laughed and the sound was oily and menacing.

"You haven't said what that is," Nathan said, forcing friendliness into his voice.

"No, sir, I haven't. Not going to either. But I'm working on it. I'm working at it real hard." Still chuckling, Charley slapped Nathan on the shoulder and strode off toward the cabin.

Nathan frowned. Whatever Charley had in mind, he wasn't working on it very fast. Still, Charley had kept peace between the Indians and the whites for quite a few years. Maybe he could do it again. Nathan climbed the steps to the hayloft to toss down hay for the animals.

Charley leaned on the top board of the fence and watched the white mare trail behind Horse, as

Horse followed Nathan toward the barn. "That's a pretty little mare you've got there. Want to sell her?"

Nathan looked at Fawn's mare as if he were surprised to see her. "This white one? No, she's not for sale. I've got a mule I wouldn't mind trading though."

"No, I'm interested in the horse. What do you want with her? She's too small for you, and you've got that buckskin you always ride."

"She's a gift," Nathan said in a burst of inspiration. "A gift for Miss Darcy. You know, Jesse Keenan's wife. Next time I go to Bancroft I'll drop her off at their cabin."

Charley's pale eyes narrowed as he considered the plausibility of this story. "Seen Jesse lately?"

"Not in the past month," Nathan replied as he automatically shoved Horse's head away as the animal nipped audibly at his shoulder. "Have you?"

"Nope. I don't get over there much." His face set in narrow lines of hatred though his voice stayed steady.

Nathan didn't miss the expression on Charley's face, but he gave no sign and asked no questions as he climbed over the fence. "I've got to run my traps this afternoon. I'll be back after dark."

"You sure must have a mess of traps for it to take so long," Charley said testingly. "Want me to go along and help?"

"No, I know just where they are, and two people cause too much commotion. Tell Pale Moon to help herself to the smokehouse and cook whatever she fancies."

"I'll do that," Charley said as Nathan went toward the cabin to get his rifle and a bag for game. When Nathan started on his trap run, Charley decided he would follow at least part of the way.

Nathan paused and listened to the sounds of the woods. Aside from the usual rustle of the wind in the reddening leaves and the raucous cawing of a disturbed magpie, there were no sounds. He frowned slightly. Everything sounded right, but it didn't *feel* right. After a few minutes' concentration, he shook his head. He was being foolish, he decided. Confidently, he left the forest and went down the trail to the deserted Pueblo ruins.

"It's about time," Fawn complained as she hugged him tightly. "A woman could starve waiting for you."

"You're out of food already? What do you do—sit up here and eat all day?"

She swatted at him and took the bag from his shoulder. "Were I a Shaman I would make a riddle about smoked meat coming from a game bag," she grinned. "But I am not a Shaman."

"There's enough to last you another three days," Nathan said as he kissed her forehead. "I sure do miss you, Fawn."

"And I miss you, too, Nathan." She put down

the sack and slipped into his embrace. "Will they never leave?"

"They have to sooner or later." He stiffened and looked back the way he had come. "Did you hear that?"

"No. But yesterday I saw a great buck and four does on the path. Perhaps they have returned."

"In the daylight?"

She shrugged. "Everything must be somewhere," she said philosophically in Arapaho.

Nathan grinned down at her. "More of your Indian wisdom?"

"Is it not true? Come look. I have seen an eagle's nest on the crag opposite." She led him across the ledge and pointed. "There. Where the dark crevasse ends. Do you see it?"

He squinted across the gorge. "I think you're right."

"Of course I am. Indians are never mistaken about these things." She put her arm around his waist and lay her cheek against his shoulder. "I will cook your supper, will I not?"

"I'm afraid not," he said reluctantly. "I told Charley I'm checking on some traps. I'd better show up with some game."

Their eyes met. Fawn tried to hide her loneliness and disappointment, but he saw it plainly.

"It won't be much longer," he told her as he ran his thumb along her cheek.

"I hope not." She forced her voice to sound brave. "Is there news of the tribe?"

"Walking Tall won't be put off much longer. He's decided the war vest was a sign to attack."

"But when?" she exclaimed. "Are you in danger?"

"No, no. Don't get upset. If I was worried, would I leave you here alone?"

"Yes. This place is safe from the Indians. They would never find me here."

"You're right, they wouldn't. I was within a stone's throw of the path a dozen times before I accidentally discovered it. But no, there is no immediate danger." He kissed her passionately with a growing urgency, but forced himself to break away lovingly. "I must go. As soon as Charley leaves, I'll come get you."

"I should hope so," she said, her eyes averted to hide the tears he might see there. "This woman does not like it here. The wind makes the windows moan."

"A woman could stay in the barn," he reminded her. "Charley never goes to the loft and Pale Moon couldn't get up the narrow steps."

"Here at least I can move around. It is safer."

"I agree." He kissed her again and held her very closely as if to impress the essence of her into his clothing. "I have to go now."

She nodded and stepped back. "Take care, my Nathan. You take my heart with you."

"As you have mine," he responded gently in the language that had once seemed so foreign to him. "Don't do anything foolish."

"Has this woman ever done such a thing?" she retorted. "Just don't leave me here for any longer than you must."

He grinned and stroked her bright hair. "I'll run all the way to get you."

She watched him go, her slender shoulders back, her head lifted proudly. No woman of her tribe would dream of sending her man away with less dignity. Only when he was out of sight did she relax and wrap her arms around herself as if she were chilled. Night would fall soon and with it would come the fearsome shadows and the wind that sang like a banshee through the open windows.

Fawn picked up the sack and wandered back to the cubicles. She had slept in a different one every night, telling herself that before she had used them all, she could go home. In a few more nights she would begin again.

Because there was nothing else to do, Fawn took a leafy branch and swept out the debris of dead leaves and twigs from the room she would occupy that night. As had the ancient inhabitants before her, she carried the debris to the deep cave behind the adobe huts and dumped it. She wondered idly how many other women had hidden their garbage in the cavern so that any bones or other food would not attract predators onto the ledge and so that no signs of habitation showed from the front of the village.

Judging by the angle of the sun, Fawn had less than two hours of daylight. The village was built into the western side of the gorge, and evening came early.

She poked disinterestedly in the bag of food. There were several strips of venison jerky, a round hump of the coarse bread favored by the Utes, a few oblongs of cornbread, and a square of dried raspberry "leather." Enough food for three days. Fawn sighed and pushed the sack into the clean corner. She was tired of being there. Perhaps, she thought, she could fast for a few days and try to see visions such as the Shaman did. But she had never heard of a female Shaman and she had only mealtimes to break the tedium of her days.

Trailing her hand along the cool, pale gold wall, Fawn wandered outside. A sudden noise attracted her and she looked up toward the path. Had Nathan returned? Her heart quickened with anticipation.

"Well, now," Charley Three Toes said as he stepped into view. "Looks like I was right. Old Nathan does have hisself a little something stashed away at the old ruins."

Fawn blanched and stepped back.

Nonchalantly Charley came onto the ledge and put his head to one side as his eyes raked over her body. "And it ain't just any Indian either." He switched to fluid Arapaho and said, "You're Fawn. Many Rivers' woman. It is said that you are dead."

"I was not his woman but his wife," Fawn stated as she lifted her chin.

Charley chuckled. "I tried to buy you once. Did

you know that?" He circled her stealthily, like a predatory beast. "I wanted you then and I want you more now."

"What of your woman, Pale Moon?" Fawn tried to reason with him.

"Pale Moon is nothing in my eyes." He was slowly closing the space that separated them. "Not like you, all soft-looking and curvy. I never had me a chief's woman before. I bet you ain't near so haughty on your back." He lunged at her and his grasping fingers closed on themselves as she deftly jumped aside.

Her heart racing with fear, Fawn spun away and crouched, ready to spring to either side until she could get a clear sprint up the path to the woods. Once off the ledge she thought she could outrun Charley and reach Nathan. "You had better leave me alone, Charley Three Toes! I am powerfully protected!" She made a sweeping gesture such as she had seen the Shaman use. "I call upon the vengeful spirit of Chief Many Rivers of the Arapaho nation, and upon the warrior spirit of my father, Elk Tooth! Protect me!"

Charley grinned and shook his head. "No good, Fawn. I ain't no superstitious Indian. This ain't Walking Tall you're dealing with." Still chuckling, he came nearer. "I killed your papa once, girl, and I reckon I could kill again if need be. So you better come with ole Charley."

Fawn gasped. "Why are you doing this to me, Charley Three Toes?" She edged closer to the brink of the ledge. If he charged her again, perhaps she could shove him over the side.

"You're gold in my pocket, girl. All I have to do is deliver you to Walking Tall, and I can name my price. If I let him wipe out the settlers, my trading days are over, but for your skin, he will declare peace. At least for a while."

"But they will kill me!"

Charley shrugged. "It's worth it to me. Besides, I plan to enjoy you first."

"Nathan will avenge me!"

"Only if I don't do him in first. And I plan to do just that. He trusts me. All I have to do is walk up and shoot him. I can fix it so nobody knows it was me." He strolled toward her, enjoying her fear and being careful to stay between her and the only escape route. "The way I look at it, Nathan won't be back for maybe two, three days. That gives me plenty of time for whatever I want to do with you. Anything at all. It don't matter how loud you yell. Can't nobody hear you but me."

Fawn felt the loose pebbles beneath her moccasins. She was almost on the edge. Already she could feel the strong updraft from the canyon floor far below.

As if he were reading her mind, Charley stopped. "Don't take me for a fool, girl. You can't trick me over the side. Tell you what I'll do." He sidled away toward the center of the ledge. "I'll give you a run for the path. Go on. Run for it!"

Not taking her eyes from his face, she bolted, her

long legs carrying her swiftly. Charley was on her at once, yanking her to him in a vise-like grip as he knotted one hand painfully in her hair. He tightened his fingers and pulled her head back in a way that nearly cracked her neck. Fawn bit back her cry of pain and revulsion as he yanked open the front of her dress and put his yellowed teeth to her tender breast. Fawn fought him wildly but his strength was greater than hers and her struggles only whetted his lust.

Suddenly there was a guttered cry and a weight fell against them. In his surprise, Charley loosened his hold on Fawn and she fell back as Pale Moon attacked him.

The large Indian pounded at him with both her clenched fists, using them clasped together like a hammer. All the years of suppressed rage at the verbal insults and outright physical abuse stood behind each blow and gave it strength. A spark of intelligence lit her black eyes as she attacked the man who had caused her so much misery. Under her furious onslaught Charley stumbled backward, trying to shield his head from the blows.

Fawn heard screams, but she didn't recognize them as her own until she felt the pain in her throat. Her eyes filled with fright as she viewed the struggle, knowing Pale Moon couldn't win if Charley gained his wits. Yet she seemed tethered to the ledge, unable to run.

Charley growled like a cornered animal and his hand flew to the knife he wore at his belt. Sunlight glinted off the steel as he threw his arm up and back. Then the deadly metal buried itself in Pale Moon's heart.

Even as death glazed her eyes, the huge woman grabbed Charley and held him to her in a parody of lust. Her bulk was such that as she teetered from the killing blow, she carried him to the precipice. Realizing what she intended, Charley howled and stabbed at her again and again but Pale Moon was past feeling. With one final effort, she hurled herself into space, still hugging Charley in a grip of death.

"Fawn! Fawn!" Nathan cried out as he ran across the ledge. He had arrived in time to see the couple fall from sight.

At the sound of his voice, Fawn scrambled to her feet and ran into his arms. "Nathan!" she screamed. "Nathan!"

"It's all right, Fawn! It's all right! I'm here. You're safe now!" He held her tightly and her trembling was matched by his own. "Did he hurt you? Are you all right?"

She nodded and gulped hysterically. "I'm not hurt. He's dead, isn't he?"

"You stay here. Do you hear me, Fawn? Stay here while I check." He turned her loose and she leaned weakly against the adobe wall.

Nathan went to the precipice and looked down into the canyon that was hazed with an evening fog. After a short time he found what he sought but quickly looked away from the gruesome sight. "He's dead," he said as he came back to Fawn. "So is Pale Moon."

"You're certain?"

"There's no mistake." He took her into his arms and let her cry against his broad chest.

"She saved me," Fawn said at last. "He was about to take me and she stopped him."

Nathan stroked her hair and listened to her sobs subside. "I guess she had finally had enough."

"Take me home, Nathan," Fawn whispered as the evening winds began to rise and moan through the ruins. "Take me away from here."

He nodded. "I'll go down into the canyon tomorrow and bury them. Let's go home." He kept his strong arm protectively around her as he led her up the path.

Chapter Nineteen

FAWN GLANCED OUT THE WINDOW AS NATHAN CAME across the yard. The majestic pines wore their unchanging green, but the nip of early autumn made them more aromatic than usual. Across the broad river she could see the riotous orange and gold of the cottonwoods and aspen. Soon it would be the month of Bears Sleeping.

As Nathan entered the cabin he brought with him the crisp fall scents. Fawn tiptoed to kiss his cheek above the golden beard and felt the coolness of his skin. He hugged her and returned her kiss but his manner was absentminded.

"What is wrong?" she asked.

"Nothing. What's for supper?"

"Do not say 'nothing' to me. I want to know

You were not gone long enough to go to both Bancroft and Fire Bluff."

Nathan sat down in his chair and ran his fingers through his hair as if he were tired to his very bones. "I didn't go to Fire Bluff."

"Why not? Was trading so good at Bancroft that there was no need?" She knew this wasn't so. He had already told her that he had only a few pelts that could be considered prime, and the traders in Bancroft were very choosy.

Nathan was silent so long, she thought he wouldn't answer her at all. Finally he said, "I was on the trail to Fire Bluff and thought I would drop by old Chester Wheatley's place. He's a trapper up around the bend in the canyon." Again Nathan was silent for a long time. Fawn came to him and knelt on the bear rug at his feet. "Chester's been a hermit for years. Half-crazy old man. Sometimes I would trade his furs for him so he could stay away from folks."

Slowly Nathan's eyes rested on Fawn's concerned face, then went back to the fire. "He's dead. Killed in a bad way." Sudden, helpless fury kindled in his eyes and they glinted like blue steel. "A crazy old man like that! Murdered! He never harmed a soul! Just wanted to be left alone!" Pain rent his voice and he clamped his mouth shut. A stinging wetness blurred his vision.

"Nathan," she murmured as she reached out to comfort him. "I'm so sorry. I will sing a prayer for his soul's journey."

He briefly rested his hand on her, but he was still

torn by the memory of what he had found. "It was awful, Fawn! Purely awful! I buried him as well as I could in such rocky ground and I piled stones over the grave so nothing could disturb him. But I think I'll see him in every nightmare I ever have!"

She stood and pulled him against her as a mother would comfort a child. For all his bravery and great strength, Nathan was frightened, and it didn't take a Shaman to know why. With every breath he drew, Fawn knew he was thinking it might have been her.

Nathan put his arms around her waist and leaned his head against the warm curve of her breast. "You stay close to me and the cabin, you hear me, Fawn? No more wandering off to God knows where. You stay here where it's safe!"

"I will, Nathan." Yet both knew it wasn't safe there. Not really. "If there's ever any trouble, you lock yourself in. Put the shutters over the windows and don't open the door for any reason. If something happens to me, you run down the mountain to Jesse! Follow the river. You know the way." He looked up at her and forced her to meet his eyes. "Promise me you'll do that, Fawn. Promise me!"

"I promise, Nathan. If anything . . . happens to you, I will go to Jesse."

Each looked deeply into the other's soul. Their love was as clear as any words or actions could ever express. At last Nathan pulled her down onto his lap and they watched the leaping fire in the hearth.

* * *

Fawn lay gazing up at the night-enshrouded rafters. Nathan's lovemaking had been especially passionate, seemingly driven by a need to prove something. She knew that he was trying to mask his concern for her safety and build her confidence that somehow he would be able to protect her. She turned her head to look at him. He lay on his side facing her, one arm across her stomach. Yet even in his sleep the lines of worry were not erased from his face.

Carefully Fawn moved his arm away and slid out of bed. For the past hour she had lain awake, trying to think of a solution to their problem. One had come to her but she had brushed it aside as too foolhardy, still it had persisted. At last she decided there was no alternative, even as reckless as it seemed.

The first step was to get out of the cabin without awakening Nathan, for he would definitely forbid her to do what she must. He was a light sleeper, at best, so she moved very cautiously lest she make a noise. She gathered her clothes and moccasins and went into the other room to dress.

Would her plan work? She thought so, but if it didn't she would never live to try another one. She put on her once-fine wedding dress with the long fringe that swung with her every movement. Then she brushed and braided her hair in the way she had worn it when she wedded Many Rivers. Taking Nathan's writing quill, she threaded it in one of her braids so that it made a splash of pure white against her dark hair. Looking around the room, she took a small honey jar from the table and let herself out into the night.

A full moon silvered the pine needles above her and made deep purple shadows on the gold carpet beneath the trees. Fawn judged it to be early still. Not yet midnight. Nevertheless, she would have to hurry.

She went to the barn and looped a leather thong around her white mare's nose, Indian style, then stood on a stump to jump onto its back.

The mare snorted in displeasure at being ridden at such an unorthodox time and without her own bridle, but Fawn kicked her forward and rode behind the barn. At the tanning shed, Fawn paused long enough to get a burlap bag and a knife, then nudged her horse into the woods.

Fawn had never ridden alone at night and she shivered fearfully. An owl hooted nearby as if it were a lost soul and she heard the velvety sound of its wings as it left its perch. A limb swatted across her face, causing her to make a startled sound. She clapped her hand over her mouth and lay low on the mare's neck to avoid any other branches.

After two hours that seemed like an eternity, Fawn rode into the open and reined her horse to a stop. She rolled off its back and tied it to a low bush. She knew this place well. Only the year before she had picked berries here with Clouds Passing and some of the other women. Just beyond the tangle of berry bushes, Fawn climbed a low cliff and with the aid of the full moon she found the large outcropping of mica that she sought. It layered easily into her hand and after gathering all she could carry, she returned to her horse and dumped the mica onto a large flat rock. Taking a smooth stone, she ground the mica into a powder as fine as cornmeal. It crumbled easily and lay like a silver dust on the larger rock.

Next Fawn cut the burlap into four squares and folded it. She tied the padding securely over the horse's hooves with strings from the burlap and led the animal around to see if the coverings would stay in place. The mare stepped daintily over the flat rocks, but her hooves were almost silent. Nodding with satisfaction, Fawn again tethered her to the bush.

Removing the lid from the jar, Fawn drew a deep breath. From this point on, she couldn't back out of her plan. At least not easily. She dipped her fingers into the pot. Cool, smooth honey flowed over her hand and she closed her eyes in a silent prayer. This had to work!

Slowly she rubbed the honey over her dress, then onto her face and over her hair. The sweetness was cloying to her sensitive nose and the stickiness was unpleasant. Still she continued until the pot was empty and even her moccasins were gooey with honey. If she went back now there would be a lot of questions to answer.

Fawn dipped her hand in the powdered mica and began to sprinkle it over her entire body. It stuck wherever it touched and in the moonlight it seemed to glow. Fawn checked for clouds that might block the moon, because for her plan to succeed, the mica must shine like silver. The sky was still perfectly clear.

When she was covered with the glimmering dust, she mounted her horse and rode toward the Indian village.

Nathan moved restlessly in his sleep, and the coolness of the sheets brought him awake. He raised up on his elbow and looked sleepily at the space Fawn usually occupied. Instantly he was alert. He swung his legs out of bed and sat up. Where could she have gone? It was unlike her to visit the shed in the middle of the night. Nevertheless, he padded barefoot to the front door and looked across the yard to the group of outbuildings.

"Fawn?" he called out. "Where are you?" When there was no answer, he hurried back inside and pulled on his clothes.

In order to quell his growing fear, Nathan grumbled angrily as he yanked on his boots and hurried to the barn. A quick look in the stalls and adjoining pasture confirmed his worst suspicions. Her horse was gone.

Nathan bridled Horse and mounted him in a leap. The large animal reared and bent his back to buck, but Nathan was in no mood for mischief. He pulled the horse around and galloped for the fence. Horse cleared it easily, and Nathan loped him in a circle as he searched for Fawn's trail. He found it behind the barn and he swore softly. She was headed straight for the Indian village. Ignoring the branches that tore at him, Nathan kicked Horse into a gallop.

Fawn paused and looked around her. She had just passed the ford where her "drowning" had been confirmed. Around the next bend lay the sleeping village. Once she rode forward, there would be no turning back. Before she could weaken, she slammed her heels against the mare's ribs and the animal lunged forward. As the first wigwam came into sight, Fawn gave voice to an Arapaho war cry.

She rode pell-mell into the quiet village, tearing the silence with her shrieks. Almost at once there were startled screams from within the wigwams as the Indians were yanked from their sleep.

Fawn thundered toward the large wigwam in the center of the village. As was customary, the wigwams were erected in concentric circles with the mightiest warriors surrounding the ceremonial ground and the chief's wigwam. She easily recognized Walking Tall's wigwam by his painted totem of a puma beneath the sun. As she reined to a rearing stop, Walking Tall stumbled half-dressed out of the opening.

"You! Ungrateful son!" she screamed in what she hoped was a banshee voice. "Disobedient serpent! I bring a message from Chief Many Rivers! He sees you from the skies and is shamed! Take no war to the whites whom he befriended! Break no treaty he has made!" She continued to kick her mare and pull back on the reins so that the animal reared and plunged in a frenzy. "If you heed not his words, *he* will return next time! Many Rivers has spoken!" With a last shrill shriek, Fawn wheeled her horse and rode at breakneck speed through the camp, her dress, skin and hair shining ghostly in the moonlight. She recognized the shocked faces of the people as they staggered out to investigate the commotion. In her hurtling flight she almost ran over her brother, and for a moment she was afraid she would fall off as the mare veered sharply. But she held on tightly and let the horse run full out down the trail.

At the river she reined her mount down hill and slowed to a more prudent canter for the horse's safety. The burlap covered hooves made little noise and the sound of the river blotted out the rest. Also the padding left almost no hoofprints on the hard ground. Behind her, Fawn could hear the confused shouts in the village and her skin grew clammy with fear. She had been so close to Storm Dancer! No one else could have seen her that clearly, but he had been close enough to reach out and touch her! He had surely seen that she was as alive as she had ever been—would he tell Walking Tall it was a trick? She looked over her shoulder but no one was following her.

A great noise suddenly came from her left as Nathan burst through the woods. At the sight of her he gave a startled yell and Horse reared high in the air, his large hooves flailing.

"Be quiet!" she hissed as she brought her mare under control. "Would you have them all upon us?"

"Fawn! What in the hell are you doing!" he demanded as he rode to her. "What have you got all over you?"

"Mica. Tonight my people have seen a ghost." She grinned and her teeth flashed in her gleaming face. "I will be talked of in council for as long as there is a memory."

Nathan stared back the way she had come as he digested her words. "Damn!" he muttered. "Let's get out of here!" Although he saw no one, the village was much too close for safety.

The horses were eager to return to the barn so they moved at a good pace down the mountain. Nathan didn't try to talk to her, but he kept a close watch on the trail at their backs. When they reached the pasture, he pulled off Horse's bridle as Fawn cut the burlap from her mare's feet. Nathan opened the gate and motioned for Horse to enter, and the mare followed.

"Now I want to hear all about it!" he growled. He had had enough time to stop shaking over her dangerous ploy and his anger was real. "Just why is it you think you are invincible?"

"What is this word?" she asked blithely. "I cannot hear it."

"You know what I mean! Why did you do this?"

"It seemed to be a good plan, and it was." Now that the immediate danger was over, she felt like dancing in joyous victory. Never had she heard of any brave scoring such a coup! "I would like to wash now." Still smiling, she started for the river.

"Wait a minute!" Nathan caught her arm and turned her loose at once. "What in the hell have you got on you!"

"Honey, Nathan," she said as if this were obvious. "The mica would not stick otherwise." She smiled at him and walked toward the river, unlacing her dress as she went.

He stared at her for a short time, then hurried after her. "Fawn, this is the stupidest, most bullheaded thing I ever heard of! What did you do?"

She pulled off her sticky dress and held it up to see the effect as she neared the river. Her bare breasts were pearly by comparison to her shiny arms and face. "I dressed as the spirit of one who is dead and rode into the village. Because my skin glowed with powdered mica and because they were groggy with sleep, they believed I was indeed a ghost."

Nathan caught her arm and spun her around to face him. "What!" he gasped.

"I told Walking Tall that He Who Is Dead—I called him by name, of course—is displeased and that he himself would come to them if they continued to war with the whites." She laughed. "He looked so frightened and confused. He was standing there holding up his leggings with both hands as his mouth was gaping open. Never have I seen him so awed." She untied the thong that held her pants and let them drop. "I hope I will be able to wash the mica and honey from my clothes. Otherwise they are ruined." She examined the smeared leather.

"Will you stop babbling about clothes and finish telling me what happened!" He took the dress from her and tossed it onto the river bank.

Fawn stepped delicately into the cold water and began sluicing the goo from her arms. "I kept my horse moving as I talked so no one could get a clear view of me. Because of the padding on her hooves, my mare made almost no noise, even though she was plunging like a wild thing. As soon as I finished threatening Walking Tall, I rode at a fast gallop out of the village." She frowned slightly and bent to wet her hair.

"What! What happened? You're frowning so I know something did!"

"I almost rode over Storm Dancer, my stepbrother. No one else was close to me as they all ran when I approached. Only he stood his ground. He was close enough to see I was no ghost."

"Damn!" Nathan exploded. "Then what?"

"Nothing. I rode out of sight of the village and headed toward our cabin. That's where I met you." She scrubbed her hair vigorously.

"What will Storm Dancer do? Can we trust him?"

She shrugged philosophically. "Have we a choice? I think he kept his silence, or else they would have been after me at once. Storm Dancer and I were always friends as well as brother and sister. I have always been able to trust him before."

Nathan kicked off his boots and shucked away

his clothes. Gingerly he waded into the river to help her wash off the tenacious mica. "I think you're right," he said hopefully. "After all, he did turn us loose when we were captured."

She submerged her head to rinse away the last of the honey. "I cannot get all the mica to wash out."

He patted her wet hair that still glowed dully in the moonlight. "Maybe when it's dry we can brush it out." He grinned. "Until then I'll have no trouble finding you in the dark."

She splashed water at him and squeezed the excess moisture from her hair. "I'm freezing. Tomorrow I will wash my clothes. For now I want only a fire."

They waded onto the bank and Nathan pulled his shirt around her shoulders. In spite of her height, it hung almost to her knees. He stepped into his pants and carried his work boots by the shoe strings. "I'll get you warmed up. But, Fawn, promise me you won't do anything like this again."

"I promise, Nathan. It would never work a second time."

He groaned but put his arm around her as they went to the cabin.

Chapter Twenty

THE EARLY MORNING BREEZE RUFFLED FAWN'S HAIR as she bent to gather the late blueberries. Sunlight caught in the dark strands, turning them to flame. She shivered and pulled her shawl more snugly around her. Fall had gilded the trees, and the lazy air currents now carried the promise of winter.

Several leaves of brilliant scarlet drifted down onto her shoulders as she worked. Fawn lifted her head and gazed up toward the snowy mountain peak that reared above the maple trees.

Two days had passed since her daring ride, and thus far there had been no reprisals. She had been bored with staying in the cabin and knew that the squirrels and deer would eat all the berries if she put off gathering them any longer. So when Nathan had left for the tanning shed, she had taken a gunny sack and come to the blueberry field.

She bit her lower lip as she let her mind ride up the mountain to the village. Clouds Passing would be sewing warm clothes for her grandchildren and probably making a pot of the elk stew that Storm Dancer loved. All the women would be readying their homes and family for winter, and the braves would be fasting in preparation for the last big hunt before the larger game moved down to winter in the lower valleys. The village horses and dogs would be furry with their winter coats and the air would be filled with the aroma of wood smoke and the happy squeals of children. Fawn felt a deep twinge of homesickness.

It took her a moment to realize she was looking straight at Storm Dancer.

"Greetings, sister," he said softly in the tone of voice he used only for her and their mother.

Fawn's eyes darted toward the underbrush and she swallowed nervously. "Greetings, Storm Dancer," she replied. "Are you alone?"

"Yes. Are you?"

She nodded. If this was an attack there would be nothing to gain by lying. She saw Storm Dancer relax slightly and she did the same. "Are you well?" she asked in polite Arapaho. "And our mother?"

"I am well and Clouds Passing is well, also." He smiled affectionately. "She has everyone running about as always. Prairie Moon grumbles almost constantly, but she is with child, and at such times she always complains."

Fawn smiled. Storm Dancer's wife had never needed an excuse to complain about anything and everything. "So I am to be an aunt once more." She gazed at him across the clearing and took a step toward him.

Storm Dancer held up his hand to halt her. "Come no closer. I know you are as much alive as I am, but a curse has been placed upon you."

Fawn stopped and clutched the sack to her as if for protection. "Why are you here, my brother?"

"I have come to bid you farewell."

"What do you mean by that? You are leaving?" she asked in great surprise.

"We all are. The council has decided this area is unlucky. It seems we were visited by a wrathful demon a few nights ago. A demon that took your shape." Even across the clearing she could see the amusement on his face. "I was closest to the demon and saw it clearly. It was riding a horse of smoke and thunder, and I could see the stars shining through it. I reached out my hand to count coup, but could feel nothing there."

"You told the council that?"

"All that and more. It was a foolish thing you did, and your man should never have allowed it. Had you ridden close to anyone else you would be dead now."

"Nathan knew nothing of it," Fawn said in his

defense. "Had he known I considered such a thing he would have prevented me."

Storm Dancer nodded approvingly. "You should listen to the words of your man and be more obedient. This has forever been a failing of yours."

She couldn't deny this so she said, "Does Clouds Passing grieve for me?"

He shrugged. "Who knows what is in a woman's mind? But she often sits alone and gazes down the mountain. I believe she knows you are alive and well, but such words cannot be spoken." He stepped back into the deeper shade and the mottled shadows made him almost invisible. "Take care, my sister. If we never meet again, may the Great Spirit watch over you." He turned to go, then paused. "I give you my blessing as head of our family. I think I would like your Nathan—if he were of the People." He faded away into the dense underbrush.

"Walk in peace," she murmured as tears brimmed in her eyes, "and may the Great Spirit know your name."

A metallic click sounded faintly behind her and Fawn whirled to see Nathan lower his rifle. He blended as well into the forest as had Storm Dancer. His expression was one of profound relief.

"Nathan! I did not hear you come to me!"

"Speak English," he reminded her as his eyes searched the woods where Storm Dancer had gone. "What did he say? The tribe is leaving?"

"Yes. They are going away." She, too, looked

after her brother. "I never dreamed they would actually leave the mountain. I will never see Storm Dancer or Clouds Passing again," she added sadly.

"You won't see Walking Tall either," Nathan reminded her.

"This is true." She sighed and made a gesture of acceptance. "Such is the way of the People. We stay awhile and then are gone. The world is our home. We are not like the whites, who think they can own a parcel of land and refuse to leave it no matter what comes." Her voice broke and she crossed her arms over her chest as if she were suddenly cold. "We are one with nature and the wind is our brother."

Nathan came to her and put his arms around her, but didn't speak. He knew that if he expressed his great relief at the tribe leaving, Fawn would be hurt and angry. She was having to give up her family forever. Even though she was alienated from them, he knew she had never really given up the hope of someday being able to visit secretly with her mother and brother. With the tribe living as it always had, she felt some sense of permanence, some innate stability of life proceeding as usual, but now the high meadow would be empty and all her traditions gone forever. He held her while she silently cried for a way of life she would never know again. When at last she lifted her head and looked up at him with her large green eyes, he brushed the tears from her cheeks.

"When did you come here?" she asked tremulously.

"I was right behind you all the time. I had my gun ready in case there was trouble."

Fawn pushed the remaining tears away with her palm. "You shouldn't creep up like that. Had Storm Dancer seen you, you might be dead now."

"Are you so certain that he didn't?" Nathan gazed down at her and brushed the hair from her face. "Come on. Let's pick the rest of these berries before the squirrels get them all."

Fawn hesitated, then bent to gather a handful of the plump blueberries. Perhaps Nathan was right. It would explain why her brother had kept a distance between them, for he had never been given to superstitions. Fawn smiled tearfully. Her brother was a brave man, a great man. Only the most fearless of warriors would stand before a white man's gun in order to tell his sister good-bye. It was the bravest of deeds yet he could never retell it in council and be honored. She felt her spirits rise and decided she would sing his song to the Great Spirit and tell of his bravery.

"Let's go on back home now, we have enough," Nathan broke into her thoughts as he dumped a double handful of berries into the bag.

"No, Nathan, we must gather more while we can," she said more sharply than she had intended. Fawn was struggling to maintain her composure and hoped that by keeping busy she could take her mind off her pain. "I want to dry as many as possible, and these are the last ones of the year."

"All right, but there aren't very many left."

"Of course there are. You just have to look for

them." She shoved the leaves aside and searched in the depths of the bush.

Nathan watched her for a moment, then sighed. "I guess there may be a few more." He picked in silence for several minutes, then straightened. "Surely this is enough for today, Fawn. I need to do some hunting before I lose any more daylight."

Fawn looked across the bushes. "I still see some more in the very back."

"This will have to do."

She bent to pick more as if he hadn't spoken.

He sighed and added a few more handfuls to the gunnysack before he frowned at her and said, "I'm losing time, Fawn. We can come back here tomorrow."

"By tomorrow they may be gone," she said stubbornly. "Besides, I did not ask you to help me. Go do your hunting." She was feeling unreasonably angry, and as he moved away she said, "Why are you not tending your traps as well? Soon the snows will fall and it will be too late to trade the furs."

Nathan frowned at her sharp words. "Those traps aren't doing any good, Fawn. Not like metal ones would. Half the time the animal gnaws his way out the side before I get to him."

She shrugged. "My father had the same problem."

"Your father didn't have to depend on trapping to live!" Nathan snapped. "We will get enough meat to eat, but not nearly enough hides to trade for staples like flour and cloth!"

"Indians do not need these things," she retorted. "We are self-sufficient without them."

"Well, I'm not an Indian and I'm not going to live on roots and berries all winter like some damned squirrel!"

"Neither do we!" she blazed back at him. She had been through far too much torment to remain even-tempered now. "My people live quite well!"

"Your people dress in hides and have been known to eat their own dogs!"

This was true, so she jerked her chin up but refused to answer. "At least," she said when she could remain silent no longer, "we never destroy the earth by digging great holes and burrows like moles! As *your* people did in Bancroft!"

Nathan scowled. "You've never been to Bancroft!"

Knowing she had scored, Fawn tossed her head. "An Indian knows these things."

He threw down the handful of berries and they glared at each other. "Back off, Fawn," he growled in his deepest voice. "I'm under a big strain, and you're pushing me mighty hard."

"*You* are under a strain? I have just said good-bye to my brother—who I will never see again—and *you* are under a strain? It is I who have reason to complain!"

"About what? You have a soft bed and a dry house for the first time you can remember! You *are* with 'your people,' whether you agree or not! I'm a good provider and take excellent care of you—even if you do throw away my best steel traps!"

"So! Again you bring up those traps!" She threw down the half-filled sack of berries and put her hands on her hips. "You are still angry about that! Did this woman not make you new traps and even help you set them out? Did she not make more after *your* friend destroyed them?" Her eyes flashed green fire and her words tumbled out so fast her English was almost unintelligible.

"And did the traps work?" he shouted. "No! They didn't!"

"It is not my fault if you have the smell of white skin and frighten away small animals!"

"Talk English, damn it!" he roared. "How can I talk to you if you won't talk English?"

"And that's another thing!" she stormed. "Why should I speak your language? You should learn to speak mine!"

"My language *is* your language! Elizabeth!" he enunciated her name scathingly.

"Do not dare to call me that! I curse the day I ever told you that my first mother called me by that name! It has been a weapon in your mouth ever since! My name—my *only* name—is *Fawn!*"

"Whoever named you that must not have known you very well," he retorted. "Fawns are shy and quiet!"

Fawn's face paled in her fury. "How can you say this to me? Always I have been good to you and respectful of you! Have I even once said your ways are strange and unreasonable, though they are? Have I ever pointed out to you that the bed you made rustles like dead leaves and smells musty when it rains, though it does? Have I ever complained about learning to cook your strange foods that even a Sioux wouldn't eat? Or the way the green hides smell when the wind shifts from the tanning shed? Never!"

"Yes, you have! I hear about that bed all the time! As for my 'strange' food, at least *I* never eat snake!"

Fawn blinked. "Neither do I!"

"I've heard tales," he disputed her words. "All Indians eat snake. Snake *and* armadillo!"

"Never have I eaten either!" she gasped. "It sounds terrible! Like something a white-eyes would eat!"

"White-eyes!" he roared at her use of the derogatory term. "Who are you calling 'white-eyes'?"

"I was not speaking to the trees!" she yelled back. "Who do you think I meant?"

Nathan forced himself to draw a calming breath. This was getting out of hand. "All right. All right! So my eyes are lighter than yours. They aren't white," he ground out with barely restrained anger, "but they are light. Now calm down."

"I am already calmer," Fawn said through clenched teeth. "My people are noted for their ability to keep an inner peace. No matter what the provocation."

"I'm sorry I said you eat snake and armadillo," Nathan made himself say.

"I accept your apology, even though I have

never heard of any *Indian* eating snake. I have no idea what you mean by 'armadillo.'"

"They grow south of here," Nathan said tentatively. "They look like groundhogs but with a hard shell."

"And you thought I would like to eat that?" she asked dangerously.

"You already forgave me for that," Nathan reminded her quickly.

Fawn compressed her lips. "I am sorry I said our bed is musty. Even though it is."

He looked at her through narrowed eyes. "I've been meaning to change the ticking and restuff it."

"When we do, could we use something besides dead leaves?"

"Corn husks, Fawn. Corn husks!" He drew another deep breath. "Maybe we could collect feathers instead."

She considered whether or not he was making fun of her. "I would prefer feathers," she said carefully.

They observed each other warily. He finally put out his hand, palm up. "I'll try not to call you 'Elizabeth' anymore if we can make up."

Hesitantly Fawn put her hand in his and he curled his fingers around it. "I no longer feel angry at you—or at least not much."

He pulled her to him and held her. After a moment he said, "My ways aren't all that strange, now are they?"

"Yes, Nathan, they are." She felt his body tense

and said quickly, "But I am becoming accustomed to most of them."

"Don't talk," he suggested. "Not yet." He held her until he felt her relax against him. "I love you, Fawñ. I guess all couples have trouble getting used to one another at first."

"You had trouble getting used to me?" she demanded. "How can that be?"

"Fawn," he said firmly as he made her look at him. "I love you."

"I love you, too," she answered carefully, and her eyes told him she meant it. "In time we will learn harmony."

He grinned. "That might be pretty dull."

She flashed him a dazzling smile and the dimples appeared in her cheeks. "It will never be dull, Nathan. I can promise you that."

He sighed and pulled her back to his embrace. "It's just that I've been so worried lately. Not only about Walking Tall—although that's been the worst part—but also about getting enough pelts to trade. We have the smoked meat and food that you have dried or gathered, so we won't have to worry about starving, but that's all we have."

"I don't understand."

"I take the pelts to Bancroft and Fire Bluff," he explained patiently, "and trade them for lamp oil, beans, corn and flour meal, bullets—all the things we need that the mountain won't give us. But this year I don't have enough trade goods to buy what we need."

Fawn tightened her arms around him. "Have we nothing else to trade? The mules, perhaps?"

"Then how would I get the provisions back up the mountain?" He rubbed his cheek against the top of her head and ran his fingers through her soft hair. "I can't think of one single thing we have that anybody would take in trade for a pot of beans."

"What does Jesse do? He is no trapper."

Nathan gave a short laugh. "Jesse struck gold. If you have gold you never have to worry about beans and lamp oil. Unfortunately, I never found a lode like Jesse and Miss Darcy did."

Fawn tilted her head back to look at him. "Even though you are no longer a prospector, you want gold? I don't understand."

"I trade the furs for gold and the gold buys the supplies. You must know that."

"Who would have told me?" She smiled and sighed with relief. "Now that I know this, I will take you to gold."

Nathan laughed. "It's not that easy, Fawn. You have to find it first, and I've been over this stretch of the river with a fine-toothed comb."

"Come, Nathan," she said confidently. "I will show you."

Slowly his grin faded. "Are you serious? You know where a gold vein is?"

"No, only some pebbles."

"How? How do you know this?"

Fawn lifted her chin proudly. "All Indians know these things."

He followed her through the woods to the hollow by the stream. She knelt in the drift of russet leaves and pushed them aside. Carefully she scooped away the dirt, exposing first the onion-like roots of the ramps, then several nuggets clothed with mud.

"See? I found these last spring when I cooked those ramps for you."

Nathan dropped to his knees beside her and plunged his large hands into the wet dirt. Even through the grime, the gold ore gleamed in the late afternoon sunset with a life of its own. As he dug further, he discovered a large, mostly rotted burlap sack full of high-grade ore chunks and handfuls of nuggets. "Why didn't you tell me about this?"

"I tried to when we went to see Darcy and Jesse, but you kept interrupting me and then I forgot about it." She picked up the ramps and patted wet mud firmly around the bulbs. "I will take these home, and when you go to Bancroft, take them to Darcy. All right?"

Nathan rubbed away the dirt and stared at the large pile of nuggets. "This is a fortune, Fawn!"

"Enough to buy supplies for the entire winter?"

"Hell, there's enough gold here to buy all of Fire Bluff and most of Bancroft to boot!" He started knocking the mud from the nuggets and stuffing them into his pockets. "We're rich, Fawn!" He grabbed her and kissed her firmly. "Rich! No more worrying about traps and wrestling with smelly hides! Honey, I'm going to show you things you never even dreamed were there!"

Fawn sat back on her heels and stared at Nathan. "What do you mean?"

He held out two nuggets the size of robin eggs. "These are going to buy us some new clothes, and these," he opened his fist to show her several more, "are going to take us to San Francisco!"

"San . . . what?"

"San Francisco. It's a city in the California territory. Right on the ocean, it is, I hear. You never saw an ocean, but they say it's bigger than anything you can imagine! We can get us a coach and four, or maybe a red buggy with a spanking pair of bays. Would you like that? And a real house, with a white fence and servants to do all the work for you." He hugged her again and she felt as if her bones would snap from his exuberance.

"You never said anything about going to this city," she said with growing alarm. "This San Francisco!"

"It's a dream I thought I would never win," he told her with his eyes shining. "Ever since I was a boy I've wanted to see San Francisco and the ocean. To really be somebody! I grew up dirt poor, Fawn, but that's all changed now! You've made us rich!"

She watched him scoop up more of the shiny pebbles and stuff them in his pocket. "Leave the mountain?" she said numbly. "Leave our home?"

"Fawn, you've told me a dozen times that you don't like that cabin. The floor is uneven and the doors stick in rainy weather."

"These are things that bother you, not me."

"The bed! I'll get you a featherbed so high you'll need a ladder to climb onto it. You'll think you're riding on a bird, it'll be so soft. Real goose down, it will be, and not a corn husk around! I *know* you want that!" He poured some nuggets into her hands. "Here. Put these in your pouch."

Slowly she dropped the gold into the small bag she wore at her waist. "I never dreamed you would want to leave the mountain," she said as if dazed.

He leaned back and gazed down at the cache. "It sure seems odd to find gold like this. You know what I think? I believe somebody hid them here and forgot where to find them. Maybe it was whoever built our cabin. See, Fawn? It's like they were buried on purpose."

"Then perhaps we should leave them, Nathan," she suggested eagerly.

"Why do that? Nobody lives around here but us. Whoever buried them must have died or moved on. Judging by the rotted sack, they've been buried for quite a while. The gold is ours now." He patted his pockets happily. "We can't carry all of it at once. Let's bury it again and I'll come back for it later." He stood up and held out his hand to help her to her feet.

Fawn let him pull her up and when he hugged her, she automatically tightened her arms around his neck as he swung her off the ground. When he put her down, he kissed her hungrily and she tried to match his enthusiasm, but there was a coldness in the pit of her stomach. Fawn grabbed up the almost forgotten gunnysack of blueberries as Nathan took her hand and led her toward home. At every step he expounded on the wonders they would see in San Francisco, and Fawn had to trot to keep up with his long strides.

Chapter Twenty-one

NATHAN POURED SOME WATER INTO THE CHIPPED enamel washbasin and started removing the muddy gold from his pockets. "Put yours in here too, Fawn, so I can wash the dirt off, and we'll see what we have."

Reluctantly she dumped the contents of her pouch into the water, then retrieved her lucky buckeye and the two bone fishhooks and string. The gold nuggets lay glittering on the blue-and-white flecked bottom of the bowl. She poked one with her finger, but made no comment.

"Light the lamp, will you?" Nathan said. "It's getting dark early these days."

Silently Fawn trimmed the lamp wick and struck a light to it. When she had adjusted the flame, she replaced the long glass chimney and sat it on the table beside the basin. Beneath Nathan's fingers the caked earth fell away and the color showed bright and true. Taking his knife, he scored one of the pebbles and grinned.

"Look at that, Fawn. Have you ever seen a prettier sight?" He looked over at her and cupped her face in his wet hand. "I can just see you now all dressed in velvet and satin, with bows in your hair. You'll never have to want for anything again."

"There's as much as that?"

"Pretty close to it. We will use this gold to invest in property—like hotels or stables. Then they will make us more gold. I've thought about it for a long time. I know what to do."

Fawn tried to smile, but her lips were stiff. Everything was happening so fast she felt dizzy. Leave the mountain? Leave the only life she knew to go to a white man's city? She couldn't think of anything she wanted less. Most of his words had made no sense to her, but she had understood enough to be frightened. It was as if a stranger had taken the place of her beloved Nathan.

"Fawn?" Nathan questioned. "Are you all right?"

She forced herself to nod and smile. But her lips threatened to tremble, so she turned away and went to look out the window. The sun was setting in a dull sky and the sentry pines whispered of approaching rain. She hadn't even noticed the clouds gathering, she thought dully. When Nathan came up behind her and put his hands on her arms, she flinched, then leaned back against him, her face still turned toward the darkening sky.

"Look at me, Fawn," he said softly. "What's the matter?"

She let him turn her face toward him and saw him blur through her tears. "This woman is afraid," she whispered. "Never have I thought of leaving the mountain."

"Now that's not being reasonable," he countered. "What about all that talk I've heard from you about the wind being your brother and how an Indian isn't tied to the land?"

"This is different!"

"If you were still with your tribe, you would have already left the mountain."

"But only to go to another one! My traditions would go with me!"

He drew a deep breath and a slight frown creased his broad forehead. "You'll go with me, won't you?"

Fawn shook her head miserably. "How can I? I would never fit in this magical city of San Francisco. People would laugh at me, and my totem would weaken and die."

"You won't go?" he repeated with astonishment. "You won't?"

"I cannot, Nathan!" she cried out in pain as she fought to hold back her tears. "I belong here! On the mountain! You and I—we could not live elsewhere!"

"How do you know?" he thundered. "You can't possibly know that!"

"I do, Nathan," she said with deep sadness. "And you do, too."

He gazed down at her frightened face, and the silence grew long between them. After a while he pulled her to him and held her close. "We will talk tomorrow. Come to bed for now. We don't have to decide anything tonight." He gazed past Fawn and out at the familiar pine-strewn lawn.

He picked up the lamp and looked one last time at the fortune in gold that lay in the old washbasin. Then he took Fawn's cold hand and led her into the bedroom.

Placing the lamp on the side table, Nathan lit the fire, then stood before Fawn. When he didn't speak, she raised her eyes questioningly to his face. The pain and love she saw there tore at her heart, and she knew he would give up his dream if she but spoke the word. Fawn kept her silence.

Slowly, gently, as if for the first time, Nathan pulled the laces from her bodice. The lamp's golden aura made molten planes of her rounded breasts and her nipples were pale copper in the gauzy light. Almost reverently Nathan brushed the soft leather from her shoulders and let it fall so that she was bare to his gaze from the waist up. Still moving as slowly as one under water, he unbuttoned his flannel shirt and shrugged out of it.

The golden fur of Nathan's chest and his close-cropped beard were topaz, and although Fawn did not lower her eyes, she could see his magnificent muscles, and her pulse quickened in spite of her sadness. Nathan loosened the drawstring of her leather pants, and a shiver of excitement swept through her as her pants fell to join her dress. Fawn stepped free and reached out her hand to untie the fastening of Nathan's trousers. They, too, fell, and he stood before her in naked glory. Still their eyes held and only several inches separated their bodies.

Hesitantly Nathan lifted his large hand and pulled a lock of her hair over her shoulder and ran his fingers down its length. He touched her cheek as if she were infinitely precious, and Fawn felt her skin tingle as his fingers caressed her. She knew he was waiting for her to speak, but she could not. To ask him to stay would be to destroy his dream. But to bid him go would rend her very soul. She had made up her mind to accept the loss if she must, but she would not urge him to go.

"I love you," she said so softly he could scarcely hear her words.

Without speaking he stepped nearer and enfolded her in his arms. Fawn lay her face against the familiar breadth of his chest and closed her eyes tightly to check the tears that stung her. She did not see how she could ever bear to lose him, yet she feared he was already planning his departure.

When he bent and lifted her, she buried her face in the warm hollow of his neck. He stood for a moment cradling her against him, then lay her tenderly upon the bed. He lowered himself beside her and held her face in his palm. Gently he kissed her, feeling her soft lips part beneath his. Lovingly he tasted the warmth of her mouth and let his tongue tease the incredible smoothness he found in her lips.

Nathan held her close as his other hand followed the satin of her skin to the pulse that raced in her throat. Gently he ran his fingers over her shoulder and down to her rounded arm. Using the sensitive back of his hand, he caressed the full swell of her breast and felt a familiar sense of wonder at its creamy texture. Her nipple was already erect and eager for his touch, and when he took it between his thumb and forefinger, she moaned softly.

He raised his head to look at her as his hand covered her breast. He felt himself caught up in the moss-green depths of her eyes and was aware of a curious sensation like a merging of their souls. For a timeless moment he lay there holding her, knowing her, then she reached up and entwined her fingers in his hair and drew him down for her kiss.

As if gates of passion had been opened, he felt a surging of need for her and his lips mastered hers as she moved eagerly beneath him. He could feel her hands running over him and urging him to even greater excitement. Skillfully he entered her willing body, and her cries of ecstasy spurred him onward.

She was so slender beneath him, as willowy as a reed and as graceful. He cautioned himself to take care, but she showed no such tredpidation and drew him to her with increasing passion. When he tried to slow down to let her rest, Fawn moved beneath him relentlessly, urging him on, as she ran the tip of her tongue over his nipples as he had done to her. Nathan heard a groan escape his throat and scarcely knew he had uttered it. With words of endearment and touches that inflamed him, she loved him with a depth of passion he had never known could exist. Although he held himself in check for as long as he could, she was insistent in the ways he had taught her, and when he felt the throbbing culmination of her release, he could no longer contain his own.

Slowly, the sensations of the world returned to him and he gazed down at her with a love that was tinged with awe. Moisture from their exertion shone on her brow and cheeks and her darkened eyes were fathomless pools. He gently touched her cheek with his fingertips and said in her language, "You have my heart, and our spirits are one."

"I love you with all my heart," she whispered. "Never will I stop loving you, my Nathan."

He lay his head beside hers on the pillow. They gazed at one another in the mellow lamplight and spoke from their hearts because no words were needed.

Fawn arose before dawn and dressed in darkness. The night before she had felt a love for Nathan that had been awesome in its intensity. He lay on his side, his face turned toward her half of the bed. Fawn repressed her urge to awaken him and love him again. She had a decision to make and to do this she must be alone.

She went out into the cold morning air and wrapped the fur cape snugly about her. Her breath made smoke in the still air, and the pine needles sounded dry and brittle beneath her feet. Soon the snows would come whistling down from the bald mountain peak to lay in deep drifts in the valleys. This meant that Nathan must leave the mountain soon or resign himself to wait until spring.

Fawn walked briskly across the yard and into the deep shadows of the forest. Only a sliver of the moon shone in the blue-black sky, but the path she followed was familiar and she needed no moonlight to guide her.

Soon she reached the fork and hesitated for only a moment before she took the trail that led to the pueblo ruins. The domed sky was paling as dawn approached, but still there were vivid stars arching in the cold heavens. Fawn hurried across the ledge and stood at the rim of the canyon. She lifted her slender arms and raised her palms in age-old supplication.

Thus she stood until the brilliant crescent of the sun appeared far away at the edge of the world. As it crept higher, Fawn sang the ancient song of her People, a song that reached so far back, even the tribe elders could not place its origin. She sang of her escape from Walking Tall and of her coup upon the tribe. Again and again she told of her great love for Nathan and of his for her and of their mutual respect and friendship. When she had informed the Great Spirit of all she felt He might want to know, she presented her dilemma—whether to stay on the mountain or to journey with Nathan to an alien land. Her song finished, Fawn stood quietly, her arms still upraised in the frosty air, and she waited.

The sun first appeared as a sliver of orange, then as it climbed higher, it became a glowing mound on the horizon, and finally, a brilliant orb. It chased the night shadows from the inky peaks and bathed the summits and slopes in golden light. The mountainside's dips and crevasses faded from black to violet and at last took on the garb of colors they wore by day. As the sky paled to opalescent hues, the hazy air of the canyon grew dusky rose, then pink, tinted with blue. Finally the trees below turned from beetle black to their fall shades of russet, orange, and yellow, and the ribbon of water that had carved the canyon for aeons, caught the light and became a course of molten silver.

An eagle soared into the space of the canyon, its feathery wing tips carrying it silently on an unseen current of wind. The cry of its mate echoed off the yellow stones, but she did not fly to join him. Circling, the eagle drifted effortlessly through the airy realm and caught an updraft that bore it aloft. Flapping its mighty wings, the eagle flew higher and higher until it vanished against the sun.

Fawn lowered her aching arms and sank to the ground. Tears wet her cheeks as she rocked back and forth in her misery. Unbidden, another song poured from her, the Woman's Song. The one that was sung when wives and mothers and sweethearts saw the warriors come home from war leading riderless horses. After a time, she stopped and let the canyon's silence wash over her and heal her sadness as well as it could.

She had asked for a sign and it had been given to her. Now it must come to pass. She stood up and hugged the cape around her as she started home.

Nathan was coming out of the barn when she arrived. He was whistling happily and seemed to crackle with health and vitality. "Hello, Fawn," he called out in greeting. "Where have you been?"

"Walking."

"It's a beautiful day, isn't it? That maple tree in the horse lot is as bright a red as I've ever seen." He paused and looked searchingly at her. "Is something wrong?"

"No, Nathan, of course not," she answered quickly. "I will cook our breakfast." She hurried toward the cabin before he could get close enough to see she had been crying.

Nathan smiled as he remembered their loving the night before. His smile broadened to a grin as he went back into the barn. "Horse," he said conversationally, "I'll bet there's never been another man in the whole world that's happier than I am." He opened the stall and let the big buckskin follow him to the tack room. He got the currycomb and brushed the horse's amber coat until it gleamed. Horse closed his liquid eyes and let his ears drop back toward his neck. "You like that, don't you," Nathan laughed as he finished grooming the animal. "We have something to do today, Horse. We're going down to Bancroft one last time before snowfall and get all the supplies we can possibly need." Nathan patted the horse and put him back in the stall.

When he went into the cabin, Nathan was still whistling. Fawn looked up at him and he broke off in mid-tune.

"Your breakfast is ready," she said quietly.

Nathan slowly sat down in his chair as she brought a steaming bowl of grits to the table. She kept her eyes averted, and he sensed something was wrong. "What's the matter? Are you catching a cold?"

"Yes. I am catching a cold."

Nathan helped himself to a slice of bread. "I thought Indians never got sick," he said to tease her.

Instead of smiling, she shrugged. "This woman must be different, for I have a cold."

"It's kind of sudden, isn't it? I mean, you felt great last night."

She glanced at him sadly and passed the pot of blackberry jam.

Nathan caught her hand and wouldn't let it go. "We both know you're not sick, Fawn. Now tell me what's on your mind."

"This woman will not discuss it."

"Fawn!"

"I cannot understand your words," she said in Arapaho. "Leave me alone."

He dropped her hand and watched as she spread jam on her bread. He frowned in confusion at her obscurity. Nathan was proud of his own directness, a trait he had also admired in Fawn. If she was displeased, she said so and didn't leave him trying to figure out what he had done to make her angry. At times, in fact she was so straightforward they had had roaring arguments before the issue was resolved. Nathan liked that about her. Now, however, she was being as evasive as any one he had ever seen.

"You won't tell me?" he demanded.

"No!"

"All right! Be that way!" He stood up and strode across the room. "I have to go to Bancroft before it starts to snow. I'll be back tomorrow. It would be too hard a ride down and back the same day. We'll talk when I get back." Out of habit Nathan had not invited her to go with him.

Fawn looked at him steadily, and he had the uneasy feeling that many things which should have been said were hanging between them. But he knew he had to leave soon or be prepared to travel at night leading two pack mules over the rough trail. His frown deepened. "You'll be all right, won't you? You remember how to go to Jesse's if there's any trouble?"

"What trouble could there be with Walking Tall gone? I will be all right." She forced a smile to her lips, but it never reached her eyes.

He crossed the room and bent to kiss her. For a long time he looked into her troubled eyes. "I'm not going," he stated flatly.

"Yes, you are. Nathan, it must be done now before the snows." She caught his hand and held it tightly for a moment before releasing it and saying firmly, "Go."

Nathan straightened and sighed. "I'll be damned if I can understand you, Fawn." He walked to the door and looked back uncertainly, but she made a sign of farewell. "I'll be back tomorrow," he said as he left.

He was still frowning as he walked to the barn and saddled Horse and harnessed the two pack mules. "Don't ever get married, Horse," he confided. "It will make you crazy. I know." The word marriage reminded Nathan that he and Fawn had never actually made it official and he wondered briefly if she ever wished they had. "Maybe next spring would be a good time for that," he said to his horse.

He swung into the saddle and tightened his knees as Horse crow-hopped in a stiff-legged circle, as he always did when he was first mounted. Then the animal flicked his black-tipped ears forward and relaxed like the gentlest of animals. Nathan leaned over and caught the lead rope of the mules. As he rode into the yard, he cast a calculating glance at the cabin. Fawn always came to the yard to see him off. He thought he saw a shadow that might be her in the window, but she remained well within the house. In case she was indeed watching, Nathan waved as he rode across the yard.

All the way down the mountain he pondered what could be troubling Fawn. She had been upset over him talking about San Francisco, but she had not mentioned it this morning. Maybe, he thought, it was the gold itself. If she thought, as he did, that whoever had buried it had died before reclaiming it, she would think the gold was tainted or at least unlucky. That was probably it, he decided.

San Francisco. His smile faded as he let Horse choose his own path toward Bancroft. Now that it was within his grasp, he wasn't so sure he wanted it. He wasn't certain just what had changed his mind. Perhaps it had been when he looked past Fawn and saw the serenity of his dusk-cloaked yard with the towering pines flanked by Wolf Creek or later when they were loving in the fire's glow of their bedroom. Certainly he had not wanted to leave when he awoke that morning and looked around at the coziness of their cabin. He had never lived in any other house he had liked as well as this one, and one of the main benefits of it, in his opinion, was its isolation. He wished he had told Fawn about his decision not to leave the mountain for good, but decided he could tell her when he returned. From her reactions, he was pretty certain she wouldn't be disappointed. Of course he never for a minute believed she had meant it when she had said she wouldn't go with him. He was positive that she loved him, and a person didn't stay behind and say good-bye to the one they loved. No, she had just been upset at the suddenness of it all.

Not that he wouldn't like to *visit* San Francisco. Nathan smiled at the thought of seeing all its wonders and sharing them with Fawn. It would make a perfect honeymoon trip. He grinned, and his white teeth flashed in his beard. While he was in Bancroft he would buy some ready-made dresses for Fawn to wear on their honeymoon to San Francisco and put their names on the waiting list for a wagon train in the early spring. Then, afterwards, they could settle down in their cabin, having seen the world, and get around to the business of raising a family. Nathan laughed happily and patted Horse's sleek neck.

Fawn waited until Nathan had been gone for an hour before she mounted her horse and started down the trail after him. For months she had watched him ride off to Bancroft or Fire Bluff, and now that their world was already shattered, she intended to satisfy her curiosity. If he did indeed have a woman in Bancroft, it might make it easier to give him up.

The path was easy to follow, having been traveled by horse and mule for several years. She kept going at a good pace but didn't rush. She had no intention of rounding a bend and coming face to face with Nathan and the slow-moving mules.

It was further than she had expected, and by the time she saw the town below, the first lights were already being lit. She slid off her mare and tied her to a pine. After looking around carefully, she took a deep breath and left the protecting forest.

She walked across a small clearing which separated the woods from the town. A rough foundation had been laid out for a building in its center. The grass was rutted from old wagon tracks, and deep furrows were gouged in the mud from heavy loads and thick traffic.

The town beyond was a contrast of newly sawn planks that still looked raw and yellow and tumbledown shacks that were weathered a salty gray. There were far more buildings than she could count, and Fawn's mouth dropped open in astonishment when even more came into sight as she approached.

Most frightening of all were the people. They seemed to be everywhere she looked. Young men and women leading children by the hand walked up and down a wooden walkway in front of the buildings. Several old men sat on a long backless bench beside a barn where a younger man was pumping a bellows to force air into a fire pit to heat a length of glowing iron.

Her eyes were large and startled as she tried to take in all the sights. Two boys were using sticks to push a hoop, much as she had done as a child in the Indian village. A group of men were gathered around a dappled gray horse and seemed to be haggling over a price or the animal's merit. Three women strolled by with baskets looped over their arms. Fawn stepped aside to let them pass, but they scarcely glanced at her.

Night was coming to Bancroft, and the mountains that encircled it were fading into an inky blur. Only the upper slopes could be seen in silhouette against the rapidly darkening sky. Fawn looked up, but she could see few stars with the glow of so many lamp lights around her. Even though shadows were darkening fast, the people carried on as if it were noon.

Fawn avoided a group of men who stood in front of a brightly lit shop. As they watched her, one made a comment to his friends that would have been obvious in any language. Fawn nervously felt for the reassuring handle of her knife and stepped into the concealing shadows of a house.

What if she couldn't find Nathan? This thought had never even occurred to her, but then who could have guessed that Bancroft would be so crowded and confusing? Fawn watched as a woman carrying a small child came to call in one of the men who had been ogling her. When he left, the others disbanded and wandered away toward other destinations. Fawn relaxed somewhat.

She was growing hungry, so she took a strip of jerky from the sack of food she had prepared for her journey. She bit off a chunk of the venison and chewed it slowly as she wondered what to do next. She had never considered that Bancroft might be so much larger than the Indian village she had known.

The house that overshadowed her was taller than any structure she had ever seen. By the rows of windows she reasoned there must be an upper level, as in the pueblo village. Curiosity overcame her fear and she stood on tiptoe to look in the window.

Some strange fabric hung like a cotton cobweb over the glass panes, but she could see through it to the room beyond. A dozen men and perhaps half that many women were eating at a long trestle table, and the man on the end nearest the window was Nathan. Beside him sat a small woman wearing a frilly pink dress and a cascading series of ribbons in her silvery blond hair. Even as she watched, the woman familiarly lay her hand on Nathan's knee beneath the concealing table. Fawn gasped and put her hand over her mouth to stifle her cry of pain and anger.

Every time Nathan had come to Bancroft for the past two years, he had stayed here at Slovak's Boarding House. It was the only place in town that served three hot meals a day and also guaranteed clean bedding. He always insisted on a room to himself, even though it cost more and had gained a reputation for gentility with its proprietor. There was, however, one drawback to Slovak's Boarding House, and that was the daughter of the proprietor, who was even now sitting by his side.

Over the past years Nathan had become proficient at avoiding the young woman, but of late she had become more and more assertive, if not down-right aggressive.

Nathan felt her hot hand on his knee and he jerked as if he had been stung. She was smiling demurely at an old gentleman seated across from them, but her palm was inching up Nathan's thigh. Without any hesitation, Nathan grabbed the errant hand and slapped it down on the top of the table. As he did, a movement in the window caught his eyes and he did a double take as he recognized Fawn. Their eyes met in stunned recognition, then she turned and bolted into the night.

"Fawn!" Nathan bellowed in a voice better suit-ed to mountains than dining rooms. The young woman squealed in fright and tried to look as if her hand had been in full sight all along. Without a glance at the other diners, Nathan leaped up, overturning his chair with a loud clatter. He mut-tered an apology to the proprietor's wife, who was all aflutter by now as he ran from the room.

On the porch Nathan hesitated, trying to decide which way Fawn had run. Where would she go when she knew nothing about the town? He reached into the door to grab his heavy coat off the hall tree and ran after her as he pulled it on. When he reached the middle of the street he looked around frantically while he dodged wagons and riders. She was nowhere to be seen.

Nathan searched the town until he had to admit she was gone. He was beginning to wonder if indeed he had even seen her at all. He could almost believe it was a trick of the light coupled with his longing for her. Almost. But he couldn't forget the shocked pain on her face. He lifted his head and frowned at the black hulk of the mountain. Would she be foolish enough to go back up in the dark?

Chapter Twenty-two

FAWN LET HER HORSE PICK HER WAY CAREFULLY OVER the rocky ground. It was difficult finding her way in the dark, but she couldn't bear to stay in Bancroft until dawn. Not only was she frightened of the men who seemed to be everywhere she looked, but Nathan could easily find her in the daylight. Besides, she had seen no place to sleep safely. When she reached the grassy plateau that overlooked the town, she stopped.

Fall had long since robbed the grass of its green, but the yellow straw was still abundant on the flat ground and would make a billowy bed. Fawn gathered several armsful and lay down, wrapping her cloak snugly around her body. Below, she could see the glittering lights of Bancroft and occasionally she could even make out people as they went about their nocturnal business. Miserably she tried to guess which building sheltered Nathan. The thought gave her pain and she probed it mercilessly.

The yellow-haired woman was exactly the sort she would have chosen for Nathan had she not desired him for herself. The woman had been as pink and white as a field flower and looked just as delicate. Exactly the sort of woman that she thought a man would want for a wife.

The thought made her ache, and she tried to turn her pain to anger. If only she could lose her temper, perhaps she could stop the misery that racked her. Maybe in time she could even stop loving him.

An owl hooted in the distant woods and a slight breeze lifted the tips of the dead grasses. Fawn lay back on her makeshift bed and curled into a tight ball. But she didn't feel angry, only hurt and very much alone.

Fawn dozed fitfully most of the night, and well before dawn she gave up all pretense of trying to sleep. A light frost silvered the weeds and emphasized the hushed silence of the slumbering town below. She wrapped the fur cloak more snugly around her and took out a strip of raspberry "leather." At the first bite, however, she put it away. Her stomach rebelled at even the smell of the dried fruit and she breathed deep gulps of air to stave off her nausea. This had happened to her every morning of late, and she wondered dismally if she was indeed catching some disease, yet by midmorning she always felt perfectly well. She tied the bag of food to her waist so that she could ignore it, and then she started back up the mountain, her horse's footsteps leaving a dark trail in the wetness.

In the long hours of the night she had decided where she would go. A Ute tribe camped on the far side of the mountain—the same tribe where Charley had bought Pale Moon from her father. Now that Charley was dead, the tribe would be in need of an interpreter. Fawn's English wasn't proficient by any means, but it was probably better than anyone else's in the tribe. The Utes were not likely to be in contact with Walking Tall, and she could always leave if her old enemy returned to the mountain. She looked over her shoulder one last time. She would much rather have stayed with Nathan, but he had chosen San Francisco and some yellow-haired woman. At last Fawn felt a spark of anger and she tried to nurture it as she continued.

Because of the deep canyon that split the mountain, the easiest way to the other side was also the most obvious—over the top. Light snow had fallen, but as yet the ground would be only partially covered. Fawn had often heard Elk Tooth talk of following the trail over the summit when he was a boy. Generations upon generations of Indians had used the trail and it was easy to follow. In some places the rocky tundra was actually worn down to a visible path by the tread of thousands of feet over the years. Fawn felt she would have no trouble finding the trail and following it to the Ute tribe beyond.

She drew near the cabin she had shared with Nathan and rode up to the pasture. Sliding off her mare for the last time, Fawn patted her and turned her loose, then hung her bridle over the fence post where Nathan would see it. She would miss the animal, but it had been a gift from Nathan, and Fawn knew she had to leave everything connected with him behind. She tried to ignore the cabin where she had known so much happiness. That was all in the past now.

As she neared the river ford, she faltered. Just beyond the bend was the site where the Arapaho village had been. She couldn't imagine its absence, and curiosity drew her closer. She brushed aside the branches and peered at the open field that had once housed all her family and friends. Slowly Fawn walked out into the clearing.

Here had stood Elk Tooth's wigwam where she had learned to tan doeskin and weave baskets of the river willows and reeds. Over there she had had an argument with another child and Storm Dancer had had to act as peacemaker. She wandered over the hard-packed ground and paused at the center of the field. A large, bare circle indicated the previous location of the chief's tent. Here she had come as a bride and here, too, her husband had fallen dead as he beat her. Fawn stared at the ground which no longer bore any evidence of all that had happened. By the time the spring grasses sprouted, there would be nothing to mark where so many people had lived, dreamed, and died.

Carefully she picked her way past the long dead ashes of campfires. She was tiptoeing as if a sound would shatter the memory of the vanished camp. At the place where Storm Dancer had lived, she paused again. Had he been the one to discard the broken pot she now saw? Had it been Clouds Passing? Fawn knelt and picked up the broken shard, but it no longer seemed to hold any essence of her family. Fawn let it fall to the dirt and turned her back on the deserted camp. That life was gone—as irreparably broken as the fragment of cooking vessel. It was time to put it aside.

She quickened her pace and turned her path toward the steep slope of the upper mountain feeling as if Fawn, the daughter of Elk Tooth, had died. If only, she thought, it would be possible to put aside Fawn, the beloved of Nathan. Far more of her spirit yearned for the cabin than it did for the campground where she had spent almost her entire life.

Once she left the village the trail became steeper. At times she needed both hands to catch at tree trunks and rocks to pull herself upward. Yet she continued to climb. She had to put as much distance as possible between the golden bearded giant and herself, before she weakened in her resolve and ran back to him.

Maybe, she told herself grimly, Nathan had already left for San Francisco. Maybe he had had no intention of ever returning to her and the cabin. This thought gave her the will to climb ever upward.

She ate sparingly of the dried meat, raspberry "leather," and corn patties she carried in her sack. She had no idea how long it would take to find her way to the Utes and she knew food would be scarce on the cold tundra.

Gradually the few hardwood trees thinned and only the shorter, gnarled pines remained. Fawn found herself gasping for air at the higher altitude and she frequently had to stop to catch her breath.

As she continued her climb, the wind-crippled trees became more scarce and finally were left behind as she reached the tundra. Rolling hills swept up to the crown of the mountain, broken only by storm-blasted boulders half-buried in the hardy bracken. To her left an ancient glacier lay in a finger-shaped gully, its perpetual snow tinged a pale ivory from the past year's dust. A light powder of new snow made a crunching sound under her feet as she trampled the wiry plants beneath. Curving up and over the bald knob of the summit was a faint line of white where snow had gathered. The Indian trail! She had found it!

Night was falling, and Fawn looked back the way she had come. There was not likely to be any shelter on the wind-ravaged height, nor would the scraggly pinion pines below her afford her any help. She pressed onward.

The trail was easier to walk upon than the rough

bracken, and the ground here was almost level. If
the altitude had not taken her breath, she would
have made even better speed.

She followed the path to a dip in the hill above
the glacier, where she stopped. A low overhang of
weathered granite jutted over the trail, and beneath it someone had long ago dug out under the
hill to form a shallow cave. Fawn bent over and
crawled under the boulder. She had no firewood,
but her body heat would keep her from freezing.
Miserably she huddled in the cave and watched a
bank of silvery storm clouds form on the horizon.

Again she slept very little, and in the middle of
the night she awoke to the sound of a hard rain
slapping against her granite roof. Fawn edged back
against the inside wall and watched the water fall in
sheets outside. Soon rivulets were coursing over
the path and streaming into the glacier to freeze.
The rain had a brittle sound like sleet. Fawn
huddled closer into the folds of her fur cloak and
buried her head against the cold.

By dawn the rain had faded to a dismal drizzle
that seemed to be freezing almost as soon as it hit
the hard ground. Fawn forced herself to eat some
of the jerky and a corn patty and hoped it would all
stay down. She was beginning to get very thirsty,
but she knew she would have to wait until she could
find a stream. With the abundance of water on the
lower mountain she had not anticipated there
would be none on the summit. She unbraided her
hair and let it hang loose for warmth.

Ducking her head, she went out into the wet air. Without bothering to look around, she headed doggedly over the mountain.

"Fawn!" Nathan's bellow rent the frosty air. "Fawn, wait!"

She jerked to a stop, then whirled incredulously to see a familiar figure on horseback a few feet away at the edge of the glacier. Quickly she turned away and hurried up the trail and away from him.

"Stop walking, damn it!" he yelled as he jumped off Horse and ran up the slope. "A man can't breathe up here!" He was gasping for air as he caught her arm and turned her to face him. "Where in the hell do you think you're going?"

Fawn looked up at him. He had obviously not been as fortunate as she in finding shelter, for his blond hair was plastered wetly to his head and beads of moisture glistened in his beard. She tried to ignore the deep anguish she saw in his vivid blue eyes. "I am leaving," she replied at last.

"I can see that. *Why* are you leaving?"

She stared up at him. "Surely you have no need to ask that, Nathan."

"I know what it must have looked like back there in Bancroft, but . . . Why aren't you wet?"

"I slept in a cave."

He studied her for a moment. "Come home, Fawn."

She looked away quickly. "I have no home. You must go and marry that yellow-haired girl—the one with the squinty eyes and the rather large nose—and go to San Francisco."

"I don't want to marry her! As for San Francisco, if you had just asked me, I'd have told you I don't want to stay there forever. I only want to *see* it."

Fawn looked back up at him. "You don't want to live there?"

"No. I did at one time, but I changed my mind."

"Nevertheless, you would be happier married to the yellow-haired one. She looks quite docile to me." Fawn tossed her head haughtily and tried to shrug off his hand.

"Damn it, I don't want to marry her! I want to marry you!"

Fawn stared at him. "I don't believe you," she said at last.

A muscle tightened in Nathan's temple and he pulled her off the trail and onto the highest summit of the mountain. He tilted his head back and threw his free arm wide as he held her wrist securely. "Hear me!" he bellowed as loudly as he could. "I call on the Spirit of the mountain, all the ancestry of the Arapaho tribe known as that of Walking Tall, and the Great Spirit to hear my words!" His Arapaho was badly accented but intelligible.

"Nathan! Be quiet! You know not what you are doing!" Fawn cast a fearful eye at the low clouds above them. They were settled almost upon the ground, and should the Great Spirit hurl a lightning bolt, He could hardly miss them.

"I know exactly what I'm doing," Nathan assured her. Looking back at the stormy clouds he cried out, "I, Nathan Stoddard, take this woman,

Fawn, to be my wife!" He looked back at her and said more softly, "If she will have me."

"Yes," Fawn said in an awed voice. Then louder she proclaimed, "I, Fawn, of the wigwam of Elk Tooth, will accept Nathan Stoddard for my husband!" She looked at Nathan as if half afraid still of what they were doing.

"I love you, Fawn," he said as the drizzle increased to a steady rain. "I'll always love you."

"Even if my hair is not yellow and I wear doeskin instead of gingham?"

"Especially because of that."

She smiled and the elusive dimples appeared fleetingly. "Come, Nathan, we will go home."

He pulled her to him and kissed her thoroughly as the rain pelted against their faces. When he raised his lips from hers, he said, "We will make this official next time we go to Bancroft."

"We?"

"You're going with me from now on." He put his arm around her and held her close as they started back down the mountain.

"How did you find me?" she asked as she leaned against him.

"You left a trail a blind man could follow," he teased. "It was just a matter of catching up with you." He whistled and Horse obediently trotted over to them. Nathan fondled the animal's ears, then lifted Fawn into the saddle. As he swung up behind her, Horse pranced skittishly and bared his teeth. Nathan reined him around and set his course homeward.

Fawn lay back against Nathan's deep chest and looked up at him. "Don't ever leave me again," he said in a voice that sounded shaken now that she was finally in his arms and coming home. "Keeping up with you is like trying to hold onto the wind."

She touched his lips gently and reminded him, "You have made an oath that you are my husband and I am your wife. I will never leave you now."

He smiled down at her and said, "Just the same, I want a promise."

"I promise, Nathan. And I, too, have been thinking. It would be nice to see this San Francisco —for a visit. I would be honored to have you show it to me."

Nathan grinned as he held her tightly. "Come next spring we are going to set that town on its ear and make love in an ocean!" He nudged Horse to a ground-eating canter and put the windswept tundra behind them.

Tapestry
HISTORICAL ROMANCES

Breathtaking New Tales

of love and adventure set against
history's most exciting time and
places. Featuring two novels by the
finest authors in the field of romantic fiction—<u>every month</u>.

Next Month From
Tapestry Romances

DELPHINE
by Ena Halliday

FORBIDDEN LOVE
by Maura Seger

POCKET BOOKS